"What are you doing?"

The words came out worried rather than calm, like Sonya had hoped.

"Right now, nothing at all." Kai grinned. "But if you take the necklace off, I'll be more than happy to give you a neck massage, or if you take the towels off, I can do a body massage, or . . . you can take off whatever you like and I'll give you whatever you like."

Sonya's fingers moved to the butterfly. "Whatever I like?"

He raised an eyebrow. "Did the masseur miss any spots?"

She wanted to squeeze her thighs together to hold back the heat that was seeping there. "It's a shame, really. You spend all that money, and you know, they do miss a few important ones."

"Imagine that," he murmured conversationally. Then with hands on his hips, he scanned her body from head to toe.

"Truth or Dare?"

TRUTH
or
DARE

DELILAH DAWSON

St. Martin's Paperbacks

TRUTH OR DARE

Copyright © 2006 by Delilah Dawson.

Cover photo © Bruce Talbot / Getty Images

All rights reserved. No part of this book may be used or reproduced in
any manner whatsoever without written permission except in the case
of brief quotations embodied in critical articles or reviews. For information address St. Martin's Press, 175 Fifth Avenue, New York, NY
10010.

ISBN: 0-312-93654-0
EAN: 9780312-93654-9

Printed in the United States of America

St. Martin's Paperbacks edition / April 2006

St. Martin's Paperbacks are published by St. Martin's Press, 175 Fifth
Avenue, New York, NY 10010.

10 9 8 7 6 5 4 3 2 1

To my editor, Monique Patterson,
Thanks for your leap of faith in me
and my dreams!

"There is nothing like a dream
to create the future."

— VICTOR HUGO.

ONE

KAI ARMSTRONG TOOK a hard look around the apartment, mentally counting down the remaining minutes left to search it. The woman's home was impeccably clean, organized to the point of insanity. Instead of making it easier, the neatness made it twice as hard to be thorough, and dammit, he knew he was overlooking something. He could feel it in his bones.

The bedroom, however, was subtly different. Although it was just as tidy, it was unequivocally feminine. The stale apartment air was faintly scented with perfume, lotions, and face powder. Her closet revealed conservative suits, but her dresser drawers held the lingerie of a first-class call girl.

His fingers twitched against scraps of black lace when he heard keys jiggling at the front door.

"Damn." Out of time. He carefully placed the garment back, closed the drawer, and in three steps had slipped into the nearby closet, melting into its depths just as Sonya Drummond walked into the bedroom.

Through the slats of the closet door, he watched the con artist drop a couple of gift-wrapped boxes on the bed, kick off sensible shoes, then shrug off a double-breasted jacket.

She sighed, looking exhausted in an all too fragile, womanly way that no thieving embezzler had the right to.

The little black number she wore was by all rights a no-nonsense sleeveless dress that was conservative, sleek, and professional. The cut hinted at soft curves and somehow distracted from the career accountant look.

Sonya unzipped the dress and started shimmying it off.

The dress made a hushed sound as it slid down her body and——her thigh-high stockings were completely unexpected. The lacy rust-and-black bra and matching thong looked sinful against her creamy mocha brown skin. Her waist was small, complementing the swell of her hips and breasts like the body of a violin.

Not one damned bit conservative!

Kai felt talons of pure desire claw into his belly. The seam of his jeans started to get snug, making him feel like a slack-jawed lecher.

Well, damn it all. . . . There on her slim neck was the butterfly necklace he'd be scouring the apartment for!

She absently touched the piece of jewelry, then walked over to the bedside radio. Moments later,

Kai heard soulful jazz crooning from the speakers.

If he didn't get out soon, his brother was going to call wondering what was up. Kai looked down to check his wristwatch, then made sure his cell phone was off. He nudged his erection to the left for comfort, but it did no good.

When he looked up again, Sonya Drummond had put her suit on a hanger and was heading straight for his hiding place.

There was no time to do more than hold perfectly still and pray.

She opened the opposite closet door—thank God!—and placed the hanger on the rail, just inches away from his face. The displaced air pushed her lingering heat and scent onto him. Licking his lips was a mistake. He could practically taste her, her essence lingering like an invisible kiss.

Forcing back the thought, he watched her return to the bed and slide the nylons from her legs in a careful, practical manner, probably so as not to get runs or some such thing. Might as well have been a Victoria's Secret model, though.

How on earth had he not seen some of this sensuality when he was building her profile? All those clocked hours had only captured the image she'd wanted him to see, making him believe that her car, her job, and her boxy, bland business suits were certifiably boring and conservative.

She'd mastered the image of prim dowdiness, from her hair to her low-heeled shoes. Even her scent reminded him of soft linen and fresh flowers.

And until today, he'd fallen for it.

This woman he was looking at now . . . well, she should've been wearing cleavage-defining, curve-hugging suits and musky perfume, and charging by the hour.

Mentally, he took a bow, admitting he would've remained clueless if not for searching her home. Almost a sucker, but not quite.

He certainly wasn't in the business to ask why cons committed crimes but to find the weakness that drove them to it. And with white-collar criminals it was usually their nature to return to the same kind of crime, which suited him just fine.

And now that he thought of it, embezzlement fit her Jekyll and Hyde act. If her lingerie revealed a weakness, his surveillance hadn't caught it. Maybe that's how she was spending her money, though. Hey, food for thought.

He shifted his head to the left for a better view and the dress on the hanger brushed his cheek like a caress, the scent of her diving south to swell his growing erection.

One thing was for sure. If her secret sensuality held the key to her weakness, it wasn't going to be hard to come up with a plan to take her down.

Home at last!

Sonya stretched her neck, then absently removed the pins that held her coiffure in place. Her hair tumbled past her shoulders and she massaged her scalp, exhaling in relief. It had been a hectic day at work and the last thing she wanted was reminders that not only had she aged yet another year, but she also still remained single and a workaholic.

And lonely.

Horny, too.

Normally, that didn't bother her, but the horniness was new on the pity list and, to her amazement, it had steadily moved up the list to the number one spot.

Happy Friggin' Birthday.

The fortune cookie that had been dessert for her Chinese lunch had promised "A wild and dashing adventure is soon to come."

In bed?

Ha!

If the Fortune Cookie Gods were listening, surely they knew that her hormones had her all but climbing the walls, yearning, waiting for sex, sex, SEX! Not the polite, stilted sex she'd had with Paul several years ago. That would be the equivalent of golf or croquet sex. What she needed was some serious tackle football sex. Some hot, sweaty, rough-around-the-edges sex. Unpredictable sex. The kind of sex that loosened headboards and made animals out of timid lovers.

She sighed. At least, she'd heard there was such a thing.

Her friends Julie and Lisa talked the subject to death every chance they got. If Julie hadn't gone to San Francisco on business and Lisa hadn't missed her plane, they'd be painting the town red right about now. OK, mostly her friends would be painting the town while she'd most likely be taking notes.

Sonya settled on the bed and apprehensively eyed the gift Julie had sent her. As crazy as she was, there was no telling what she was up to. Especially when she had warned Sonya to "keep an open mind."

Sonya crossed her legs, reached for the box. Inside, she found a card along with what looked like a plastic butterfly-like apparatus. What was it with butterflies anyway? Just days before, her uncle had surprised her with a gorgeous butterfly necklace she'd finally worked up the nerve to wear and—

"Oh, my goodness. . . ." At closer inspection the plastic thing looked like . . . a sex toy? Sonya gaped at the package for a moment before opening the card.

What can I say? Gift certificates are too predictable. This should be much better anyway. Fresh batteries included. Have fun and try not to go blind! Happy Birthday!

Julie

The nerve! Sonya giggled. Were confessions among friends no longer sacred? All she'd done was mention that her sex-o-meter was revving high these days. How could Julie jump to such an outrageous conclusion?!

Sonya examined the toy more closely, then tore the wrapper off. The plastic wings were pliable and soft, and it even came with controls. She inserted her finger into the space provided; then, with a touch of a switch, Sonya turned it on. It began vibrating with a low hum.

"Oh!" She shivered when the tiny tremors traveled up her finger like fluid lightning. Moving the control lever higher increased the humming, and by the time she maxed it out, her whole hand was all but shaking.

A delicious sensation snaked up her arm and nestled deep in her breasts, tightening her nipples and kicking her sex-o-meter up several notches. God! She needed to get laid often and supremely well if she was getting turned on by this clever little insect.

A very vibrant, humming insect. Plastic and batteries. Who knew?

The longer she sat studying the toy, the more the crazy vibrations against her finger thickened her pulse and made her want more. . . . Would it be just as good against the aching part of her sex? As it was, she was slowly melting. And leaning toward myopic.

And now what?

The jazz from the radio took on a sultry rhythm, and she balked, stunned that she was really contemplating using the gadget.

Hell, why not? It was just a . . . a thing. What harm could it do? Better yet, what thrills could it bring?

She counted to ten; then closing her eyes, Sonya touched the butterfly to her face, cheeks, and lips, hissing in a breath at the odd contact. The touch felt almost electric, especially beneath her jaw. Experimentally, she took her time zigzagging a path downward to the rust-and-black lace that covered her breasts.

Hey, that wasn't so bad. Not at all.

So maybe if she touched . . . Oh yes. There. . . . She licked her lips and drew a lazy design over her bra, moving inward until the butterfly lingered over her nipples, delving into the valley of soft curves between.

Oh yes . . . that was . . .

"Mmmm." She grinned. The sensations shimmied up her back, making her arch slightly. Why on earth hadn't she thought to test-drive one of these toys before?

She found herself hesitating with the butterfly against her belly button, feeling suddenly prudish. Silly, really.

The trick was to simply take action and go where no vibrating butterfly had ever gone before.

Don't think about it. Just do it!

She uncrossed her legs and tugged the scrap of garment down to her knees, then sank backward into the soft comforter. With the butterfly in her hand, she undid the front clasp of her bra and pushed the delicate material to the side, still debating for a moment before testing the lovely tremors against her bare skin.

Oh, Lord. It sure beat blowing out candles.

She skimmed her other hand over her belly again and slid south until her fingers made contact with the small thatch of pubic hair.

Catching her breath, she touched herself, delving deeper. Oh yessss!

Paul, her former boyfriend, had never cared to touch her there. And before him there had only been those awkward first- and second-base touches back in high school, which were *nothing* compared to this.

If a man was to master this touch, she'd be putty in his hands. Hell, she'd become his sex slave, his love concubine, anything he wanted.

Her fingertips were already slick with her wetness, but she kept the slow tempo, anticipating the spiraling rush of sensation. She licked her lips and shifted her hips, thirsting for a kiss that would never come.

When the ache threatened to get the best of her, she switched the vibrations into a higher gear, then brushed the toy against her clitoris. The initial fluttering vibrations simmered on her skin, and she gave in to the sensation with a gasp. Each touch, each delve into her wetness made her body flush hotter, sending shivers of fluid pleasure clear down to her toes.

God, she wished for a dream lover, right there, right now! Hard and ready to mount! She needed the weight of skin and muscles, of tangling legs and wide-palmed caresses, of breathless, tangled kisses from someone who knew exactly where to touch . . .

Under her fingertip, the pleasure rose rapidly, and Sonya groaned, tipping her head back and riding the throb of each pulsation. Her orgasm loomed, whirling and racing in her blood like a glowing surge of energy trapped inside a crystal—

A loud ringing noise blared and Sonya jerked in a blind panic, nervously yanking the butterfly from its precarious perch. Disconcerted, her eyes darted around her until she realized the noise was only the bedside phone's ringing.

She glared at it. "Goddammit!"

The dumb instrument responded by shrilling back.

She dabbed her forehead with the back of her hand, but after the third offensive ring she snatched the receiver and put it to her ear, prepared to vent.

"Sonya? Hi. Hope I didn't catch you at a bad time."

"Um . . ." Jeez, not the boss! Not now! The laziest two-bit, bad-breathed, water-cooler clueless wonder who always seemed to think she never had enough of a workload.

"Sounds like I woke you up?"

Sonya cleared her throat, hoping her voice would sound less husky. "No, I was just . . ." Reaaaally *getting it on with a toy . . . um, having my way with a vibrating, plastic insect . . . riding an electric butterfly. . . .* "Um, unwinding."

"Well, say, I was just calling to see if you were able to handle the Nelson paperwork I left on your desk. They're gonna send someone to pick it up first thing in the morning."

Ugh! Such a micromanager! "Yes. It's all taken care of."

"Excellent. Great. Well, I'll be in midmorning tomorrow. Crawford and Associates wants an early game of golf, so," he chuckled as if he'd cracked a fine joke, "I'll be *losing* to Craig again. You're in charge while I'm out."

Yeah, whatever. Don't call me at home ever again, you moron!

If there was ever anyone who could successfully ruin the moment, it was Lester Werner. All the fizzing arousal from moments earlier dissolved. In the span of two seconds, she just knew what he was going to say next. *No, don't ask me out again. Nooo!*

"If you're free tomorrow evening, I—"

"I'm sorry," she interrupted. "I've already made plans."

"Oh. Of course." He sounded genuinely perplexed, which summed up how amazingly clueless the man was.

By the time she hung up the phone, Sonya was frustrated in more ways than one.

Alone with her butterflies.

Older. None the wiser. Successful, sure, but even that hard-earned achievement wouldn't keep her warm at night. As it was, the loneliness had begun to fester nightly, forming a hollowness in her chest that gaped wide open. . . .

Her birthday was definitely *not* going to turn into another pity party. She wanted sex, and in a more personal and intimate manner than a tiny battery-operated vibrator provided. Preferably at an exotic location where a muscular cabana boy would serve her cute umbrella drinks right along with hot, sweaty sex! *That* was exactly what she needed.

Sonya inhaled a deep breath, feeling slightly dizzy and exhilarated. Hey, a birthday resolution!

A raunchy fling? The idea seemed so perfect she wondered why it had never occurred to her before!

What better way to celebrate entering her thirties than shedding her inhibitions, discarding her old image, and becoming a whole new-and-improved thirty-year-old Sonya!

One who apparently wanted to do it with poolside help.

She groaned and flopped back on the bed.

It sounded crazy, but other than the constant loneliness and sexual frustration, what was there to lose?

She dabbed her forehead again. This was it. No backing away from it now. Besides, it beat the usual try-to-shed-ten-pounds routine she'd been promising herself on birthdays and New Years.

A vacation was just the thing. Somewhere with anonymity. Preferably without interruptions. And who knew, maybe after the sex madness wore off, she'd come back to San Diego and hunt down a husband in time for her next birthday.

Thirty and crazy.

Thirty-one and married.

It was a plan.

Sonya squeezed her thighs together and tried to ignore the thick heat that still lingered like a dull throb between her legs. She sat up and the bra straps slid from her shoulders.

The sight of the elegant vibrator suddenly embarrassed her and she knew this wasn't going to be the night to short out its poor circuitry.

All in good time. The thought of her boss was still present enough to taint the mood anyway.

For now, she'd settle for the comfort of a hot shower.

Setting the item aside, Sonya retreated to the bathroom, humming "Happy Birthday" along the way.

Kai couldn't believe it! He felt as if he was trapped in an erotic version of *The Twilight Zone*!

It had to be every male fantasy: seeing a woman please herself like Sonya Drummond had, making those small moaning noises, seeing her body's blatant response to that little device. There was a carnal innocence in the way she'd used it, in the exploratory way she'd fumbled, then unexpectedly held off, looking oddly embarrassed.

Man, he'd never envied a vibrating unit more! It didn't change the fact that he would've traded places with it in a hot second, kissing her where her fingers played or invading her with his body, with his mouth, until he felt all her tremors dancing against him, around him, gripping him. . . .

Holy Hell, it was all he could do to keep from ripping the damned closet doors off the hinges and storming her while she was so thoroughly lost in the groove.

Instead he continued to hold the closet knobs in a death grip, breaking out in a sweat, head bent against the wood. He peered out while the sultry images replayed in his mind, mingling with the distracting perfume of her clothes, damn near bringing him to his knees.

If he ever found out who'd called to interrupt the final moment, there would be hell to pay! He still was having trouble with the fact that she'd stopped masturbating to answer a phone call! Christ, who does that?!

Sonya stirred and Kai leaned back far enough to watch through the slats as she stood and strode naked to the bathroom. After a few quiet noises, the sound of water came from the shower, followed by more sounds of her stepping in.

Kai eased his hands from the closet doors, took a steadying breath, then stepped carefully out. His erection bordered on painful, straining his pants like Italian salami.

Nudging it left or right didn't matter at this point.

He closed the closet doors and began to move away.

The room smelled of sex.

Incomplete sex.

Don't be a pervert! Move on!

He hesitated a second longer, then left out the front door. He locked it then as casually as possible and strolled down the street.

TWO

"NOW, SONYA, I am your personal image consultant, and this is exactly why you hired me, right?"

"Right. But when I said I was looking for a change—"

"Ta-dah! Is *this* not a change?"

Sonya looked up at her dear friend and makeover artist, Lisa. The short dynamo had indeed transformed Sonya in the last week. Drastically. And with military precision. Lisa had launched a commando raid on Sonya's closets, tossed out the old wardrobe, bought new clothes, added makeup to the mix, and was now giving a firm nod to the hairdresser. The silver scissors glinted and came dangerously close to snipping off Sonya's waist-length tresses.

"Girl, you gotta believe me, this is going to look fabulous!" Lisa insisted. "Close your eyes and when it's over, I assure you, you'll be happily surprised with the results. Jose here works miracles with hair."

"Short hair? Like supershort hair? I don't think it's for me," Sonya argued weakly.

"You told me you wanted to take risks. Make a new you, find a new look. Now is not the time to chicken out, girl. This man knows what he's doing, OK?"

Jose's grin widened with masculine appreciation. He wiggled his eyebrows and Sonya cringed deep in her gut. Her hair! Unchanged since high school! The only reason she'd cut her hair then had been to rid herself of the nightmares where her mother would yank on her pigtails. Cutting her hair now would mean a new liberation again.

She suppressed the old instinct to run, gulped, and said a firm, "Do it."

He winked. She closed her eyes as the first snip marked the point of no return. So much for bravery.

She hoped the light-headedness was from the missing hair and not quivering panic. At the moment, it was a little hard to tell.

The chair was swiveled away from the mirror, further security to keep her from peeking. With every snip of the scissors, Sonya dwelled on the chunk of money she'd invested in her new image. When that didn't comfort her, she went through the mantra that had guided her since her birthday.

New image. New choices. Life's just too short.

If Jose didn't stop cutting, her hair *was* going to be too short. She heard a sigh and felt a tap on her knuckles. Jose chuckled.

"No need to tear out the armrests, sweetie," Lisa

reprimanded in a soothing tone. "Relax. It's looking beautiful already."

Sonya eased up on the armrests and tried to believe Lisa. But who was she kidding? She wasn't aiming for beautiful. Being plain was nothing to be ashamed of. Actually, it suited her just fine.

It was attitude that mattered. The new change of clothes *had* made her feel much more feminine and sexy. And maybe it was her imagination, but it seemed as if men noticed her more now. Some even greeted her. Maybe that accounted for the ghostly feeling of being watched every now and then. It certainly took some getting used to.

Oh, the price of high maintenance!

After yesterday's experience at the spa, it would be ice-hockey season in hell before she underwent another wax job, that was for sure!

For the first time since the third grade, her toenails and fingernails were painted fire-engine red. Sexy.

But her hair . . .

"Aren't you excited about the cruise?" Lisa said perkily, keying Sonya to the fact that she was digging her nails into the armrests yet again.

"The singles cruise? Of course!" But her excitement was laced with apprehension. It had been that way since the day she'd signed up for it.

"She's gonna have herself a Sex Fest," Lisa confided.

Jose made a humming sound of interest.

"I never said that!" Sonya defended herself. "I said I was hoping to meet a guy."

"Sex Fest," Lisa repeated in a whisper.

Sonya huffed. "I read somewhere that people go on vacations to have flings all the time."

"Nightclubs are cheaper," Lisa replied dryly.

"Besides," Sonya could feel her face heating all the way to her ears, "I'm sure Jose is not interested in this topic for discussion."

"Of course I am interested in people's sex lives," Jose replied. "I'm a hairdresser, aren't I?"

Sonya groaned.

Lisa cheered. "I personally love the idea of kicking off a thirty-year-old you with a quick fling or two . . . or three. . . . It's an excellent idea."

Jose made another sound. "You would."

"What? You've never hit your midlife crisis?"

"It's not a midlife crisis," Sonya said defensively. She wasn't even midlife . . . yet.

They ignored her.

"Of course not." Jose snipped away, sounding like a scholar. "Myself, I looked for the meaning of life for a couple of months. I even thought of buying a really fast car, but to each their own, eh?"

"Sex *is* the meaning of life," Lisa countered before Sonya could respond.

"It's not like that," Sonya interrupted, smelling an argument about to start. "I mean, I'm not looking for anything deep or emotionally investing. Just something mutually enjoyable."

Man, that sounded so much worse than when she'd rehearsed it. How exactly did a woman proposition a man anyway?

"She psychoanalyzes everything," Lisa whispered.

"I like to call it analytical preparation," Sonya muttered.

"You're taking the fun and spontaneity out of it," Lisa insisted.

"What's wrong with planning my spontaneity?"

"Sonya." Jose's accented voice rolled past her left ear. "Whatever your reasons, the men on this cruise are going to go loco over you. And with your hair like this, well, they will not stand a chance, eh?"

She blushed at the tone of his voice. "Lisa is overexaggerating, Jose. I'm a sensible woman. Do I look like the kind to do something crazy? Sex Fest? Not likely! I'm just taking a cruise and hoping I'll get to meet a nice guy."

"Nice guy?" Lisa scoffed. "Forget nice guys. Bad guys are more fun. Ignore your psychoanalysis and take my advice. That cruise will be the perfect opportunity to wreck some beds and slay some hearts."

Sonya smiled and began to relax. "Leave it up to you to treat a cruise like a tournament for the deprived."

"Starting tomorrow, it will be. When you're surrounded by single men, that boat—"

"Ship," Jose corrected.

"Whatever," Lisa said dismissively. "How much do you want to bet the guys will have the same agenda you do? Just cut loose and show a little of that wild side we know nothing about."

Jose simply tsk-tsk'ed and kept his scissors snapping.

"Wild . . ." Sonya repeated, her mind skittering over Julie's outrageous birthday gift. Like a creature, restless desire stirred inside her, but Sonya *still* wasn't sure how to go about seducing a man.

"This new you needs more confidence," Lisa observed.

"I'm leaving tomorrow, Lisa," Sonya reminded her. "This is as confident as I'm going to get."

Lisa made a long thoughtful sound. "Then we're going to have to go shopping today."

"I already have all the clothes I need for—"

"Not that kind of shopping. You need bedroom kind of confidence."

"Caramba," Jose muttered. "Here she goes."

"It's all about what happens in the bedroom," Lisa breezed right along. "Let's pick on Jose for a moment. He looks like the type to put notches on his bedpost to track his sexcapades."

Sonya cringed.

Jose simply chuckled. "It's too hard on the furniture. Makes more sense to notch a belt." He sounded so amused, Sonya was tempted to peek at him.

"Well, it's the equivalent of women keeping little black books and battery-operated devices," Lisa pointed out. "Same difference. Sonya, you need to start with a battery—"

"Hello! Can we just focus on the haircut?" she interrupted, not liking where the subject was headed.

"Multitask with me, honey. When you walk into a room and a man looks at you like he's got notches on his bedpost—"

"Belt," Jose interrupted.

"Whatever, you look right back at him with the confidence of a woman who can get her own satis-

faction from devices guaranteed to function anytime, anywhere. Low, medium, or high speed."

Sonya couldn't suppress the new flush on her
cheeks. Had Julie blabbed about the butterfly gift?

"Anytime? Anywhere?" Jose questioned, sounding only mildly annoyed. "Are you saying you pre-
fer batteries to the services a man can provide?"

"As a matter of fact, yes," Lisa continued blithely,
"Everyone knows sex can be enhanced by lotions,
lubricants, restraints, toys. . . ."

"Wow. So many things to keep track of." Jose
sounded suitably impressed. "Maybe you should
invest in a tool belt to hold all your gadgets and
still keep track of your notches? Something with
studs."

"I am *not* hearing this," Sonya commented loudly.

"You should take notes," Lisa scoffed. "We're
giving you excellent pointers."

Sonya stayed out of the conversation as the two
began to discuss the pros and cons of resorting to
"toys" and how they could possibly be used for
"confidence." The blow-dryer made most of it impossible to follow. Thank goodness.

By the time the debating had stopped and the two
agreed to disagree, Sonya was more than ready to
hear the last of it and open her eyes.

Lisa's murmur of approval came at her left and
Jose fussed at her right. Both sounded like fairy
godmothers putting the final touches on their handi-
work.

Jose said, "Now, open your eyes . . . and look at
you."

Sonya did, apprehension tightening in her gut. "Oh, my goodness," she whispered, not truly believing her own eyes. "It's so beautiful!"

The reflection showed her stunned expression. The hair was short, true, but sleek, sexy, and modern. It was a style she'd envied but been far too afraid to try. It was bolder and as different from her old style as her old wardrobe was from her new one. It transformed her completely!

Sonya smiled.

Jose clutched his chest in mock heartbreak. "No doubt. You're gonna slay someone's heart!"

🦋

"Where is that woman?" Kai Armstrong grumbled under his breath as he massaged his left knee. An old college football injury made his knee ache if he sat in cramped quarters for any length of time, and at the moment it was complaining loud and clear.

He scanned the street again. To his knowledge Sonya Drummond kept a daily routine he could set his clock to.

Today she was twenty minutes late.

If Dre had let Kai hire another person, he wouldn't have had to take off the last couple of days from this surveillance to finish up their last case. . . . But what else was new?

At least he'd been able to verify that the final paper trail of money was tied to her bank account. The account she'd held with her uncle, another accountant, since she'd been eighteen. She made the deposits, he made the withdrawals. The money was often replaced, then extracted again. Except none of it was their money.

Kai sighed and held off using his binoculars. He squinted at the woman walking up the street.

Nope, the hair was all wrong, but—

The clothes were not her usual business suits, but—

OK, definitely not her. This woman had the kind of walk that would've made a blind man gape.

Kai raised the binoculars and focused.

He started from the bottom of her luscious red nail polish peeking out from the open-toed low-heeled shoes and moved on up. She had sexy arches on her feminine feet. Not bad legs, either. Shapely. Too bad the denim skirt started at her calves, but the way it cupped the curve of her buttocks made him sigh in appreciation. Nothing but bounce! And although her denim jacket hid most of the view, the lovely set of breasts made sitting in the car for the past hour worthwhile.

Then there, between the magnificent jiggle of her barely revealed cleavage, gleamed the small piece of jewelry she never left home without.

"Well, I'll be damned." He frowned and focused back on Sonya's face. She hadn't suddenly become drop-dead gorgeous, but she'd definitely been made over. Stunning. The new haircut accentuated her understated beauty and made her look even more sultry, bringing the attention to her lips and eyes.

Unfortunately, his penis was obsessed with a more uncensored memory of Sonya on a bed, and as if on cue, an erection started to firm up in his pants.

Hell, she'd pulled a fast one on him with that dowdy accountant look, but this look made him worry more. It galled him to see her strutting around with the stolen loot hanging from her neck like some kind of Medal of Honor.

Kai lowered the binoculars but kept watching as she entered her apartment. He ran through the information he'd gathered, trying to decipher what it meant. The first clue had been sniffing her mobile phone conversation and finding out she'd booked passage on a singles cruise. Add to that the new look, the recent purchases that had popped up on her credit card, and, the most incriminating of all, her relationship to Otis Drummond. If she wasn't involved in her uncle's embezzlement schemes, Kai'd eat his socks.

What now?

Kai ran his hand over his clean-shaven head and groaned.

Could he hope that after two years of sleeping in motels, hunting and bar-busting his many prey, he was going to finally get a cushy job? It didn't hurt that Old Lady Miller was willing to pay all the expenses.

But a seven-day singles cruise? None of his buddies would fall for that trick after Ken had made that painful mistake last year. As the story went, there had been nothing but women, on a desperate hunt for vows, rings, and/or babies.

Lord save him from the mess!

Nope, he didn't need or care for that type of situation. It was always best to keep things simple, up-front, and honest. He'd sooner take a woman who could slug a beer than one who sipped a froufrou drink from a glass with its own umbrella.

God bless smart, independent women who appreciated one-nighters and liked hot sex without expecting anything in return! Women who knew what they wanted in bed, even if it did involve an electronic device.

"Shit." *Focus!*

If they pulled this assignment off on schedule, the money was going to be good. Better than good. First he had to recover the jewelry and, with any luck, charm the truth out of Ms. Suddenly-Sexy-Thang about what Otis had done with the money he'd stolen from Old Lady Miller.

Kai grabbed his mobile phone and dialed his brother's number. Andre always answered with his trademark, "Hey."

"Dre, where are you?"

"On the road to Vegas," came the grudging reply. "Where it's friggin' nine hundred degrees in the shade."

"San Diego isn't much cooler. Any luck with Otis?"

"Getting closer. He was here yesterday. Used his credit card to pay for gas. Must've been out of small bills. Why else would he pull out the plastic again?"

"Because he's an idiot?"

"That's one distinct possibility. How about you?"

"Something fishy's going on with Ms. Drummond. The accountant's got a very sexy new look and is about to begin a singles cruise tomorrow. Guess where I'll be for the next week?"

Kai counted two seconds before he heard Andre mutter a profanity. "No, Kai, don't tell me what I think you're about to say! While I'm going through this hot, dirty desert trailing a thief, you're—"

"Going on a cruise. That's right, Bro, but don't congratulate me yet. It's a singles cruise, full of gold-digging, commitment-bound women on a mission to do something about their biological clocks. You know I'd trade places with you in a hot second if I could."

Andre laughed. "You actually trying to make me feel sorry for you? Are you kidding me?"

"Glad you understand," Kai noted sarcastically.

"Don't even get me started, Bro. *You* try spending two days hiding in a trailer park—"

"Been there, done that."

"—digging through garbage—"

"In a hot second, Dre. Seriously."

Dre muttered something incomprehensible, which was just as well.

"It's not all going to be fun and games. I'll hunt down the Romero kid while I'm down there, but there's no time to swap jobs now," Kai noted. "Old Lady Miller was pretty clear about the payment plan. I'm just making sure we get paid, and as the motto goes, delivery equals payment."

Dre snorted. "Since when do we have a motto?"

"Since Old Lady Miller hired us."

Again Dre muttered something incomprehensible. "Try not to work up a sweat while you razzle-dazzle Ms. Drummond, will you?"

Kai thought about Sonya Drummond. He would've felt wrong trying to schmooze the dowdy woman she'd been a week ago. But the foxy con lady who had just stridden up the street, well, she was fair game. "I'm no Shaft, but I'll give it a shot. A man's gotta do what a man's gotta do."

"Right." The word dripped sarcasm.

"You know the saying. Don't hate the player, hate the game."

"Swear to God, I'm gonna kick your ass when I see you."

"You've been in the sun too long, Dre. You're getting delusional. Head indoors, grab a beer, and call me when you're back to normal."

"I'm supposed to be the computer surveillance expert and you're the skip tracer! Why am I the one who's dragging my butt across this desert?"

Kai grinned, knowing his brother was venting and working himself up. "Timing. Otis was in your neck of the woods and Sonya was in mine. Besides, remember how Mom used to say what goes around comes around?"

Andre, who was clearly guzzling something, sputtered. "Karma? What a crock of—"

"Circle of life. Your time has come, dude. Take it like a man. I pretended to be a dopehead bum during the Anderson case; you had me wearing friggin' fishnets for the Wilson case. Remember how you kept heckling me?"

"It's your job, man! It's what you do!"

"And now, it's time for some karma."

"Your argument blows. I'm hanging up now."

"Hey, wait."

"What?"

"You think my red Hawaiian shirt is too much to take on a cruise?"

Dre responded by biting off yet another profanity, then abruptly disconnecting.

THREE

SONYA STOPPED STYLING her hair and tried to view it from all angles of the small bathroom mirror. This was it. The first six hours of the cruise!

It was hard to believe that it was already the first day at sea and the sexy reflection in the mirror was really and truly her. A whole new woman. A far cry from the desolate future she'd imagined for herself as a child, thank God.

The cabin was a little smaller than she'd expected, but this bathroom was completely tiny! She tugged up at the low cleavage of the black formal dress and in the process bumped her right elbow against the wall.

"Lisa, I swear!" she muttered, wondering how the dress had ended up in the luggage a size too small.

She gave up on the material and instead covered the exposed view with a pale yellow shawl.

As was her habit of late, her fingers went to the beautifully designed butterfly dangling from her necklace. Delicate trelliswork of gold held few but carefully placed stones that gleamed eloquently, even in the dim light.

Initially, she'd been flattered by the birthday gift her dear uncle Otis had given her. He'd been the clean-cut father figure who'd rescued her when she'd been a young, jaded child, working scams with her drug-addicted mother.

He'd stepped up to the plate and adopted Sonya, raising her as his own daughter, teaching her that she *could* be respectable and upstanding. He'd simply been her hero.

But sometimes, in her sleep, she'd still remember the faces of the people she'd scammed. . . .

Sonya sighed. Those were the bad old days.

Now, her uncle liked to spoil her with extravagant gifts, even when she told him it wasn't necessary. Thinking the necklace too expensive, Sonya had put it in her jewelry drawer for safekeeping. That was until Lisa's Massive Makeover Raid had uncovered it again. She had demanded Sonya wear it "every day, at least through the summer."

Well, maybe not all summer, but definitely for this week, she'd told herself.

Sonya returned to her room and checked the seven-day itinerary that had been left on her bed stand. The night's main event was the "Break the Ice and Start a Fire" dinner. Yikes, seating arrangements were blind-date style. Her suitor was going to be at table fourteen.

Matchmaking at a whole new level.

A wave of uncertainty swamped her. It was one thing to go back into work with a new look, but it was infinitely more nerve-racking to stick to the new agenda of tracking down a Mr. Right-Now. It could very well turn into the longest dinner—if not week— of her life.

For a cowardly moment she craved an escape, a good book or movie, where she could curl up alone, without hassle, company, or forced conversation.

No, no, no. Seize the day! Carpe diem!

What she needed was confidence. Although she obviously had some of Lisa's brand of confidence in her bedroom drawer, hidden among her lingerie, she pulled on all her skills that had come in handy at an early age. Acting.

All she had to do was think like a vixen and play the role to the hilt! Bolstering up her courage, she opened the door, charged out, and promptly slammed into a very firm, very nice, muscular chest.

❦

Kai barely managed to brace for Sonya's momentum when she crashed into him. Her body filled his arms, soft, warm, all woman, assaulting him like a breath of tingling fire. Her delicate perfume brought a heated rush of closet memories into the collision and his body immediately responded.

The assault was overwhelming. Her full breasts cushioned against his chest, and her cheek bumped into his chin, carrying to his ears a husky, feminine "ummph" from her lips. For an endless moment he simply held her, his thoughts completely tied and intimately muddled.

Time slammed to a halt and for half a breath Kai fought a shameless desire to push her against a wall, lift her satin dress, and ease his erection into her luscious body.

"Sorry, I . . ." Her words faltered as she looked up at him. The depths of her eyes darkened and her lips parted, the light catching the lip gloss to perfection. "Oh, hello . . ." she whispered.

"Hello."

If there was a chance that she couldn't feel that his dick had suddenly become a steel pipe in his pants, he'd eat his shorts.

For a full two seconds she remained in his arms, her face reflecting emotions he knew he was feeling. Damned if her mouth hadn't been parted in the same way when she'd been masturbating in bed. A wicked flick of her tongue brought him to the present and she gingerly regained her balance, then peered at him through her lashes.

"Sorry, I usually don't barge out that way," she said, her face transforming to one of confidence.

Neither do my pants, he wanted to quip. Instead he shoved his hands in his pockets as if nothing out of the ordinary had happened. "No problem. In a hurry?"

Her delicate shawl slipped off one shoulder in a shimmer of satin, revealing the delicate butterfly necklace. The sight helped drag his thoughts back on track. Just barely.

Kai realized he'd been staring at the necklace nestled between her fantastic, nipple-perked breasts.

Sonya cleared her throat and quickly put the shawl back in place.

"That's a pretty necklace," he managed.

"Thank you." The blush that rose to her cheeks made him think of raspberry chocolate and other intimate indulgences. Her skin would tempt a man to paint sinful flavors in naughty places and take his time tasting . . .

Her blush darkened and she glanced away, licking her lips again.

Honey, pleeease don't. . . . I can hardly think!

"I should've watched where I was going," he finally said.

"No, no. It was my fault. I was looking down," she replied, her chuckle fading into a fidgety smile.

"Actually, I was heading to the main dining room for the 'Break the Ice' dinner. I think I was going in the right direction."

She seemed to relax a bit. "Oh, I know exactly what you mean. I get turned around and my internal compass goes off. Funny how that happens, huh?"

"Yeah." Although, at the moment, his internal compass was pointing in one direction only. Skyward.

"I think the entrance is up ahead," she said.

He cleared his throat, hefting his mind from the gutter. "Sounds like you know where it is."

"Not yet, but," she tapped the folded paper in her hand, "I have my trusty map, which should get me there."

He eyed the paper with a sheepish grin. "Is that a dig on men and directions? Wait, don't answer that."

She chuckled with a stilted feminine sound that was polite but held a soft huskiness to it that was completely unexpected. In the recesses of his mind, the devil leaned forward with interest.

"Care to join me?" Kai asked.

"Yes." She smiled, willing herself to stay confident. "Don't mind if I do."

Thank God for tuxedo jackets. He offered his arm and she sidled next to him with a soft rustling of sound.

"Lead the way," he said, glad that he sounded calmer.

As they walked, he reminded himself that this sheep, in all her sexy wolf's clothing, was deceptively good at her game.

It was time for him to either own the playing field or she was going to exploit him and use him like she used everything and everyone else.

With every step, the sexual tension billowed, and when they approached the entry line, the murmur of conversation around them grew, as they were serenaded by a classical string quartet in the background. The captain shook hands with people at the open French doors of the restaurant while sharply dressed waiters organized the lines and escorted individuals to their assigned tables. And still Kai couldn't get over the impact of her filling his arms, the way her lips gleamed with gloss, the fullness of her breasts . . .

"Beautiful," she commented.

Kai glanced around the spectacular room. Twinkling lights overhead gave the room a mellow ambience. Large ice sculptures reflected the glow of candlelight like frozen flames, and bright bouquets dotted the linen tablecloths. Silverware and white porcelain clinked quietly, adding more luxury and formality to the room.

"Yes, beautiful," he agreed, but she happened to look at him when he was watching her instead of the room.

The blush that came and went on her cheeks threw him for a loop again. If he didn't watch it, he'd soon be drooling and wagging.

The devil in him tallied up the score. So far, Kai Armstrong, zero. Sonya Drummond, ca-ching! Touchdown! *She's kicking your ass, man!*

How the hell did she keep doing that? He pasted on a smile and nodded as one of the expeditious waiters approached. " 'Number fourteen'?" the man read from Sonya's papers. "Yes, right this way."

As she was escorted away, she politely turned, then waved good-bye to Kai. "Nice bumping into you."

He returned the brief wave, admitting it had been a very long time since he'd felt like the world's most tongue-tied, inept skip tracer.

FOUR

"THAT WAS STRAIGHT-UP robbery," Kai muttered as, a short while later—and half a wallet poorer for the bribe—another waiter led him to Sonya's table.

He couldn't have picked a better spot if he'd tried. It was slightly more secluded from the other tables, offering more intimacy and an endless dusky ocean view. Nearby, a piano player was skillfully tickling some blues from the ivories, a saxophone skirting the notes.

"Here you go, sir," the waiter said, pulling the chair out for Kai.

Sonya's face brightened with recognition, and then a glint of suspicion formed. "*You're* number fourteen?"

"Small world, isn't it?" Kai tried to show an equal amount of astonishment. "Kai Armstrong," he introduced himself.

Her smile widened as she accepted his offered

hand. And just like that, the contact of skin on skin
sent his pulse thumping again.

"Sonya Drummond," she said after the slightest
pause. "I guess this means I won't get a chance to
make a great first impression."

He took his seat. "Oh, I think you've already made
one. Besides, lasting impressions are more important
than first impressions, don't you agree?"

"Absolutely." She took a sip of water and the
shawl shifted on one side. She efficiently adjusted it.
Kai damned himself for immediately looking at
her cleavage.

The waiter appeared and rattled off the menu spe-
cials. Kai studied Sonya as she listened to the waiter's
selections. Her skin sure was flawless. Topping the
list of flavors to slather on her skin, Kai mentally
added Dollops of Whipped Cream and Caramel,
which he would place on the tips of her breasts, allowing her body heat to start the white foam to slowly
melt—

"And you, sir?"

Kai realized the waiter was ready for his order. Kai
randomly made a selection, reminding himself once
more that Sonya was guilty as sin of stealing from
helpless little old ladies. Perversely enough, that only
made him want to handcuff her to the bed before
delving into the whole whipped cream fantasy. He
sighed and shoved the tempting images away.

So what if she was sexy and the attraction off the
scope? He was a professional. He could handle it.
He would definitely handle it.

Once their orders were taken, they were left alone again.

This time when she smiled, the devil had switched the fantasy, making Kai the one with whipped cream on his body while she licked it off.

He groaned and tried to cover it up with a cough. *Enough.*

Playtime was over. He needed to get down to business. Whatever her game was, he was ready to play hardball—and win!

❧

Since it was taking all her acting skills to portray such sophisticated nonchalance, Sonya sincerely hoped Kai couldn't tell she was gawking. The handsome Mr. Armstrong was a far better candidate than she'd ever expected.

Approximately six foot four, with wide shoulders, a voice like bourbon, and a face that showed off his African ancestry like elegant art. A dimple on his right cheek begged to be licked, and to top it off, the man had a warrior's body that wouldn't quit. He filled out his suit like a bodyguard in a tux. And more than all that combined, she kept replaying the moment she'd felt his arousal nestled against her.

It had been so natural and spontaneous that instead of revulsion or panic, she felt . . . desired.

By far, it was the sexiest, most stimulating embrace she'd ever been in!

Lisa would absolutely flip.

If he looked this good in clothes, what would he

look like with them off?! A tiny part of Sonya was panicking. Men like him probably had closets full of notched belts.

So what? Wasn't she here to notch her own belt? And the man was practically heaven-sent. Lord knows his sex factor was off the chain, and ever since she'd first crashed into him her breathing kept doing a silly fluttering thing, refusing to return to normal.

Sonya glanced around nervously, her fingers toying with the confetti of Break-the-Ice questions that littered the tabletop, obviously provided to prompt conversation. She absently wondered if her acting skills were still as bad as when she was a child.

"Makes you wonder who came up with these questions, doesn't it?" he said, looking amused. "Want to take turns asking each other, 'What's your sign?'"

"My sign?" She couldn't even remember the last time she'd looked at a horoscope. "I don't know."

"Me, either. All right, then let's go with this one." He touched one with his long fingers. "What do you do for a living?"

Easy enough. "I'm an accountant. Not very exciting stuff."

"An accountant," he repeated, and for the life of her, it sounded like an exhilarating, daring occupation. "Taxes or bookkeeping?" *Silk or satin? Velvet or lace?*

Another blush threatened to blow her cool composure. "A little of both."

"Do you enjoy it?"

"I do, actually. It's sometimes tricky to make numbers balance. But on the positive slant, some of my clients are surprised by how mismanaged and unorganized their accounts were before they gave me their business."

He nodded and rested his fork on his plate.

"How about you?"

"I'm in the repo business."

"Repo?"

"Repossessions." He shrugged. "It pays the rent." But he didn't expand further.

Sonya took a sip of chilled wine, trying to imagine Kai on the job. Exactly how did one confront strangers to inform them they'd defaulted on payments and would now have to return their goods? She'd bet he could look like an intimidating brute if he wanted to. Just the thought of him doing some sweaty roughhousing was enough to—

"How's your salad?" an inquiring waiter interrupted.

Sonya kept her gaze on her plate, aiming to look glamorous rather than guilty of an illicit mental quickie. "The salad is delicious. Thank you."

Kai murmured a similar comment.

The piano and sax music filled in the brief pause with a Sammy Davis Jr. tune while the waiter proceeded to serve the main dish with professional exuberance.

Sonya caught Kai's gaze over the candle and felt a flutter in her gut. The dark hues in his eyes changed so suddenly, she searched again, wondering if she'd imagined it.

"Is this your first cruise?" he asked.

She sipped more wine, hoping she oozed calm

sophistication. "Actually, I've never been on a cruise before, but it sounded much more adventurous and exciting than the stay-at-home vacations I normally take."

"And how exactly does an accountant define 'adventurous and exciting'? Do you let the numbers fall out of balance a little, move the decimal point over too far, or forget to carry the one over?" His smile was full of teasing charm.

She clung to her wineglass with one hand while strangling the napkin in her lap with the other. "I guess it's the equivalent of all that."

Putting on her best performance, she continued, "And if the numbers fall out of balance, so to speak, then so much the better, right?"

The way he watched her lips was almost tangible. "Anything I can do to help you out?" he asked, his dimple showing.

His eyes held hers and Sonya's heart skipped a beat. Could he mean what she was thinking? "That depends. How do *you* define excitement?"

He took a moment to think about it. "Fun. Memorable. Wet."

"Wet?" A myriad of implications blazed through her mind.

The candle between them flickered. "I could define that for you if you like."

She managed a careless chuckle while holding down her anxiety. *Think sexy!* "I sure hope you don't mean scuba diving."

Man, she sounded like one of those 1-900-number girls!

His left eyebrow went up and his look became so heated, she felt as if he'd moved to just inches away from her. "Depends on the body of water."

Breathe. . . .

His smile crept into a more intimate grin. "I'd say that most men's fantasies have to do with some form of moisture. Sweat, for example."

The wine she'd been sipping pooled in her mouth and she had to remind herself to swallow.

"Am I being too forward?" he asked.

Yes! "Not at all. Your boldness is refreshing."

"So is yours."

"Although," she ran her fingers up the stem of her wineglass, "I have to wonder whether your, um, services are exaggerated or if you're just quite the smooth talker."

"Worried I'm all words and no action?"

The urge to fan herself was overwhelming. By the intense gleam in his eyes she knew he was testing her, so she replied, "Well, the kind of action I enjoy requires stamina."

He did it again, moving his thumb over the crest of the glass as if it were her breast. "Glad to hear it."

Go, girl! Double or nothing. "Can you handle seven whole days?"

"And seven whole nights."

"Verbally impressive."

"Ms. Drummond. I promise you I don't start anything I can't finish."

She didn't care if he noticed her gulp down her wine that time. "I may have to hold you to that."

"I'm looking forward to it."

The tension in her gut fluttered. Was she out of her mind? How was she ever going to go through with this?

The wine was all but buzzing through her veins, the world was fading behind her boldness, and she was acting out her role for all she was worth. "Mr. Armstrong, just to be perfectly clear, does this mean you'll provide, um, stud services for the duration of this cruise?"

With a slight flick of her wrist, the wine in his glass started to spiral a ruby funnel. "That's correct. With the condition that we feel free to indulge in each other's fantasies, Ms. Drummond."

It was an absolute crime that the waiters interrupted to serve the meal.

❦

The trapped look in Sonya's eyes intrigued Kai more than her words had jolted him.

She smiled ever so carefully. "Mr. Armstrong—"

"Kai," he corrected. How many fools had gladly handed over their money when she'd flashed that sultry smile?

"Kai." She peered at him through her fabulous lashes. "I have so many fantasies. Where do I start?"

The devil in his pants suddenly came to attention like a student raising his hand, desperate to shout the answer. *Pick me! Pick me!*

Once again, the waiter chose that moment to appear and serve up a side dish, which, for all Kai cared, might as well have been imported Norwegian chalk.

He eased back in his chair for marginal comfort, waiting for the man to leave, but when he did, only the soft piano notes filled the tension.

"Well?" Kai prompted.

"Unlike your, um, wet fantasies, Kai, mine have to do with hard heat," she confessed huskily.

Kai wanted to pull her into his lap and make her whisper her fantasies into his ear, detail by detail. Hot. Hard. Heat. Slippery wet. *All* of them!

Her scarf slipped a little, framing another golden wink from the necklace. Yeah, that too.

"Kai . . ." She seemed to have trouble saying his name. "I think we should also discuss any," she paused, "basic restrictions. Limitations."

"Such as?" He glanced at his plate and tried to show interest in the tiny salad.

"I'd like to restrict this game to only ourselves. No third parties."

"Not a problem."

She poked her fork at the beautiful layout of her meal but only took a small bite. "And if one of us doesn't like where things are going, we have to respect that."

"I would never make you do anything you wouldn't want me to." For as much as his mind was barking orders about business, Kai knew he couldn't walk away from her without sampling what she was freely planning.

The soft candlelight played against her face, enhancing a ghost of a flush that made her look both demure and seductive. Man, oh, man.

"Want to add anything?" she asked, shifting the damned scarf again.

"Sure. How about we up the stakes with a prize?"

"Such as?"

"The first one to back down from a challenge automatically forfeits and loses, and has to give the winner a token of his—or her—choice."

She seemed to be thinking about it, then asked somewhat breathlessly, "Define *challenge*."

He shrugged. "Truth or Dare?"

She paused, and he watched her exhale slowly. "OK."

He winked. "Glad you agree to the terms."

She caressed the rim of her wineglass. "I can be quite competitive."

Maybe so, but this was one game he planned to win. "I'd like to think that I am as well, Ms. Drummond. You'll find that I'm the kind of man who finishes what he starts."

A fragile chime of clinking glass called their attention to the captain, who stood and raised his wineglass and toasted everyone to a "fun and romantic cruise."

"More wine, ma'am?" the waiter asked.

Sonya was about to murder him. Why did he keep showing up when she needed him not to?

She checked her attitude and returned his smile. *Absolutely my last glass of wine,* she told herself.

She made one more stab at keeping the shawl in place. Taking her wineglass, she raised it. It was now or never!

"To stud services," she murmured confidently.

Sonya felt as if the world had stopped in shock at her boldness, waiting on the edge of their collective seats for his reply.

The slow turn of his lips made a formidable smile. " 'Stud services' gives the impression that you have the edge in this game, and the truth is . . . I always play to win."

Ha! Sonya could practically hear herself panting. As horny as she was, he would need good medical coverage and a skilled chiropractor by the end of the week.

He leaned back, too. "That OK with you?"

There was the million-dollar question. The answer trembled on her breath for half a second. "Yes."

By his cocky expression Sonya could only assume that he was already daydreaming about accepting his trophy.

She touched her wineglass to his. "A toast then. To our special game."

"May the best lover win." The pristine clinking of their wineglasses punctuated his comment.

Sonya felt trapped in his gaze, the murmur of conversation around them faded for a pause. It was done!

Her teeth clicked against the wineglass when she sealed the toast with a nervous sip of wine. She hadn't really believed she'd do it, but there she was, the fling all but inked on paper!

The bubbly excitement kept expanding in her. As the chilled wine made its way down her throat, Sonya suddenly wondered if she'd just sealed a wet deal with a hot devil.

FIVE

KAI CAUGHT THE moment of uncertainty as it
crossed her features. Perfect. As long as she didn't
know he had the upper hand, this was going to be fun.

"Tell you what," he said, playing his next card.
"I'll even let you go first."

She paused from drinking, savoring it. "How
very kind. Thank you."

"You're welcome."

His gut clenched again when she licked her lips
and narrowed her eyes at him. The mental image of
her on the bed, eyes closed in near ecstasy, flashed
through his mind.

"OK, Truth or Dare?" she asked politely.

"Truth." Not that Dare was out of the question in
a public restaurant, but . . . *Let's see what you've
got, sugar.*

She paused. "I need to know about your bill of
health."

"Ah." Well, that wasn't what he'd been expecting.

It was smart, though. Caution trumped recklessness any old day.

"We did agree on truth, right?"

The fact that she, a lying thief, could say "truth" without wincing was to be admired. Regardless, her eyes searched his.

"Yes," he replied. "The *truthful* answer is I'm healthy. Never had an STD and I donate blood regularly. I'm not allergic to latex, either."

Sonya smiled in what could only be controlled relief. "The same goes for me. I work near a blood bank, so I go whenever they need me." She eyed her wineglass. "I'm on birth control pills, too."

"Hmm. Good."

"OK, Kai." Her chin raised a tiny bit. "Your turn."

The devil in him hovered gleefully over the scoreboard. "Truth or Dare?"

Kai could see the pulse beating right next to her dangling earring as she undoubtedly contemplated her answer. "Dare."

Several risqué scenarios piled up on the tip of his tongue, but he discarded most of them, deciding to start things off slowly. "The shawl. Let it go."

After the slightest hesitation, she raised her hands to her shoulders and parted the overlapping shawl, allowing it to slide to her elbows. Like an opening stage curtain, it revealed the elusive butterfly necklace right in the middle of the lickable smooth skin he couldn't get out of his mind.

He marked the rise and fall of her elevated breathing, admiring the way the deep-cut dress damn near revealed all but her perked nipples.

At this rate, his erection was going to have serious seam marks. "Thank you."

Her breasts were outstanding, lush, with a cleavage that made him want to dip his tongue there.

With the slightest movement of air, a waiter was
back at their table. After a noticeable pause, the
flustered man immediately turned to the ready-made
tray of desserts he carried and began to describe
them.

Kai selected the melon dessert.

So did Sonya.

The waiter departed.

Kai watched her eat the dessert without saying
another word. The way she held her spoon between
her lips kept the devil in him straining at the chains.

"Nice weather we're having, don't you think?"
she asked politely.

Small talk. Great. Well, in light of their earlier
conversation, it would help bank the embers a bit.

🦋

" 'S a beautiful night," Sonya mumbled.

"Yes, it is." Kai managed to stifle the uncomfortable emotion that kept nudging him. Ms. Sonya
Drummond didn't quite stagger, but she was being
very, *very* careful with every step she took.

After leaving the dining room, he'd put his arm
around her shoulders, more to keep the danged
shawl from showing her goods to the world than
anything else. If she couldn't remember him in the
morning, that would work to his advantage if he

needed to establish an alibi. The less conspicuous they were strolling out on the deck, the better.

Besides, the way she was moving was distracting him plenty. He felt like he could use two extra hands to keep her walking in a straight line and still keep her shawl in place.

After all, what were stud-service providers for?

They strolled the outer decks, their bodies brushing, the chill of the night barely cooling his body heat.

When they came to the outer hallway of the cabins, she paused by the railing of the deck. "Dare?"

"What, no Truth?" he teased.

The paleness of the moon spilled in and illuminated her smooth skin, turning it into a sepia temptation. His mouth went dry, hungry for the taste of her, to nuzzle her skin, there in the arch of her cheek, at the pulse at her throat, and most definitely in the decadent display of cleavage. He'd bet the warmth of her blushes made her skin taste like sin. How could a woman who was so unethical and devious blush like such a saint?

"I want youuuu to take the Dare."

Oh yeah, she was slurring. "Dare me, then."

Sonya peered up at him from beneath her long eyelashes, causing his smile to slip.

The devil went on a rampage. Hell, she was lit. Some women looked cheap and tired when they were lit, but Sonya looked like she'd just had a quickie in a coat closet. Sexy and soused. A dangerous combination.

Still, the chemistry between them was like a live wire. Her eyes hid none of it.

She whispered something he didn't catch.

He leaned toward her. "What was that?"

She tucked a lock of hair behind her ear and he noticed her hand trembling slightly. "I dare you to kiss me. Right here, right now—"

Kai sucked the last word right off her lips, his tongue delving against hers, her breath trapped. She instantly reacted by clutching him and responding.

Her weak moan drove him to sink his fingers into her hair with one hand and pull her closer to the planes of his body with the other. It was an effort to try to get a grip on his desire and set the pace.

She tasted even better than he'd imagined . . . wine and melon, heat and need. It was like tasting something forbidden. The world receded until he couldn't hear anything but her single soft moan, could feel nothing but her subtle surrender, until time whirled around them and they were both gasping for breath. A slight tremor transferred from her body to his, settling into the tightening, hard weight of his arousal.

"Oh my. . . ." She blinked dreamily at him, a drowsy, drunken expression on her face.

Oh, shit! Kai closed his eyes and tried to force the blindsiding passion from searing through his remaining logic.

Attraction or not, he wasn't about to take advantage of a drunk woman. He was willing to be her stud-service provider, but he sure as hell wasn't going to cross the line and take advantage of her this way. If she were much more sober, he'd have no problem, but she was completely lit.

However . . . it didn't mean he couldn't take strategic advantage.

He nestled his face into her cleavage, inhaling, then licked the soft, perfumed display. His tongue flicked under the crest of skin, nuzzling the swell of flesh, kissing toward the left mound until the dress slipped and the nipple slipped into his mouth.

"Oh . . . !" It was barely a sound.

He sucked gently, then harder, enjoying the tremor he felt coursing delicately through her body. Earlier, he'd imagined the taste of her breasts, but now, with her warm skin under his tongue, he realized he hadn't counted on whatever peach-and-vanilla lotion she'd rubbed on her body. The combination was more wicked . . . far more decadent than any five-star dessert.

He searched out the flavor, indulged in it, licking, kissing, and suckling a path to her other breast until he'd tasted that nipple, too.

"God . . . oh . . . Kai. . . ." Her fingers flexed against his chest.

The remaining logic was steadily slipping into the haze. He reined it in and kissed her on the mouth again; this time he brushed his hand casually over the back of her neck, trying to place the clasp of the gold chain.

Sonya arched against him, her hips rocking slow and urgent against his erection in the timeless, unmistakable invitation for sex.

He hadn't meant to utter an expletive, but in the heat of the moment he'd reacted instinctively, returning the pelvic motion, but the movement caused his fingers to fumble the necklace and the jeweled butterfly fell neatly into her cleavage just as he pulled her in tight.

"Ow!" Sonya pushed back, bare breasts heaving, eyes still glazed with passion. She looked down, blinked in confusion, then rescued the necklace.

Pulling on all his acting abilities, Kai frowned as well. "How the hell did that happen?"

"Don't know." Her other arm was still around his shoulders, and the sex-crazed part of him knew that in a few calculated moves he could have the upper hand again. If not for her inebriation, he could have her dress up, his pants down, and be buried deep inside her. . . .

He bit back a groan.

One-handed, Sonya gathered the necklace into her palm.

Kai jerked his mind back on his job and gave her an innocent look. "Want me to hold it for you?"

She was still breathing pretty heavily, obviously working hard to recover. "No, that's OK."

Damn!

She reached up to kiss him again, but he avoided her, blaming himself for not having slowed her drinking earlier.

"What?"

"You're drunk, honey."

Sonya immediately tensed, her expression changing to cool indignation and embarrassment.

"Nope. Jussa little tipsy," she said quietly. "I feel fine. Honest."

The devil in Kai was continuously smacking its forehead against a granite slab. "Honey, you *feel* so much better than just fine, but we both know you're not."

Sonya eyed his lips, her own still puffy from the hard kisses. "But—"

Kai touched a finger to her lips, detaining her from her mission. The contact was warm and her remaining words trembled there.

He pulled his hand back. "I started this, and I intend to finish it. But you made the rule about respecting each other and we agreed to play by the rules."

With the necklace in her clutch, Sonya tucked the stubborn strand of hair behind her ear again, and a gem in the dangling butterfly pendant caught the light again. "Of course."

An icy trickle of guilt came at him from nowhere. The words *Truth or Dare* mocked him. How far was he bound by the truth? How much did he dare to venture into the gray areas of ethics?

In that instant he dearly wished she were the kind of low-life crook he could've physically taken down, wrung the truth out of, then hauled back to San Diego. If she'd been legally convicted of a crime, he wouldn't have been wrestling with the logical or ethical aspects of innocence.

"I guess this is good night then," Sonya said.

Kai ignored the parts of his body that screamed for reprieve. He regretfully looked at her lovely breasts, then adjusted her clothes into some semblance of propriety. "Yeah."

He rubbed his jaw, the sensuous taste of her still lingering on his tongue. Their eyes met again and he held the look, reveling in the sweet need there.

Sonya blushed and looked away, panting quietly, with such polite restraint that it tied him up in slip-knots.

Echoing down the hallways, the pounding of some far-off conga drums escalated and a woman's squeal was followed by laughter and cheers. Kai felt like growling as he stepped back.

"Let me walk you to your room."

She shrugged. "No need to." Her eyes sparked soberly even though she seemed to hold on to the stair rail for dear life.

"I insist."

This time, their clothes didn't so much as touch. Even her walking was defiant. By the time they reached her door, Kai was sure he'd done the right thing. Only morning would tell.

He brushed his lips against hers. "Good night, Sonya."

"Good night."

One last kiss, he told himself. One last one to let her know he hadn't lost interest. He brushed her lips again, just long enough to hear her sigh of longing. The very tip of her tongue flicked over his bottom lip, starting to pull him under again.

It wasn't until she'd disappeared into her room that he deciphered the words she whispered before the mind-altering kisses.

Carpe diem.

SIX

EARLY THE NEXT morning, Kai finished his sit-ups, flipped, and did push-ups, then reached for his phone to check in with his brother.

"Hey," Dre answered.

"How's it coming along?"

Dre yawned loudly before answering. "Sampling Margaritas."

"Great. Drinking on the job. What else you got?"

"I wasn't talking about drinks," Dre chuckled, and in the background a woman giggled. "But on to Otis. Found his Visa was used at a casino on the outskirts of Las Vegas."

"Where the Margaritas are?"

"Yup. In any case, he's in his room now and I'm a couple of doors down. I'm putting together the Plan A Nab Attack."

Dre, always the man with a plan. "Try not to let your Margaritas get in the way."

"Never do."

Kai nodded because it was true. Dre always got the job done. "Think you'll wrap it up soon?"

"By tomorrow for sure."

"Cool. I'll let you do your thing. Call me when you have Otis in custody."

"Alrighty."

Kai hung up, trusting that his brother had the situation in control. It would be nice if one of them was in control of something. If last night was any indication, Kai wasn't sure he was in control of very much at all.

❧

Next Kai made the obligatory call to Old Lady Miller to update her on the case.

"Andre has followed Mr. Otis Drummond's trail into Las Vegas, but I wouldn't be surprised if Otis was making his way to Mexico," he explained.

"I'd like those plans thwarted, you understand," she said haughtily.

Thwarted? He'd have to use that one on Dre. "We aim to please."

"Good. And the necklace?" her voice demanded over static.

"It will be delivered by the end of the week," he promised.

"I certainly hope so."

He grinned. The old biddy always had to have the last word, but she had a heart of gold. Ever since her home had burned down months ago, she'd become fiercely protective of her remaining items, which made the crime of stealing her necklace seem even worse.

They agreed on the next date and time to call, then hung up.

With the phone back in its cradle, Kai's thoughts turned back to Sonya like a message in a bottle carried by waves back to shore. Last night he'd tossed in bed, replaying her replies to questions, looking for clues in her answers, but had come up with nothing. His body, however, had been stuck on aroused with Kai unwilling to take matters into his own hands.

In the end, he'd handled it, feeling weak for giving in and annoyed with himself for not being able to figure out why Sonya Drummond triggered such a strong physical response from him.

He hadn't drunk too much wine. She wasn't a dazzling beauty, although there was something beautiful and alluring about her features. And despite how hard he fought it, she was steadily becoming more tempting.

Kai absently massaged his bum knee.

Aw, hell. She was simply a project and he'd do what he needed to in order to get his job done. She was a means to an end, nothing more, nothing less.

The purpose of the cruise was to get to the necklace and maybe steal a few secrets and kisses along the way, the latter being fringe benefits.

But it was her kisses that stuck with him the most. What was it about the way she'd done that licking

thing with her tongue, then softly bitten his lower lip
when they'd paused for breath? Just thinking about
it was stirring up the latent passion.

Kai pushed off his bed. It wasn't the time to ap-
preciate Ms. Drummond's kissing skills. Enough
was enough.

It was Day Two. Time for a new and improved
plan. A simple plan. To steal the necklace, search
her cabin for a cash-flow clue, and then split. If that
didn't pan out, he'd be back to square one.

Kai threw on a tank top, running shorts, and
shoes, quickly checking the daily schedule for the
gym. Five minutes later, he had warmed up but decided to leave the meat-market atmosphere of the
gym in favor of the running track on deck.

Despite his sunglasses, the daylight was almost
blinding. Under a sky that was like hard blue ice, the
ocean rippled silver-black, flowing like mercury as
far as the eye could see.

When Kai was on his fourth lap around the deck,
he spotted Sonya through one of the large windows
of the buffet room. She was standing in line, wearing a blue sundress and dark sunglasses. From his
angle, it looked like she wasn't wearing the necklace, but he couldn't be sure. Still, it gave him a sudden spurt of hope.

Next to her, a muscle-head with a flattop and
neon white smile was telling her something that
made her laugh. He leaned closer as she served up
something on her plate.

Kai came to a stop and huffed in air, annoyed

with himself for wanting to walk up to the idiot and knock him overboard. Instead Kai looked away, pretending not to see her.

Kai stretched his lats and quads before he became aware that a female jogger had also stopped to stretch beside him. Stacked. Definitely cute. Her clothes and body were tight, and everything about her said she was interested.

He smiled politely and moved on before she could start up a conversation.

He rushed back to his cabin, grabbed his electronic skeleton key card from where he'd hidden it in his suitcase, and went around the corner to Sonya's room. A sense of déjà vu came over him at the memory of their bodies colliding outside this very door. Worse, his ever-aroused body responded to the memory and he could've sworn her scent still lingered in the air.

Suddenly worried that she might be back from the buffet, Kai inhaled, testing the air, but could no longer detect her scent.

"Mind's playing tricks on me," he grumbled in disgust.

He checked up and down the deserted hall and then slipped the skeleton card into the slot. The unlocking mechanism engaged and he pushed the door open.

Once inside, he gave himself only a few minutes to search. Sonya was organized to the point of being neurotic. Everything seemed to have its place. He thought how naive it was to leave her suitcase unlocked, making it easy to rummage through. Or was that all part of her plan?

Her suitcase was new, her clothes folded as neat as layered tiles. From the bottom a gold-and-peach patch of lingerie caught his attention, and he tugged it out. It was a hot lace number that would hide absolutely nothing from view. Classy, yet elegant and sexy. A con artist with expensive taste. But then, he already knew that.

He put it back, but the image was already burned into his mind.

Business, dammit!

Under a few more clothes, his eyes lit on the yellow satin shawl from last night, and he couldn't resist rubbing the fabric in his hands, raising it to his nose, and inhaling.

Ah, yes. There it was. Her damned scent. Linen, vanilla, and cream. The flavor had been calibrated just right by the heat of her skin and tasted like . . .

His penis twitched.

He carefully repacked the items and moved his fingers around to the back of the suitcase, searching with his fingertips for any hidden latches. Instead he found a Bon Voyage card with the message: "Don't forget to rock the boat while you are carpe dieming!" scribbled on the inside next to the signature "Lisa."

So there it was. *Carpe diem.* Seize the day. Did this mean there was yet another accomplice in the embezzlement venture? It was something to consider. He looked for more notes but couldn't find any.

Kai searched the rest of the room, checking everywhere, from the light fixtures to her shoes.

Nothing.

He frowned, looked around one last time, then left to finish his laps around the deck.

SEVEN

SHE WAS STANDING in the buffet line when she spotted Kai out on the deck and quickly realized she'd seriously underestimated him. Last night, Kai Armstrong had looked impressive in a formal suit. This morning, in his jogging attire, he was just plain sinful.

With the cop sunglasses, angular features, and clean-shaven head, bare chest, and dark shorts, he looked like a special-ops marine in training. His strides were long, his pace hard. He looked mean and lean.

Subtly dangerous.

It was a pleasure to just sit back and watch him run. The pain of the hangover receded, so, hidden by a leafy plant, she watched him. Once. Twice. And after the third lap around, he disappeared.

She waited awhile, but when it became apparent that he wouldn't show, Sonya reluctantly returned to her cabin.

The message light on her phone welcomed her, announcing itself like a tiny lighthouse. Sonya picked up the phone and pressed the necessary buttons to retrieve the message.

"Hi there." Kai's voice was deep and gentle. She smiled. "Thought you might have a bit of a hangover, so I booked a masseuse for you at the Golden Starfish Spa. Starts at, ahh . . ." There was a pause and the sound of rustling paper. ". . . three o'clock. Afterward, if you feel up to it, we could do dinner?" Another pause followed, as if he was uncomfortable with answering machines. "OK. I'll call ya."

Sonya's stomach did a silly flutter and she replayed the message. This was about the sweetest, most thoughtful thing a guy had ever done for her.

Either that, or the man was more desperate than she was to get laid.

Hours later, Sonya had managed to shed her inhibitions and now lay in the center of a petit silk hammock that was suspended in the middle of a deep hot tub. Small towels covered her breasts and hips, and a masseur was working her arms while aromatic water filled the specialized tub. There was the delicate chime of water drizzling over copper bells that was almost ceremonial.

And what a tub! It had been fascinating to watch the huge cling wrap used on the interior of the tub before it had been turbo-filled. Every customer got the plastic job, for their "hygienic protection," the staff assured her. A tub condom.

It was hea-ven! If this was Kai's idea of a wet adventure, she was all for it.

Before being taken to the hot tub, Sonya had been stretched on a massage table, and every kink, joint, and muscle had been soothed and melted until she'd felt like a boneless blob. And now this? How much had Kai spent?

She was half-awake, half-asleep, when the tepid water rose to cover her all the way to her chin. The wet towels, along with the weightlessness of the water hammock, gave her a sense of intimate serenity.

The masseur said in a whispering tone that he would be back in fifteen minutes, then he left her alone with the soft trickle of water for company.

Moments later, when the door opened, Sonya opened one eye a peek but wasn't prepared to see Kai saunter up to her in swim trunks and one of the thin shirts that the spa provided. Shocked, Sonya almost sat straight up but remembered in the nick of time that she was supposed to be in the Skilled Seductress mode.

"You sure look relaxed," he said into the quiet.

"Thanks to you." His shirt was parted and she could see the contours of his chest. His breathing was steady, but his eyes were making her hot and tingly in a whole new way.

He pointedly looked at her necklace. "You were supposed to be completely naked."

Sonya resisted the urge to squirm and make sure the tiny towels were still covering her privates.

"Yes, well, this may be a fine establishment, but you can never be too careful. I would've hated for it to get misplaced or stolen, so I asked if I could wear it and . . ." She ended there rather than embarrass herself further by rambling on like an idiot.

Kai's smile widened further as he stepped into the tub until the water reached his waist. He stood just inches from where she was lying. The water settled around her in ringlets of tiny eddies.

Muscles that had been as limp as a noodle earlier now began to tense in anticipation.

"What are you doing?" The words came out sounding worried rather than calm, like she'd hoped.

"Right now, nothing at all." He grinned. "But if you take the necklace off, I'll be more than happy to give you a neck massage, or if you take the towels off, I can do a body massage, or . . . you can take off whatever you like and I'll give you whatever you like."

Sonya's fingers moved to the butterfly. "Whatever I like?"

He raised an eyebrow. "Did the masseur miss any spots?"

She wanted to squeeze her thighs together to hold back the heat that was seeping there. "It's a shame, really. You spent all that money and you know, they did miss a few important ones."

"Imagine that," he murmured conversationally. Then with hands on his hips, he scanned her body from head to toe. "Truth or Dare?"

She should've known he would sneak in his turn! What would she answer? A Dare was simply too blatant. It would be like begging for sex, and Lord knows a sophisticated woman would take the more intriguing, tantalizing route.

Chicken. . . .

"Truth."

He lifted her foot from underwater and held it just barely over his waistline, hovering over the bulge of his crotch. "Is it true that feet are one of your more sensitive erogenous zones?"

Maybe. She wiggled her toes. They sure felt sensitive when they were being scrubbed, cleaned, and massaged earlier.

"Come on, lady. The truth."

The towel covering her hips shifted slightly when the low-level jets cycled on. "The contact borders on ticklish."

Kai lifted her foot higher and placed it against the sprinkling of hair on his chest. He kept massaging her foot. "More ticklish than erotic?"

"I've actually never—"

He placed his mouth against the instep of her foot and sucked gently.

"Oh!" The contact sparked a jolt of tingles that arrowed right up her inner thigh and straight to her vagina.

"Did that tickle?"

"Oh, um, no. . . ." *God, no!*

He licked the arch of her foot, then sank a soft bite on the sensitive nerve there. Sonya bit back a groan and reflexively tried to pull her foot.

"Relax," he coaxed.

As if she could!

"Tastes minty."

"They did this peppermint foot therapy thing that . . ."

Kai kissed the arch of her foot, his tongue making swirls and licks, his lips moving as he whispered things against her skin.

Sonya shifted in the hammock, her hands shifting against nothing but water when what she really wanted was something more substantial, like bedsheets. Or manly muscles.

Kai's mouth slanted at a different angle to her ankle as he slid one hand down her calf . . . to the back of her knee . . . then lower . . .

"Oh-ummmm—" Sonya covered her mouth with the back of her hand. Her shifting motions had caused tiny waves to tug the towels away from where they should've been.

Kai went on his knees in the water, placing her leg on his shoulder and continuing to work his mouth from her calf to her knee, licking and lapping his way to the delicate skin there.

Meanwhile, his hand gathered water and leisurely dripped it over her thigh, then slid over the slick surface, upward, then downward, slowing until his knuckles brushed her pubic hair.

"Kai . . ." Sonya closed her eyes and waited, aching, barely breathing. She heard a cranking sound and felt the hammock lift her body above the waterline.

When she dared to look at him, his gaze fused with hers, the intensity of need unmistakable. He reached toward her and removed her hand from her mouth, letting it fall back into the water.

He knelt back down.

Oh, Lord!

Sonya closed her eyes again and couldn't help tensing as his lips and nibbles led him down her inner thigh, to the spot where her leg and hip met. Oh, heavens, he was less than an inch from it. When he exhaled, she could feel the warmth on her sex. It was almost intolerable to have to withstand his open-mouthed kisses when all he had to do was move his tongue around just a little bit more . . .

"Please, please, please," she begged.

Suddenly she was shifted on the silk with both her legs on his shoulders and his hands moving over her outer thighs to her hips. His mouth! Oh, his sensuous, clever mouth sealed over her sex in the most intimate kiss.

"Kai!"

Sonya arched, colors whirling behind her eyes when his tongue delved past the folds of her sex and stirred her senseless. He licked and kissed her as if she were a pot of honey, tearing her breath with each lick, curl, and roll of his tongue, rocking her in the water to create waves that could only be broken one way.

"Oh—" His tongue teased her clitoris, swirled around it, then lapped it up like a cat. His shoulder muscles tensed and bunched. "Kai— Jes— Oh!"

The weightless rhythm was devastating. Sonya grunted, her legs gripping his head when she tried to hold back.

Kai hummed or growled, doing something that vibrated right from his mouth and lips to the tip of his tongue as it still penetrated her. The orgasm yanked right through her, trapping her, suspended on the water, his mouth completely dominating her.

Her whole body trembled, quivering . . . quivering . . . soundlessly exploding in a million tiny waves . . . floating away.

Like ripples of water settling, Sonya became aware of what had just happened.

From the haze of serenity she heard Kai's strained grunt, too, felt the sharp gush of his breath, and felt the tremble where his mouth still kissed her.

For endless seconds all she could hear was their harsh, raspy breathing and the water lapping against the edges of the tub.

She didn't even protest when Kai tugged her from the silk hammock so that it caressed her back when she tumbled limply into his lap, still straddling him. The towels had long since fallen away, and the fact that he was clothed and she was wearing nothing but a necklace made her feel vulnerable and overly exposed in his arms.

Kai sighed into the crook of her neck.

Two sharp raps on the door startled her. "Sir, two minutes!" came the stage whisper.

"Damn," Kai mumbled.

Between their bodies, Sonya felt the slinky trail of her necklace as it fell over her breasts and into his shirt.

"My necklace!" She reached down and retrieved it, his hand briefly covering hers.

The mood suddenly turned, leaving her feeling awkward, trying to think of some way to cover her body from view. It was easier to study the clasp than to wonder why she felt the need to immediately find a large towel.

"Don't know why this thing keeps falling off. Must be the clasp."

Kai kissed her on the lips, brief and hard. "If I'm not out of here in the next minute, I'm going to be in some deep trouble. I'll pick you up for dinner and jazz at eight."

"Um, that sounds great."

He got out of the tub, grabbed a towel, and was gone.

Sonya sprang into action, too, and bundled up in a robe, knowing it was impossible to let anyone else touch her at this point.

Blushing furiously, Sonya made her apologies to the masseur for having to leave early. It probably didn't help that she couldn't even make eye contact with him, for crying out loud.

So much for cool sophistication.

Kai paced the confines of his cabin, absently rubbing his chest, wondering how he could've fumbled the necklace *again*.

It had been right there in his hand. Perfect for the picking!

By all rights, it should've been easier than that. She should've taken it off along with her clothes for the initial massages, but then, wouldn't you know it, she got twitchy.

He sighed and scratched his chin. The chemistry between them was crazy. Wild-humping crazy.

Maybe it was because he finally had his chance to live out part of the fantasy that had obsessed him since the day in the closet when he'd seen her pleasuring herself. He'd been able to kiss some of the places that devious plastic butterfly had taken, and it had only made him ravenous to taste the rest.

And she'd been deliciously wet.

He'd taken a sweet satisfaction in knowing that no matter how good an actress she was, there was an unrehearsed innocence in the way she'd enjoyed the sex. There was a newness, a virginlike surprise, to the way she'd cried out and trembled. She'd cried his name, husky and desperate. It made him hard all over again just thinking about it.

If he could've had about half an hour more . . .

His mind veered away from the thought.

It was enough to know she'd been his. Her limbs, her taste, her unraveling control. His hunger should've been sated, but now he was intrigued, his appetite rearing up again.

He wanted more.

And as long as she didn't have too much wine at dinner to compromise his principles, he planned on getting his fill of her tonight, once and for all.

And this time he wouldn't fumble the damned necklace, either.

🦋

A sense of déjà vu overcame Sonya when she found herself under the cold spray of the shower, berating herself again. "What a tramp!"

There had to be ten thousand ways to say, *Forget jazz, Kai. Please, come to my room and make love until we're ready to pass out.*

By the time she'd finished showering, she'd come up with twenty lines that would have worked.

She took extra pains with her appearance. Her hair, for one thing, was driving her crazy. There was no choice on what style suited her best, really, but agonizing over it kept her from wondering what she would say when he knocked on her door.

Thanks to Lisa, there was a large selection of gowns to pick from. Snug, clinging gowns. Way-too-small gowns.

Sonya tried several on before settling on the plum gown with a high collar and swooping low back. From the front, it looked conservative, elegant, and the butterfly necklace stood out nicely. The gold work of the butterfly trailed around the gems and displayed them beautifully.

From behind, the dress was as daring as she could ever hope to get, sloping against the very crest of her butt.

She only prayed that there was no acquaintance from back home to see her flaunting herself.

Those days of working out before the cruise now paid off with the exception of a couple of stubborn pounds on her hips. Those, she figured, had been handed down through generations and, well, were something she was just going to have to be proud of.

Besides, this wasn't about free milk and a cow, so to speak. It was more like no fence and a bull.

She grinned before remembering she still hadn't done her makeup. Lisa's instructions, which had been so painstakingly taught, only made Sonya feel like a clown. So after the third time of removing and applying the makeup, she settled on a swap of lipstick and a touch of eye shadow.

A dab of musk-based perfume went on each of her pulse points, from ankle, to wrist, back of the knees, front of the elbows, then the base of her neck.

Don't think. Just do it!

After a brief hesitation, she rubbed a tiny bit on the topmost part of her pubic hair, then avoided her reflection as she put her makeup case away.

What next?

Condoms. Shopping with Lisa had made Sonya overly optimistic, so she'd purchased a variety of them. Probably more than she needed. She shoved four into her purse, then added another one, just in case.

All her swirling, pent-up cravings simmered just under her skin.

As if on cue, a knock sounded at her door.

One quick look in the mirror confirmed she was the new Sonya, sleek and stylish, each hair in place.

Her eyes, though, were the old her. Nervous and unsure. Closing them briefly, she eased herself into the role of the cool sophisticate.

"It's just a little jazz, maybe some dancing," she whispered to herself. "And please-oh-please, a whole lotta sex. . . ."

She reached for the knob and opened the door.

Kai had his hand raised as if to knock again. At the sight of him, Sonya's heart started double-knocking against her ribs. Here was the man who had kissed her the night before, the hunk in a classic suit. The gentleman who had been considerate and kept a cool head even when she'd thrown herself at him. This man, bold, black, and beautiful, barely resembled the marine jogger she'd seen that morning. Nor did he really look like the lover who had seduced her in one of his wet oral fantasies in a hot tub, a man with almost savage passion.

This man could easily break her heart.

"Hi," he said.

"Hi."

His gaze swept over her, from the straps of her shoes to the loose shift of the plum-colored dress where it gathered over her hips. He openly studied the way it draped over her unbound breasts, and his gaze kept going upward, past the dignified collar. The hues of his pupils changed as he looked at her lips, nose, then eyes.

Oh, my . . .

Sonya felt the burn of intent clear to her bones. He knew what she wanted and was going to give it to her, pure and simple. Her nipples became hard and tingly, and her mouth went dry.

"Beautiful," he murmured.

Sonya felt it. Natural and womanly, alive in her skin the way no man had made her feel before. His gaze shifted to a place over her shoulder and she heard his groaned intake of breath. She turned to look, and their gazes collided in the mirror that revealed her naked back.

"Truth or Dare?" she managed, turning to face him.

If possible, the heat in his eyes doubled. "Dare."

"Come in here . . ."

He waited.

". . . and give me . . ." *my fantasy.*

Without a word, Kai stepped inside, slowly took the knob from her hand, and deliberately closed the door. He stood behind her, unmoving, and she simply couldn't make herself turn around to face him.

Kai's breath brushed over her skin, and peripherally she could see the mirror reflect his image as he lowered his head to place a raspy-soft kiss on her shoulder.

It was like lightning and frost on her skin, both sensations trapping the breath in her lungs and sending a shiver of pleasure spiraling down her back.

"Say it." He whispered the words and they danced there before fading into the unbearable silence of the room.

She breathed, inhaling his cologne, his very presence, hearing him shift closer. "I want you to touch me."

Another kiss touched her, this time closer to the back of her neck. She shuddered and a soft moan escaped her.

"And?"

"More."

"Say it."

"I want to . . ." Make love. Have sex. The only word that defined her need seemed too crude to be uttered. It faltered on her mouth, tangled up in embarrassment.

"Fuck," he finished for her, breathing it into her ear.

Yes! She shivered again, wondering if he made love in the same way he delivered the hard word on such a soft sound. "Yes."

"Look at me," he coaxed, his deep voice sounding even more gravelly with need. His hands slid over her hips, over the shifting dress, turning her until she faced him. There was no way she could pull together the barest air of cool sophistication now.

"I won't do anything you don't want me to," he promised.

"I know."

Kai raised her right hand to his lips and placed a tongue-flecked kiss in the hot center of her palm.

Sonya swallowed audibly.

The look in his eyes damn near smoldered. He pulled her in for a kiss that was nothing like the night before. There was no soft prelude, no gentle control, just a mouth-plundering, neck-bending kiss that left her weak. He invaded her mouth with his tongue, making her aware of every luscious bit of contact.

There was a decadence in the way he kissed, taking and teasing her for more, for angles of his mouth, for breath, for licks, for lips. Deep within her, the sexual ache expanded, driving her to pull her body tighter against his, fitting her pelvis against his blatant erection just as he gripped her hips and held her fast against him.

Oh, dear Lord, he felt so very hard. . . . In that wordless, timeless moment, she knew she was out of her element. Whatever happened, she wasn't drunk, wasn't irrational. It was obvious that Kai was skilled at seduction. She desperately hoped she could give him as much pleasure as he was giving her.

Kai's hands roamed her bare back, caressing the exposed skin so that she felt already naked in his arms. Sonya held on to his shoulders, the world tilting behind her eyes as his kisses grew more urgent, sucking her breath away.

"Oh," she moaned. "Kai . . ."

"I want you naked," he breathed against her ear. "I want you hungry for me. Wet. With me deep inside you."

His teeth sank into the earlobe, then his tongue licked and whispered into her ear. "I want to feel you wrapped around me. Feeling me . . ." His mouth trailed along her jawline in tiny heated kisses.

Oh yes, yes, yes. . . .

Kai's arms moved away momentarily and Sonya opened her eyes just in time to see his jacket slide off his shoulders. The scent of his fresh starched shirt blended with his deodorant and body heat.

In the soft light, his devilish smile was twice as sexy, his voice as deep and gruff as she'd ever heard it. "Undress me."

Her fingers shook with the novelty of it. She unbuttoned an onyx button by his Adam's apple, the pristine white of his shirt a sharp contrast against his dark skin. A second button followed, and she impulsively kissed the flesh she revealed, unwrapping

him, button by button, like a gift, reveling in the
heady power of hearing his unsteady breathing.

Kai's chest was all sinewy muscle covered with a
sprinkling of hair. She touched him with her hands,
tasted with her tongue, exploring as she saw more.

Kai groaned and abruptly cupped her head for another hard kiss. By the time it ended, she realized
he'd undone her gown and it now sagged as if prepared to faint to the floor.

He cupped her breasts over the gown, and the exquisite imprint burned clear to Sonya's bones. His
thumbs trailed over her sensitized nipples as he
watched her with a look full of carnal anticipation.
When she moaned, he slanted his mouth over the
sound and swallowed it.

She'd never felt so molten inside, like she would
implode if he didn't kiss her again.

Little by little, her gown shifted beneath his palms,
gravity taking it down.

"Please." Her weakened knees threatened to
buckle.

"Yes," he agreed, and released the gown so that
she stood before him in nothing but the heels and
plum-colored French-cut panties.

"You're so beautiful." He looked awed, yet fighting himself from savage action. She found herself
tumbling with him onto the bed, his mouth swooping down for another kiss.

Sonya yanked his shirt from his pants, and he
made short business of taking it off and flinging it
into the air. His belt buckle jingled in midair and
then, to her nervous delight, his shoes made two dull

thuds as they, too, hit the floor. His trousers followed. She kicked her high heels off.

Time froze as they looked at each other. Sonya surprised herself by not wanting to cover up her breasts. It was powerful and intoxicating to watch his desire so openly revealed in his face.

The flat of his hand spanned over her belly button and, with a circular movement, began a clockwise trail. The fluttering in her gut turned to simmering honey with each caress. Kai lowered his head and kissed her left nipple in a thorough, open-mouthed kiss that left it feeling tight, moist, and achy.

He returned the favor to her right breast but stopped when his nose bumped into the butterfly pendant. He paused to look at her, the depths of his eyes dark as shadows.

"Don't stop," she told him.

"Tonight I want you completely naked," he whispered. "For me."

Her fingers fumbled to remove the necklace, and she carefully placed it on her nightstand.

"Thank you."

"You're welcome . . . oh!"

Kai's mouth went back to work on her breast again. His hand explored more freely as it circled south. She tried to endure the pleasure without embarrassing herself but ended up moaning like some creature in heat, the sounds escaping of their own volition.

The feel of his fingers cupping her sex was intimate and jarring. Despite her firmly pressed thighs, he persisted, massaging over her skimpy underwear and murmuring against her moans.

"Open."

"Kai . . ."

Her thighs quivered as prudish instinct momentarily took over.

Sonya could've sworn he whispered, "Carpe diem," before slipping his hands farther underneath the lacy trim with determined presence. Any remaining shyness dissolved when his fingers invaded her wetness, stroking as if he were sampling the texture of satin.

Sonya was locked in the gaze of his maple dark eyes, panting when his fingers delved again, deliberately skimming the folds of her sex before slowly, slowly, slowwwwly . . . returning to surround the sensitive bud of her clit.

"Oh, my . . ." She squeezed her eyes shut, but that only intensified the sensations when he did it all over again . . . so very insanely slow.

With more control than she'd expected, he explored her sex, maintaining a shallow contact but using every one of her reactions to perfect the rhythm.

"Sonya?"

Don't stop! Don't talk! Don't make me beg. . . .

"Protection?" he breathed.

"Birth control pills," she managed.

"Condom?"

God, if he had to move, she was probably going to scream. She opened her eyes to look into his eyes, knowing she had to. "Yes."

"In a minute." His fingers invaded. "Do you like this?"

"Ohhh, God . . . yesss!"

He dipped his head and a gust from his staggered breathing warmed her neck, his fingers never stopping. "Good."

She squirmed.

He eased off.

"Please."

His words were gruff. "So polite. Who would've thought?"

The need kept feeding on his touch, burning through her. "Kai . . ."

"Tell me what you like," he whispered hotly.

"I-I . . ." She stalled and rode the pad of his thumb as it brushed over her clit.

He kissed her chin, then nibbled her lip, his fingers halting.

"No!"

"Harder?"

"Yes. . . ."

"Like this?"

"Oh . . . please, yes. . . ."

"Soft, then hard?"

"Mmmm. . . ."

"Tell me."

She couldn't. Words escaped her.

"Lower?"

"No, don't . . . oh, wait . . . oh, God . . . yes . . ." *And yes . . . and yes . . .*

"Higher?"

"No! . . . Wait . . . oh. . . ." *Perrrfect!*

He whispered over her, his words streaming, implicitly blending with his actions.

"When I saw you in the spa, I wanted to take you right then and there."

His fingers edged into her sex more possessively.

"To bend you over the edge of the spa . . ."

His fingers cleverly slid farther into her sheath.

"And ease myself between your sexy thighs. . . ."

She arched.

"Next time . . ."

Oh! Oh!

"I'll blindfold you."

He kissed her cheek and jaw, licking when he strategically paused.

"Would you've done that for me?"

All the answers seemed to be "yes!" He kept the murmur of words as he moved to her collarbone, until the meaning of his words blurred and she could hardly think.

"Please, Kai . . ."

"Shift like that . . . yes . . . trust me."

At the time, his lips hovered right over the valley of her breasts, above the region of her heart.

Trust me. Oh yes, yes, yes. . . .

"Open for me," he whispered gruffly.

Sonya parted her thighs even wider for him, and his fingers surged deeper, causing Sonya to clutch his shoulder in one hand and the bedsheet in the other, arching against the steady magic of his touch in an attempt to ease her body's cravings. He prolonged the torture, memorizing the flower of her sex by touch alone, dipping, trailing, circling . . .

Every time his mouth suckled her breast, it tugged urgently at the tremors in her gut, linking fluidly to the intimate place his fingers touched. He was like a cellist, his fingers pressed, playing her through all the fine notes, stressing and fine-tuning the sounds in search of the perfect strokes.

She wanted to shred his clothes off his body, wanted to shred something . . . anything . . .

Sonya gasped, involuntarily clamping her thighs together and trapping his touch there. The action caused a quiver that drowned her ever so slightly in lightning and weakness. Sonya licked her parched lips and opened her eyes to find Kai's taut face watching her closely.

Without stripping her underwear, he used his fingers in a slow outward drag until only his fingertips touched her, then he resumed his upward massage to the topmost ridge of her sex, focusing solely on the clitoris.

"Now!" she breathed.

His fingers slid inside her slick passage again.

She heard her underwear rip. The new freedom allowed him more access, and Sonya suddenly felt off-balance, teetering on the brink of a new, edgier kind of release than she had ever experienced.

"Oh, no you don't," his voice rumbled like warning thunder. "Not yet."

She cried out when he removed his hand. "No! No, no, no—"

"Shh. Hold on, sugar." He kissed her and she finally realized he was stripping off his remaining clothes.

"I have to feel you, skin to skin, remember?" he whispered urgently.

She shimmied her torn underwear off her hips and kicked it down and off her feet, visually taking her fill of Kai's muscular naked body. His blatant erection thrust out, a damn fine specimen of primal maleness.

Tentatively, she touched it, and he hissed as if in pain. When she would've pulled her hand away, his own covered hers, the scent of her wetness still in his hand and blending with his distinct male arousal.

Sonya palmed the length and breadth of him, fascinated by his size and shape, her weakness turned into control in a shift of power.

Although her heartbeat seemed to have lodged between her thighs, she planned to torture him with the same open-handed, circular motion he'd used on her body, getting bolder with each of his groans.

She experimented with hand movements, stroking him more thoroughly, making it last the same way he'd worked her just moments before. Not too tightly. Just snug enough. Back and forth, gliding.

His body tensed with each movement. She could see he was clenching his teeth, watching her through half-open eyes, his hand in sync, over hers, guiding, yet trapped. When he tugged her hand away, she knew he'd had about enough.

"Hold up," he whispered, then kissed her hard, rolling a condom on.

He tried to wrestle control back with the kiss, but she refused and turned her head against his shoulder, gasping and kissing the faint perspiration from his collarbone.

She worked her mouth up the muscular column of his neck, his heartbeat pulsing beneath her tongue, matching the throbbing in the center of her palm where she defiantly continued to stroke him.

Every inch of skin was alive, anticipating the friction of light sweat and need. She held the back of his shaven head for another kiss, her breasts against his, putting their bellies into closer contact.

"Enough." He reached down to extract her hand, but she fought him.

"No, Kai. I need—"

A split second later, he had her pinned to the bed, arms by her head, his body hovering over hers. His eyes gleamed with passion. "I know exactly what you need."

"Then give it to me!" She shimmied her hips and parted her thighs, giving his body no choice but to settle more intimately against hers. Oh, so close, so close . . . !

"Not yet," he breathed. She moaned and squirmed to maneuver a more strategic closeness. He groaned, rocking gently in mock intercourse. "Don't rush me."

"Don't make me wait!"

He kissed her again, then with a careful thrust, the tip of his erection slid inside her, more virile and thicker than his fingers had been, but still not enough! Dammit!

"Don't do this to me!" she pleaded.

His chuckle was a half-broken, half-strangled sound. And when she least expected it, another of his kisses smothered her lips, her breasts cushioned his weight, and another inch of his length slid inside her.

She tried to arch her back for more, but he was too heavy, too in control. She felt desperate and light-headed. "Now!"

Kai licked the slope of her breasts, the dip at the base of her throat.

Another inch slid in.

She cussed between broken breaths, wrestling with desperation.

"Sweetheart—"

"Now!"

Two inches that time. She wasn't sure if it was his body shuddering or hers. It didn't matter. All that mattered was knowing she was infinitesimally closer to exploding and close enough to kill him if he denied her again.

This time, their mouths didn't even touch. The kiss was a shared breath between them, a place to gasp when he settled farther into her, sliding in thickly.

Oh, so perfect! There! Yes, yes, yes! That was it! She clutched him. "Do it. . . . Oh!"

He flexed his hips, initiating the oldest, most intimate dance of time, docking in the rest of the way, until he was filling her to the hilt.

Quickly releasing her hands, he used his own to hold her closer, to thrust deeper again, slicker.

Sonya wrapped her legs around his hips, his thighs hard and sure against her inner thighs, grinding against her sensitive clit. His rhythm was controlled slowness itself; the moist sounds of sex came together to the tempo of racing heartbeats. . . .

Behind her eyes, the world dimmed, and as Sonya struggled for breath, the sharp orgasm suddenly overtook her from deep inside, ripping through her like an explosion. It stripped her mind of thought, of sound, of everything but the feel of Kai gripping her, rocking deep inside her, impaling the small, fiery shudders in her womb.

Even his name was trapped in her mouth without breath. There was only the moment frozen in time, her soul bared to him.

Complete.

An endless moment later, the muscles of his inner arms trembled where they brushed the sides of her breasts, and his forearms flexed against her shoulder blades. His fingers twitched where they cradled her head, and from that cherished position Sonya inhaled and felt the heat of Kai's ejaculation inside her.

He whispered her name and buried his face on the side of her neck.

For an eternity it seemed to Sonya that there was only the sacrament of skin on skin and the jumbled rhythm of breathing.

Nothing felt so right as his weight on her. Nothing felt so safe as falling asleep in his arms.

Nothing had ever felt so utterly perfect.

🦋

When Sonya finally awoke, nestled in the warm bedsheets, she felt like she'd endured a marathon. Her muscles were warm and hummed with latent energy. She felt completely seduced and lazy. Half-awake, she tried to nuzzle into Kai's chest, but she found empty bedsheets instead.

"Kai?"

She looked around the room, seeing her gown neatly draped over a chair and not on the floor as she'd expected. All traces of Kai, however, were gone.

Her smile faded.

Suddenly apprehensive, Sonya wrapped the bed-sheet around herself as she got up from the bed.

Her hand went to her neck for her necklace before she realized it wasn't there, and turned to the bedside table.

Instead of the necklace, she saw the remains of her underwear, which had been turned into a French-laced rosebud. The pit of her stomach tightened, and as she lifted the makeshift rose, the first tendrils of dread began to unravel, raising the possibility that perhaps her magnificent lover had been nothing more than a clever, seductive thief.

EIGHT

KAI FELL IN line with the rest of the passengers who had chosen to set foot on Puerto Vallarta. The sea was unusually restless, frothing against the ship. The wind blew like soft hair against his skin. Even the sky, usually as bright as the city, was a murky gray.

His bulky camera hung on a cord and bumped against his chest. It felt like Sonya's necklace was burning a hole through the secret compartment of his camera, branding his skin. The tour group moved around him, pointing out landscapes and architecture, but Kai didn't bother looking at any of it.

The salty air reminded him of the taste of Sonya's skin when it had glistened with perspiration. The murmur of the wind replayed her voice, in that quiet way she had of gasping, of saying his name like it was a rarely spoken profanity.

There was a part of him that had sorely wanted to see her gradually awaken in the morning, maybe even reaching for him in her sleep the way she had the night before.

Just thinking about it was beyond pointless. There was no bounty for her. Legally, she was clean and clear, even though she was guilty by association. And who could overlook the undeniable evidence?

As far as the job went, it was mission accomplished. Touchdown. Score. He'd won the big game, so why did he feel like he was forfeiting the game? Technically, it wasn't a loss. It was a stalemate. He hadn't backed down from any sex challenge, and he hadn't issued one. He'd just walked away from it.

Forget it. It's over.

He shouldered his backpack and disappeared into the crowd, leaving the tour group behind. No matter how many times he'd visited Puerto Vallarta, he'd always felt the excitement of the town. At this moment, however, all he wanted to do was find the nearest airport, head straight back to San Diego, grab a tall, ice-cold beer, and watch sports on TV until his mind went numb.

Instead, he walked down a traffic-jammed road to where the cracked asphalt turned to a sea of cobblestones. The honking and cursing were less hectic and a little less crowded. On one side of the street, vendors guarded their stands in the open-air market, selling crafts that were as bright as parrots. When Kai's phone rang, he stopped beside a fruit booth to answer it.

His brother's voice was a mixture of anger and distress. "I lost him!"

Kai squeezed his eyes shut. "Tell me you don't mean Otis."

"No, I mean his grandfather. Shit, Kai, of course I mean Otis!"

Kai looked around, cussing under his breath. "What happened?"

Dre grumbled and a knot started forming in Kai's gut.

"Louder, Dre. I can't hear you."

"I said he threw a can of beer at my head!"

Kai prayed for patience. "And?"

"He knocked me out. I was going in as room service, and, well, he opened the door, took one look at me, and bolted. Ran across the room, grabbed one of his beer cans, and . . . Hell! Who knew he could pitch like that?"

"Yeah, who knew?"

Dre paused. "Damn, Bro, I'm sorry."

Kai's sigh turned into an exhausted gush. "A beer can? Are you serious?"

"Right on the head. I didn't have time to duck or anything." Dre sounded just as angry with himself.

"It's done. Did you double back?"

"Yeah. By the time I came to, he was long gone."

"Any leads?"

"No one's talking."

"Did you get your head examined?"

"Don't start on the mental jokes, OK?"

"Just answer the damned question!"

Dre sounded like a six-year-old. "Look, I'll find him, don't worry. I wasn't out that long. He couldn't have gone far."

Right. Sure. Hell, having Old Lady Miller's plans thwarted was going to cost them. "Dre, call me when you're back on track. And if you get dizzy or nauseated—"

"—go see a doctor. Yeah, yeah." Dre grumbled. "Thanks, Mom."

"I mean it, Dre."

He mumbled some more, said good-bye, then hung up.

Kai snapped his flip phone shut, his gut telling him it should've been him taking down Otis instead of Dre. He was used to the hunted suddenly hurling objects at him, not that they did that very often. On the other hand, he didn't even want to think of how Dre would've handled Sonya Drummond.

Kai brutally shoved the thought aside and pushed his phone back into his pocket.

Kai flagged down a taxi, stopping halfway in when he heard a woman calling his name. A cold premonition snaked down his chest right before he spotted Sonya running and waving at him from among the street vendors.

Kai stepped the rest of the way into the cab, closed the door, and commanded the cabbie to jet.

"Kai!"

The cab shot into traffic, just before she could get any closer.

In the driver's side-view mirror, Kai focused on the wavering sight of her. Sonya looked tousled and angry. Royally pissed, actually. She looked like a curvaceous Hollywood diva in her tight blue tank top, snug khaki pants, and sassy large purse.

Everything that was so right was also so wrong! Her lushness would be a magnet to every macho creep in the district. And how the hell did she expect to catch him, wearing those impractical, sissy-heeled sandals? Worse than all that, her oversize purse was a pickpocket's dream.

Leave it to him to deal with a white-collar con who had no blue-collar skills. The taxi swerved dangerously close to a donkey cart and Kai tried to convince himself it was the jarring force of the taxi that caught in his gut instead of the devastated look he'd seen on Sonya Drummond's face.

❦

Twenty minutes later, Sonya was fuming in the backseat of a taxi, angrier than she could ever remember being.

Kai had seen her and left her standing there.

That goddamned-low-down-no-good-bastard!

She'd quickly flagged another cabbie, and the driver had been happy enough to give chase. She gripped the seat and tried to keep her cool, almost landing in the front seat when the taxi came to an unexpected halt.

"*Aquí, señora*," the cabbie announced cheerfully.

"Here, indeed!" she agreed.

In her hurry to exit the taxi, Sonya handed a bunch of bills to the cabdriver, certain she was overpaying

him, but it would take too much time to calculate the
dollars into pesos at the moment.

"Your *amigo* is in the bar," he said with a thick
Mexican accent, nodding at her in the rearview mirror. "You want I should wait? Follow him again?"

"No, that's not necessary. Thank you."

She hurried into the bar, barely registering the
clay moldings and colorful baskets of flowers draped
from the windows.

Maybe she should give him the benefit of the
doubt. Maybe he'd meant to play a game by taking
the necklace. Maybe he hadn't really seen her running to him.

Whatever.

Curbing her anger, she hoisted her purse on her
shoulder and entered the small establishment, pausing for a moment behind a big potted plant to let her
eyes adjust to the dim interior.

The tables of the patio setting were half-filled with
patrons. At her right, there was a loud group of college
students, their muscle shirts announcing they were
from the USC volleyball team. One of the players
raised his shot glass at her, recognizing her for the
American tourist that she was. After ogling her with
an overfamiliar leer, he grinned and downed the drink.

It wasn't even eleven in the morning.

To her left was a lone stretch of bar, where Kai
was leaning forward and showing a camera to the
bartender. The man paused from wiping down the
countertop and adjusted his bifocals to look at a detail Kai was pointing out.

Sonya watched, wondering what was going on.

The bartender pressed something and suddenly a shimmy of gold spilled out and was quickly caught in midair. He tilted the object to catch the light.

Her necklace!

Fuming with indignation, Sonya found herself storming up to Kai, her painful sandals clicking all the way.

"You conniving, thieving bastard! You . . . you . . . How could you!" She poked him in the back with her finger, checking the most unholy urge to slap him in the back of his head.

He turned and frowned at her in confusion.

"Is that what you were after all along? That piece of jewelry? Why me? Why did you have to pull that stunt and—"

"Do I know you?"

Sonya choked and fell back a step, reeling as if he'd punched her. The world contracted sharply. "Know me . . . ?"

The bartender smiled amicably, pure Mexican charm oozing from his sun-creased face. "What can I get you to drink?"

Sonya glared at Kai, while at the same time feeling as if somewhere in her chest something was bottoming out. "My necklace. I want it back."

"Excuse me, lady," Kai said politely, "but I think you've got the wrong person."

Blood roared in her ears. "Like hell I do!" She ground her teeth and poked him again in the chest several times. "How could you do this to me?"

"Look, I don't know who you think I am. Maybe I look familiar or—"

Her heart flinched. "Don't you dare! After all we . . . After you and I, we—"

"What?" The depths of his eyes were cold and hard, challenging.

She didn't realize she'd actually tried to slap him until his hand clamped over hers just inches from his cheek. His grip was strong and uncompromising.

Sonya tried to pull free, but when she couldn't, she stuck her nose right in his face and snarled, "You're the lowest possible kind of slime."

"Pot calling the kettle black, huh?"

She twitched with indignation.

"You bothering the little lady?"

The voice from behind had her looking over her shoulder to find a few members of the volleyball team at her back.

Some of the patrons were already glancing nervously in their direction, and more than a few were not-so-subtly heading for the door.

The leader of the valiant pack swayed a little, but surely he and his burly teammates could easily teach Kai a lesson. A painful lesson, she hoped. Sonya turned back to Kai, looked pointedly at her captured wrist, and smirked. "Well?"

"This is just a misunderstanding, boys," Kai said smoothly, releasing her wrist, his dimples flashing and his teeth gleaming in a smile. "I don't know this woman."

"He's a liar and a goddamned thief," Sonya repeated emphatically. "He stole my necklace . . . and my camera!" she added impulsively.

"No fighting in my restaurant! Take it outside, please," the bartender said, pointing toward the exit.

"Look, guys," Kai shrugged as if he were confused but trying to be generous and understanding, "the lady seems a little—" He whistled a loony sound.

Sonya almost snarled again but suppressed the impulse when the inebriated players started to look indecisive.

"I am not crazy and I'm telling you he did steal from me!"

"I don't know, lady. Can you prove it?"

"Prove it?"

"Yeah."

What were they expecting?!

"He, ah . . . He's got a birthmark on his, um, left butt cheek that looks like a goldfish." Sonya could feel her cheeks blazing at the lie, but thankfully no one seemed to notice. Their interest was now on Kai's rear assets.

"Oh, that's just . . . classic." Kai chuckled. "You don't think she's serious, do you, boys?"

They glanced from Sonya to Kai.

"Goldfish," she stressed. "Big eye and all."

Someone chortled.

"You gonna show us your butt, mister?" a short, burly player jeered. "Or are we gonna have to make you?"

"The proof is right there," she urged.

"Sonyaaa." Kai's eyes narrowed and a hard edge entered his voice.

"Aha!" She poked at his chest again. "I thought you didn't know who I was."

"Said he didn't." Beside her, her volleyball knight-in-shining-armor cracked his knuckles. His friend stretched his neck like a sumo wrestler. By now the tequila fumes from the team filled the air.

"Know what ah think? Ah think the little lady here is telling the truth," the leader said.

"Guys, come on," Kai chuckled, obviously trying to play it off as if the whole thing were absurd. "I'm not going to show you my ass to prove—"

"You don't have to," Sonya interrupted quickly. "Just give me back my necklace."

"Yeah, and that camera," a dark player with a ponytail added.

"Sorry, wish I could help." Kai tried his charming dimples again.

Ponytail said something inaudible and the rest of his buddies chuckled, nudging one another.

The hairs on Sonya's neck sent off an eerie warning. "Kai, please!" she whispered. "Hurry."

Kai's smile slowly faded, his maple brown eyes becoming as hard as flint. He stood up to his full height, the slight shift putting him in a subtle fighting stance.

The bartender slid over the bar looking for all the world like an interfering referee, except for the steel bat in his hand. "I don't want trouble here. You want to fight, go outside!"

"No, we'll take it right here, right now!" Short Burly Guy slurred, stepping up.

"Sweet Sonya," Kai called to her. "Last chance to call off your dogs."

"Who're you calling a dog?" Knuckle Cracker wanted to know.

"You can avoid this if you just give it back," she urged, holding her palm out to Kai, willing him to obey. She sensed it was too late to turn things around, but if only he'd try!

The bartender fretted in rapidly deteriorating English.

"Sorry, Hector," Kai said. "It's a little late for that."

Sonya didn't see which one of the players threw out the first punch. All she saw was Kai deflect it with one hand and respond with a flash of his own fist. It was as if a bell had sounded at a boxing ring.

All hell broke loose.

Sonya was knocked to the side just as Kai dodged another punch and threw a fist at Second-in-command's face. The meaty thud clocked the guy backward and over a table. Furniture shattered, dishes crashed to the floor. From somewhere behind her, a stool was hurled, crashed against the bar, and one of the legs used as a bat. Several punches connected, followed by grunts and heartfelt profanity.

Oh no! No, no, no!

"Wait! Stop it!" she yelled frantically, but was shoved from behind, regaining her balance against a wall. The camera landed nearby, spilling the necklace, and Sonya scurried after it. Kai briefly caught her gaze when her fingers finally snatched it from skidding past her. He started toward her, but one of the players flew through the air, tackling Kai in the nick of time.

If Kai caught up with her, she knew there was no way she was going to keep the necklace.

Next to the arch of the door, a huge potted plant survived the brunt of a shove. After quickly glancing around, Sonya hurriedly crawled behind it, then shoved the necklace deep into the cleavage of her bra next to her underwire and ducked out of the way of a flying plate.

The bartender shouted at her in Spanish, then grabbed her hand and began to drag her in another direction. Something hit her right shoulder hard, causing her to drop to her knees and gasp in pain.

The bartender's language got sharper and angrier as he swung his bat around, dragging her to the shelter of an upturned table. Sonya looked over the rim in time to see Kai drop-kick yet another one of the players.

Suddenly, behind him, the doors swung open and several policemen stormed in, whistles blowing and batons out. She scurried to find another exit, but the only two doors left were already covered by unsmiling cops.

🦋

The small jail cell stank of urine and desperation. Sonya tried not to think of the alarming variety of bacteria she inhaled with every breath.

Her motto popped into her head: *Carpe diem. . . . Take risks. Take a vacation. Meet a guy. Have wild sex. It had all been so simple.*

Kai had been pacing back and forth, not so much as sending a glance in her direction. He kept one hand on his hip and the other tapping his lips. She hated that he only had a couple of scrapes on his knuckles to show for the team brawling. By all rights, he should've been sporting a bloody bandage around his head, a broken arm, ice on his testicles—something!

Instead, he paced at a healthy stride, giving Sonya a sinking feeling that he was planning her murder right along with his escape.

Sweet Jesus. Had she surrendered herself so completely to this stranger just the night before?

She jerked her chin up. Although it was eating at her, she *would not* apologize! So what if she was in this godforsaken place, listening to roaches tap-dance over inmate hieroglyphics?

Kai had robbed *her*! Now that she thought about it, he'd probably been trying to rob her all along! Hadn't her necklace mysteriously slipped from her neck several times?

And even though he'd committed the premeditated crime, what did she get? The humiliation of being booked like a common criminal, forced to await justice in the tiny, unhygienic, germ-infested cell!

He should be the one apologizing! Groveling and begging her forgiveness on his damned knees!

A moan from the neighboring cell immediately made her feel guilty. Oh, those poor volleyball players, jumping in to help her, and look where it had gotten them.

Kai turned on his heel and walked past her again.

"Would you just stop?" she finally snapped.

He glanced at her, eyes full of murderous intent. Then he glanced away, never once breaking his stride. His anger was raw and tangible. She'd been bristling from it since she'd been dumped with him to wait in the cell from hell.

"This is *all* your fault," she reminded him as he neared her again.

"Sonya, I swear if you—"

"Oh, so you're admitting you know me now?" Sonya couldn't help poking her finger into his chest again. "Thief! Liar! There is nothing you can say to justify this, so don't even bother!"

He growled, a muscle jumping in his jaw, "*I'm* the thief?" His forced chuckle was nothing short of harsh and insulting. "Why did you go through all this trouble to hold on to that little bitty piece of jewelry when you could've had your uncle steal another one for you?"

Sonya shook her head, feeling disoriented, as if she'd unexpectedly inhaled fumes. "My uncle? How do you know I have an uncle? And what does he have to do with this?"

"Otis Drummond. He's your uncle, right?"

"Yes, but—"

"But what? Did you think I didn't know of your family scam, embezzling little old ladies out of their measly income? You know, embezzling itself is pretty pathetic, and when that victim is a little old lady without much to begin with . . . ? Well, in my book, that's a whole new, *reprehensible* low."

Sonya was stunned. What was going on? Who was this man? She was sure she'd never told him her uncle's name. And what was this nonsense about embezzling? What did any of it have to do with her?

"Exactly who are you?" she managed.

"Kai Armstrong. Bail enforcement agent and part-time defender of little old ladies."

Sonya took a step back at his vehemence, stammering as she tried to understand. "B-bounty hunter? There must be some mistake. I don't know anything about an embezzlement, and Uncle Otis would never break the law! He didn't steal the necklace. It . . . it was a gift."

"Right. And I'm the tooth fairy."

"This is ridiculous—"

"Just knock it off. That won't work on me."

"I don't know what you mean! This whole story you're telling me is crazy! I don't know where you got it, but—"

He cut off her words with a swipe of his hand through the air. "Unless you're about to fess up to how you and your uncle ran the scam, you can just zip it. As far as I'm concerned, I'm almost down two clients because of you *and* that damned necklace. At least there'll be some justice in knowing you'll be trapped here for the next couple of years to contemplate the error of your ways!"

"What?!" Her blood ran cold at the thought.

"Who knows, maybe more."

God, he was kidding! Had to be!

His smile was feral and he pulled her close. Pain shot through her shoulder from when she'd been injured at the bar, and she let out a small cry of pain.

The anger momentarily left him and he looked at her with concern before his eyes narrowed again. "Don't play your con jobs here, Sonya," he warned. "I swear to God, I'll make you regret it."

"Go to hell!" She turned her head, blinking back the tears of pain. Having nowhere to go, she turned back, refusing to cower.

"Where's the necklace?" he asked.

"Get me out of here and I'll give it to you."

The muscle in his jaw began to pulse again. "Do you realize you fidget with your hands when you lie? If you want to improve in the con business, you should really watch that. A blue-collar con would never do that. But you work with computers and all that. No one sees you when you lie, huh?"

She clenched her hands into fists. "I'm not lying!"

He gave her a disgusted look and turned his back on her.

A jangle of keys down the hall drew her attention. She recognized the bartender approaching. He ignored the pleas from the other cells and walked up to them, escorted by a uniformed guard. When the bartender reached them, he and Kai put their heads close for discussion, causing Sonya to strain to hear their conversation.

"Hector, you know the deal. Just get me out of here."

"It's going to be more than I thought, amigo." Kai's friend smiled congenially.

Both men exchanged a look of compromise, then shook hands. "Do it," Kai said. "Whatever it takes."

"It is not going to be so easy."

"Make it easy."

Hector glanced at the guard, who was adeptly playing deaf.

"Tomorrow is Cinco de Mayo, and the big rock concert begins," Hector confided in low tones. "Likely, they want you out by tomorrow, but they need . . . what you call it, Cheddar cheese?"

Cheese? Money? Sonya glanced at Kai.

"But?" Kai prompted.

Hector rubbed his chin. "This is confusing," he whispered. "They want to know if you are a stranger to this lovely señorita or not. If you're a thief who stole something of hers, then it don't look so good, you know? They must find some justice, no?"

Kai muttered a single loaded profanity.

"But perhaps she's your woman, eh? And you and her . . . well, you just had a little lovers' spit?"

"Lovers' spat?"

"Yes, yes. You quarrel. She's angry, but now you are forgiven and back in love, otherwise—" He made a gesture of confusion. "They don't know if you are a thief or a bad lover."

This time the vulgarity Kai uttered matched her sentiments exactly.

"You want to think about it?" Hector inquired.

"Screw it. Lovers' spat it is," Kai announced.

Sonya gasped. He glanced at her.

"May I have a few minutes please?" he asked the guard.

"Sure," the man replied with a heavy accent.

Kai nodded to his friend in another of his unspoken agreements, then Hector and the guard departed.

Kai smiled coldly and Sonya barely held back a nervous twitch. He looked like he was trying to talk himself out of strangling her.

He stepped up to the bars. "We don't have much time, so let me break this down for you," he said, speaking softly and slowly. "Option A. You and I are an item. A hot item. Make believe we are back on the damned cruise ship. Turn up your con factor and make them believe you *were* pissed at me for whatever harebrained female reason you want. Insist on dropping all charges, and with a little luck and a lot of money we will be out of here today. Maybe in a few blessed hours."

He let that sink in with a tiny nod. "Or option B. You keep sticking to your guns, claiming I'm a thief, and we'll both rot here long after our teeth have. Although the perk for you will be that I will more than likely strangle you before midnight, just for kicks. So, go ahead, make up your mind. How do you want to play this?"

She focused on the faint bruise forming on his bristly jaw. Beneath the rough smells of dust, sweat, and anger, the light scent of his cologne still clung to him, reminding her that she'd licked his neck and jaw the night before, snuggled and strained her belly against his, begged him to slide harder and deeper into her body, again and again . . . *God!*

"I think I hate you," she whispered, her eyes stinging with sudden tears. No. She was absolutely not going to start bawling like a baby. He'd just think she was trying to win his pity. Or worse, he'd think it was a con.

If ever there was a time to be the bold, adventurous, and sophisticated woman she'd pretended to be, heaven help her, it had to be now.

A shadow flitted in the depths of his eyes, ghosts of a lover past, but it disappeared when he shrugged, his eyes still locked with hers. "What's it going to be, sweetheart?"

NINE

BY THE TIME they made it through the paperwork and personal property, Kai noticed that Sonya's anger was tightly suppressed, her face an inscrutable mask.

Like the pro she was, she played her role of a wronged woman who had seen the error of her ways. It wasn't until they were finally on the sidewalk that Kai allowed himself to really breathe deeply, inadvertently inhaling the secondhand cigarette smoke from two cops who loitered in front of the station.

"Well, wish I could say it's been a pleasure," Kai bluffed to Sonya as he flagged a taxi down.

She looked up from her empty wallet, the panic in her eyes blazing once more with the anger she'd shown earlier. "You can't leave me here without a dollar in my wallet!"

"I'd love to give you some money so you can catch the cruise liner back, but I seem to be missing a particular piece of jewelry."

"You are despicable!"

Man, she had that digusted look down pat. "Yeah, well . . ." He glanced at Hector, who had been patiently waiting for them in the cab.

Her chin jutted out again. "I need some sort of a guarantee that I'll get back to San Diego. I wouldn't trust you right now as far as I could throw you."

"Doesn't bother me one way or another. I've got the time, but do you?" He stopped halfway in, the taxi door between them.

She bit back a shriek and her hands twitched as if she barely restrained herself from launching at him.

With a mutter of disgust, he glowered at her. "Oh, for the love of— Don't even think it! Get in the cab!"

She angrily shoved past him and slid in. Kai followed, slamming the door. The cramped quarters weren't helping the pain in his knee any.

The cab lurched into traffic.

Kai gave Sonya his most menacing glare. "You have about thirty seconds to tell me where the necklace is."

"So you can leave me in this city without a dime? Don't think so. Your mama must've raised a fool." She shook her head.

Hector kept glancing at him, but Kai was intent on avoiding him. "Like I said before. You give me the necklace, and I'll make sure you make it back to San Diego."

"Why should I believe you?"

"Hector can be my witness."

His friend shrugged, still looking confused.

Sonya toyed with the zipper of her purse, her voice rough with edginess. "No offense, Hector, but I have no reason to believe either of you."

A lengthy pause followed while Kai tried to calm himself.

"Believe it or not, Kai, I'm just an accountant who works in midtown San Diego." Her voice was still gritty but oddly vulnerable. She took a deep breath and her voice softened just a bit. "The necklace really was a gift from my uncle Otis. And neither one of us is an embezzler or even a thief. It's completely ridiculous!"

What a moving performance! Brilliant. "Of course you are." Kai flashed his most charming smile and winked, relieved when her eyes sparked with anger again.

With his finger, Kai tapped his wristwatch. "Time's a-wasting. The ship is bound to sail soon."

Her chin went up and she turned to Hector. "How can you do business with this man?"

"Mr. Armstrong is a man of honor," Hector said with conviction. "He is only teasing you about leaving you here, señorita. He is a kind—"

"Hector!" Kai groaned.

"You are." It was followed by a quick diatribe in Spanish asking him why he was harassing the lady.

"It's a long, involved story," Kai responded, also in Spanish. "Just let it go."

"That may be so, but a deal is a deal, yes?" Hector insisted. "And you Americans are always talking about getting more bees with sugar than vinegar."

"Honey," Kai corrected, slipping into English.

Sonya turned and glared at him. "Don't call me that."

Kai groaned. "Fifteen seconds left."

"This is definitely not an honorable man," she said to Hector, gripping her purse tightly.

Kai was betting she'd tell where the necklace was. What other choice did she have? She couldn't speak the language, she was out of money and was so desperate to make it back to the cruise liner that he could practically feel it.

"Don't try to play me on this," he warned, then glanced out the window, trying to figure out what else she was plotting.

"Raul Romero knows you have come to town," Hector said, perhaps in an attempt at breaking the tension.

"Great, just what I need," Kai grumbled.

"It's a big city." Hector smiled, ever optimistic.

"Yeah." And it would be that much harder to find the conniving Romero kid, especially if his family was jumping in to protect the sneaky little bail jumper.

The plan had been a slam-dunk. Grab the necklace, send it to Old Lady Miller, grab the Romero kid, and take him to San Diego to face his justice. Bingo. Done deal. Two for one. Cash in the bank.

To say the least, things were not going as planned. Kai was already down on the cash flow, Dre wasn't doing too well with Otis, and Raul Romero had probably disappeared into thin air.

Then, for added aggravation, Sonya had the necklace in her possession.

Shit.

"You need supplies?" Hector asked. God bless him, the man never missed an opportunity to sell weapons and ammo.

"The basics will do. I'll let you know if I need anything."

"Juan has some very nice butterflies."

Fancy switchblades that practically required martial arts to figure out how to use them? "No, thanks."

"Sticks?"

Hector supplied everything from batons to collapsible rods. "I'll pass."

"How about—"

"No. . . ." Sonya bolted upright, her quiet gasp slicing through the conversation.

The taxi had crested a hill, and there, framed by a perfect sunset, the bulky cruise ship—Sonya's one-way ticket home—was steadily sailing out of the bay.

🦋

Sonya felt as if she'd turned to stone. Hector and Kai spoke at the same time.

"We'll try the airport—"

"It's OK, señorita."

She screeched, her hands clenched into fists. "*It is not OK!* I'm stranded in a friggin' foreign country with . . . *you* and not a dime to my name! *It . . . is . . . not . . . OK!*"

Her words echoed in the following silence, and the taxi driver scratched his head.

"I don't have . . . spare clothes, money, and . . ." She took several hard breaths. "I don't even have my passport!" She glared at them, trying to hold down the hysteria. "I spent serious money on my new clothes! All that shopping, money I spent on . . . Do you realize I paid full price for the cruise?" she yelled. "No bargain deals! Full. Price!"

One of her out-of-control curls dropped over her eye.

"I had places waxed! I cut my hair!" She punched the seat in front of her. "And what for? So I could be stuck in the backseat of a forty-year-old taxi without a penny to my name!"

Kai and Hector shared a worried look. The taxi driver glanced away from the rearview mirror, then slunk down in his seat. The coward.

She was feeling dizzy, finding it hard to breathe. "I just wanted to travel for once, meet a guy, have a little adventure. . . . I didn't sign up to get arrested! I'm only an accountant, for Crissakes!"

Hector had a combo frown and smile of concerned sympathy like one has for injured creatures. Kai's expression barely hid a mask of cynicism, and Sonya realized he didn't believe her!

"Kai gave you his word, señorita." Hector patted her hand. "Mr. Armstrong will get you home."

"Yes!" She clung to that like a vise. "We do have a deal! You don't get the necklace until you keep your end of the bargain."

That took the edge off the panic, opening other secondary worries. Such as, with her clothes, shoes, and everything else on the cruise ship, how was she going to groom and dress without money? Was she doomed to the next couple of days wearing painful sandals and the same old clothes? She'd look like a prostitute in no time. Damn Lisa and her notions about tight clothes!

Suddenly a thought hit Sonya.

Plastic! She dug her credit cards out of her wallet, almost trembling with relief. The hell with him. She could do this on her own.

She tapped the cabdriver's shoulder. "Pull over."

He did, leaving her the problem of how to move past Kai to get out of the cab.

"What do you think you're doing?" Kai asked.

"Parting ways. I've decided to get myself out of this mess."

"Can't do that," Kai said, his right arm resting on the open window. "Are you trying to skip out on your end of the deal now? No necklace, no travel. I don't have the damned thing in my hand, and until I do, you are staying put."

Sonya blinked, hearing the words and knowing only the urge to whack him on the head with her purse.

"And before you do anything hasty, let me remind you it's Cinco de Mayo, with the annual rock festival in full swing. I'm betting every hotel and motel on this strip will be booked solid."

Sonya absorbed the words through a haze of renewed panic. She took a quick look around and noticed the decorations up and down the street. There were colorful ribbons tied to lampposts, huge banners, and even a few piñatas. The carnival-like atmosphere of the people mingling in the streets said it all.

Hector rattled off something to the cabbie, then patted her hand again. "We will go to my house, *sí*? It will be OK, señorita."

❦

They arrived at Hector's house just as night turned as dark as water, punctuated by the bright fireworks of celebration. Rosa, Hector's beautiful wife, was the soul of efficiency, struggling to put together sentences in English. Their two small boys obviously adored Kai, launching themselves at him until, despite their mother's reprimands, they hung like monkeys on his back. All traces of Kai, the rough and tough bounty hunter, were gone, replaced by the laughing, charming man Sonya had flirted and made love with on the cruise.

Sonya tried to ignore the tightness in her chest at the sound of his laughter and the way it caused the annoying sensual flutter in her gut whenever he teased. For the attention anyone paid her, she might as well have been invisible.

The kids eventually settled down, eyeing Sonya shyly. Although Rosa was unfailingly polite, Sonya sensed the disapproval from Hector's wife and found herself self-consciously tugging at her snug clothes.

With minimum fuss, Rosa fed Kai and Sonya, showed them their room—one tiny room!—usually reserved for the mother-in-law who was out of town. Rosa provided them with towels and sleepwear, then smiled and nodded.

"*Pues, buenas noches*," Hector said, his arm around Rosa, who wiggled her fingers at them.

"Good night to you, too," Kai said. "And thanks, for everything. I definitely owe you."

Rosa responded quickly in Spanish, waving her hand as if to dismiss Kai's comment as ridiculous.

Sonya was sure he replied in Spanish just so she wouldn't understand, because both Hector and Rosa got soft-eyed by whatever Kai said before they headed out.

Kai closed the door behind him and it was like being back in the jail cell again. He was the bounty hunter once more, and one look in his eyes made that fact perfectly clear.

"I'd like to have the bathroom first," she stated.

"No."

"No?"

"You'll give me the necklace right now, or I'll strip you naked to get it."

She raised her eyebrows. "You wouldn't dare."

He moved in with hard determination in his eyes.

When he reached for her, she dodged, skirting the bed.

"Kai, I'll scream," she warned.

"Go for it."

She tried to dodge him again, but he faked right and cornered her between the dresser and the wall.

"The hard way or the easy way, Sonya. Your choice."

"What kind of a choice is that?" she asked through clenched teeth.

He started to tug her shirt up and she instantly pushed and slapped at his hand, but the look on his face told her he was dead set on stripping her clothes off, just like he'd threatened.

"Wait!"

The thought of suffering more humiliation made her realize she really didn't have a choice. Angry with herself and him, she lifted her bra from below and extracted the necklace, feeling the sting from where the underwire had pushed it against her skin.

Oddly enough, he didn't look triumphant. "You did the right thing."

When he took a step backward, she brushed past him and into the bathroom with a retort. Her one-way ticket back was now gone. Without a guarantee, what was to stop him from leaving without her?

Much like the bedroom, the bathroom was small, with a tiny shower stall, a tall rack that held green towels, a dainty sink, and a toilet. And, surprise, surprise, no lock on the door.

Sonya bit her lip and kicked off her ruined shoes without whimpering, for the first time allowing herself to look at the blisters that had formed on her feet. They were going to be worse in the morning.

She pushed away from the door and approached the mirror, utterly dumbfounded by her reflection. Not only did her hair look like a vulture had nested in it, but also her clothes *had* apparently shrunk, sealing against her body like a second skin. For heaven's sakes, she could see her nipples pushing through! It was a miracle Rosa hadn't taken one look at her and kicked her out. What must the woman think of her?

With a sigh, Sonya began to disrobe. The pants came off easily enough, but the tank top didn't. The blow she'd sustained in the bar fight had sweltered into a deeper pain. Although she gritted her teeth and managed to slip off the clingy top, she didn't dare reach behind to unclasp her bra. As long as she didn't move her arm at that odd angle, it would be fine.

A knock sounded on the door. "Ten minutes."

She stiffened. What was it with that man and countdowns? "OK."

She turned the shower knobs and waited for the water to heat up. Sonya tried one more time to reach the clasp, feeling angry with herself and hating the inescapable shoulder pain.

She looked like hell. Tomorrow looked bleak, and at the moment she couldn't even undress to take a shower.

A rap sounded on the door. "Hey, can I come in? Rosa dropped off a nightgown for you."

"Sure. Why not?" Sonya replied sarcastically. "Why pretend I'm allowed any privacy at all!"

To her surprise, the door opened.

Sonya snatched a towel and held it in front of her. "Goddammit!"

Kai held up the garment but froze when he looked in the mirror behind her. Sonya's first thought was that he was checking out the back view of her thong underwear, but when his frown darkened and he moved closer, she stiffened and held her ground, starting to worry.

"What do you think you're doing?" she demanded.

His voice was suddenly deadly quiet. "How did you get that bruise on your shoulder?"

Oh, crap. That. "How do you think?"

He placed the nightgown on the toilet lid. "Turn around."

"Like hell."

"Dammit, Sonya, I'm not here to cop a feel!"

"It's nothing. Just get out. Please."

"It sure doesn't look like nothing. . . . Is that why you cried out when I—" His frown cleared, and he paused to rub his jaw, the tenseness of his features softening.

"Right now, Kai, I'd *love* to have some privacy. Please?"

"Tell me how you got the bruise and I'll leave."

"The bar fight. Happy?"

"Not even." He kept his gaze on the mirror, but he didn't leave. It figured. "You having trouble getting the bra off?" he asked after a pause.

"I'll manage. Alone," she hinted again. The drizzle of shower water filled the silence, punctuated by the city's far-off fireworks. Steam started to lightly fog the air.

"Let me help."

"No!"

Suddenly he was right in front of her, mere inches away.

"What are you doing?!"

It was a mistake to look into his eyes. They were a melting maple honey color again, concerned, unthreatening, but this time tinged with regret.

"Don't touch me, Kai."

"Shhh."

With infinite care, his arms wrapped loosely around her body, and she stifled a wave of panic by holding perfectly still. A shiver chased down her spine when his fingers brushed her skin, working the clasp in the back, unsnapping it with barely a touch. It seemed forever that his hands trailed down to her waist, before moving back to his side.

"I'm sorry," he said, his voice low and gravelly, made for pillow talk and intimate confessions.

Sorry? For what exactly? she wanted to retort, but was unable to even look away. He was back to being the lover she would've done anything for. She wanted to hold him, to let the weariness slip from her shoulders, to trust him to embrace her, skin to skin, to soothe her with sweet, languishing sex.

But damned if recent facts hadn't proven he was only a bastard in disguise. Definitely not her dream man.

She tore her gaze from his, waiting for him to leave.

What she least expected was the soft kiss he placed on her cheek before he stepped back. Sonya glanced up, holding the towel in place as her bra straps slid from her shoulders.

Kai turned and left. The door closed with a barely audible click.

If only . . .

Chucking that thought with the last of her underwear, Sonya stepped into the shower and let the tepid water drizzle over her, each droplet on the sensitive bruise reminding her of how wrong things had gone.

Why had he kissed her like that? In light of all that had happened, Kai wasn't going to let the fact that she was injured, stranded, and had no money stop him from doing his job. No doubt about that. There had to be a way to get that necklace back. It was the only real leverage she had to guarantee passage back to San Diego.

The day's events refused to wash down the drain, but it was the coarse sage-scented soap that made it hardest not to think of Kai, not to remember his body sliding over hers, his mouth-devouring kisses, the way he'd felt when they were locked in a tight physical embrace, the moment of thick mutual release dissolving deep inside her. . . .

Sonya lowered her hand and touched herself for a moment, remembering his fingers, clever and slick with her wet arousal. He'd made her feel like a real woman, whole and unashamed. Then he'd stolen from her and fled.

Reluctantly she withdrew her fingers, unwilling to submit to a fantasy of a man who had betrayed her so thoroughly. Still, she ached.

She'd never felt so completely like a woman, so in tune to every nuance of sex. Was it that sex before had been so incredibly boring and bad? Or was sex with Kai just that amazingly good?

And how could he be such a perfect lover and yet such a harsh, frightening stranger?

TEN

KAI'S HAND WAVERED over the doorknob. He'd knocked twice already, but the shower was still going and there had been no reply. So he walked in again and quickly replaced the nightgown Rosa had loaned Sonya with the pajamas Hector had loaned him. It wasn't like Sonya had the mobility to raise her arm to put on the nightgown anyway. The pajamas, with their button-down front, would be easier.

Besides, he liked to sleep naked.

Sleep? Not likely. On one hand, he had the craziest, absurd guilt that made him want to nurse Sonya's bruise, to shelter her and make sure she would never get hurt again. On the other hand, he knew better than to let down his guard. He had the necklace and he fully intended to get it back to Mrs. Miller.

He could handle another night of crazy sex. Heart-stopping, nut-twitching sex. It didn't help that at some level, he *knew* she felt the same way, too. He wanted to hear her swear using his name again, wanted to fall on his knees and venerate her with intimate kisses, to taste her until—

Rubbing his forehead, he stopped, abandoning the sentence in a fit of frustration. Instead he nudged his erection into what he hoped was a less obvious angle, but it remained locked and loaded.

He exhaled, facing the grim truth. The erection wasn't going to go away.

But what was he supposed to do with Sonya? He'd been so sure she'd been trying to trick him somehow by pretending she was injured back in the jail cell, but now, seeing that awful bruise on her shoulder, it made him wonder if he was losing his edge. He had to close the case and move on soon.

From the bathroom he heard a metallic groan of the shower knobs. Sounds of running water stopped, and just like that, Kai imagined her patting her body dry with a fluffy towel, stroking the terrycloth over the back of her neck, over the flatness of her belly, down between her legs.

He groaned and wiped his forehead. His dick was never going to go limp at this point.

Kai exhaled and paced some more to kill time, pausing to study the photos on the large dresser where Hector's family, along with a saintly figurine, were grouped in still-life harmony.

The more Kai stared at the figurine, the more it seemed like the safest place to hide the butterfly necklace. At least temporarily. Not that he didn't trust Hector with it, but the fewer people involved, the better.

Working quickly, Kai retrieved the necklace and fitted it through the small hole at the bottom of the figure. When he placed the figurine back, the saint's face didn't look quite as serene anymore. More like constipated. And the eyes were unnerving.

Kai turned the figurine slightly so the saint's gaze faced the wall. Lord knows he was in enough trouble without the religious aspects of what he was doing.

When the bathroom door opened, Sonya stepped out smelling clean and looking rosy. Her pajama shirt dropped to mid-thigh and the bottoms sagged around her toes.

"About time," he growled, then moved past her before she could detect his condition. At least he hoped her quick inspection was inconclusive.

She'd opened the small window, which helped to evaporate the steam, but on the towel rack her satin peach thong and bra were hung out to dry like Christmas ornaments.

Kai stared at them for almost a full minute before he realized what he was doing. He was going crazy imagining the mingled scents of soap, lace, and woman.

It was sick to want to grab the garments and sniff them, wasn't it?

"Christ!" Turning his back, Kai stripped and stepped into the shower stall, but the lukewarm water was steadily sliding into frigid levels, proof that she'd emptied the small water heater. That should've been effective to reverse his erection, but strangely enough, it didn't.

Taking a stance, he abrasively lathered himself, head, chest, legs, everywhere. When ignoring his penis didn't work, he reached for his erection and stroked the length with soap, imagining Sonya doing the task. He imagined her wet shoulders and breasts. Remembered the way her sex was hot, slick, and tight, God, so tight. And her mouth . . .

Kai clenched his teeth, trying to hold back the rush, prolonging it, but the ejaculation snaked from deep inside, causing his scalp to tingle with the effort it took to keep it from jerking through his body. A few more hand strokes and he felt empty again. He leaned an unsteady hand against the stall to keep his knees from buckling. The cold water gradually began to register as it trickled down his spine.

So much for having the upper hand.

He began to straighten, then there, in the shift of light, he saw a movement.

🦋

Sonya tiptoed into the bathroom, intending to put the pajama bottoms on the toilet seat. It had occurred to her that Kai's thoughtfulness—giving her the pajamas—meant he'd have to sleep naked.

Either that or he intended to sport the nightgown, and she knew him well enough to know *that* wouldn't happen. She'd deal with showing her legs, just as long as he had *something* to wear to bed!

She'd just placed the pajamas on the toilet seat and turned to leave when a low moan from the shower stopped her in her tracks. There it was, that rhythmic lapping sound.

She turned toward the shower curtain, her mind putting it all together.

Startled, she covered her mouth, then three seconds later, she moved a little closer, looking through the tiny space at the edge where the curtain hung partially open.

The wispy steam barely veiled Kai's reflection in the tile, head back, hand stroking his erection. The suppressed sounds he made were stilted and erotic, entirely too intimate.

The steam was hot against her lips as she watched the movement of his grip, hearing the sluicing water, straining to see the bulbous weight of his testicles and the watery shine on the length of his erection.

Sonya's breasts ached and tingled. Between her legs, the heat of need resurged, and she gripped the edge of her shirt, tempted to touch herself again.

For a maddening second she did, watching him do the same, then she swallowed dryly and pulled her hand away.

What was she doing? Kai could get out at any minute! Was she nuts?!

The sound of soap tumbling in the shower jolted her and she quickly scrambled out of there. Back in the bedroom, she breathed a sigh of relief to hear the shower still going.

Oh, this was bad!

She was hot and bothered and confused and there was no relief in sight. If Kai walked into the room, he'd be able to tell at a glance that she was hot to trot. How was she supposed to sleep with him in the same bed in this condition?

The only option was to take care of it. What was good for the goose, yada yada yada. Quickly!

She'd slid under the covers and started touching herself, her fingers dipping past the folds of her vagina, pushing a little deeper to where the empty ache throbbed. She stroked upward, all the way to her clit and back, mentally replaying the sight of Kai's grip, his shoulders back, his eyes closed, fist pumping.

Come on, come on! Who could compete against such a deadline?

It wasn't working!

She huffed and tossed. When she turned her head, she found herself looking directly at the figurine of a saint. She slammed her eyes shut.

Perfect. Just perfect. Now getting off was going to be nearly impossible. Lightning would surely lash out from the sky and fry her on the spot for masturbating in the presence of a saintly figurine.

She hastily wiped her hand on her shirt and went to move the tiny statue to another location. She'd just lifted it when her necklace partially tumbled out of the bottom.

Yes! Sonya enclosed it in her hand, still not quite believing it.

The thrill of victory and possession was soon followed by brief doubt. Suppose Kai was right and Uncle Otis truly had stolen the beautiful piece of jewelry?

Impossible. Irrelevant now. This was as good as getting her passport back.

The minute they were back in San Diego, she'd tell Kai where the necklace was. Who knows? By then she would finally be able to prove to him that both she and her uncle were innocent!

Heaven had smiled down at her.

Correction, more like a saint. The patron Saint for the Desperate, Horny, and Hard Up. She made a mental note to light a candle for it tomorrow. Maybe even two.

Now, where could she hide the necklace?

A quick look around the room inspired nothing, but then her gaze went to Kai's wallet, wristwatch, and belt, all tucked tidily next to his shoes. Mid-large shoes.

OK, so they were large. Whatever.

A quick peek in his wallet revealed about five dollars' worth of pesos. Upon closer inspection, she noticed a barely discernible zipper hidden in the seam.

She tugged it and gaped when she saw good old American money. Large bills, no less!

Why, that scheming, no-good, lying . . . The sight of a long, razor-thin blade at the back of the belt brought her thoughts to a halt. A blade? It looked dangerous enough, but the thought of Kai using it made her shudder. This had to be his extreme emergency pack.

What to do?

If she took the money and ran, she'd never get far. She might even end up in a far worse scenario than in a Mexican jail. As much as she hated to admit it, for the time being, sticking with Kai was the better of two evils. And this was the most foolproof place to hide the necklace.

Sonya quickly unzipped the belt beyond the point where the money lay and past the tip of the thin, flexible blade. She laid out the necklace inside the zipper, arranging it carefully so she could zip up without feeling any obvious lumps.

Kai would never think of looking at his own things. At least she hoped not. It was perfect.

The pipes in the walls creaked, indicating Kai was getting ready to step out of the shower. Hurrying, Sonya put everything back the way it was, then scrambled into bed.

🦋

Wearing nothing but a towel, Kai strolled to the foot of the bed, glowered at Sonya nestled under the bedsheets, and tossed the pajama bottoms on the chair nearby. "I'm not wearing those."

Sonya's heart lodged for a second before ka-plunking into motion again. Was her face hot? Did she look like she was guilty or, Lord forbid, dying to get laid?

"Why not?" she demanded.

"Too small and too tight where they shouldn't be."

Was that a bulge under his towel? No way. He had just taken care of business in the shower! She'd seen and heard it herself!

"And women complain when we stare at their breasts," Kai noted. "Lady, my eyes are up here."

She snapped her eyes back to his face, feeling the second wave of a blush take on her whole body. Her breasts, which *he* was openly ogling, perked up, all but straining for his touch.

His glower was gone, his pupils changing to a darker, more sensual hue that she was quite familiar with.

Sonya tugged the sheet to her chin. "You can't sleep naked!"

"Don't have much of a choice."

"You are a guest in this house. It's indecent!"

"Indecent? Right." His hand went to tug at the towel and Sonya quickly closed her eyes, then as casually as possible, turned to lie on her injured side, ignoring the pain from her protesting shoulder. The alternative meant watching him, and that was out of the question.

There was a definite slumping sound when the towel hit the floor.

"Well, good night," she said, a little too brightly.

He chuckled and seconds later the mattress behind her sagged with his weight.

The man had some nerve! A nice, sexy nerve. And if she were bolder and braver, she'd turn around and get freaky with it.

"Take your shirt off."

Her eyes popped open. "You have *got* to be kidding!"

"Of course I'm not kidding." He tugged at it. "Rosa gave me a homegrown remedy to put on your bruise and I intend to use it."

She looked over her shoulder at him and he

wiggled a blue-tinted jar at her. To keep from kinking her neck, she rolled to her back and put out her hand, not looking farther down than his chest. "I'll do it."

He shook his head, his eyes steadily holding hers. "Nope."

"Then no deal." Man, he smelled good. Clean, fresh-out-of-the-shower, lick-me-wherever-you-like good. Even his five o'clock shadow looked sexy. It blew apart the whole conniving bastard image she was trying to hold on to. Of course, how could that image compete?

"I already have two deals going with you," he reminded her. "One was made under blackmail and duress, binding me to take you to San Diego. And another, made under much more suitable circumstances, guarantees me all the fun I can get until you can't stand it anymore."

"Oh! That's . . ." *So true? On the money?* ". . . beside the point!"

❦

The look of surprise on Sonya's face was followed by a flash of excitement she couldn't quite hide with her fierce glower. The logical thing to do was to forget the sex, and just handle this like any other case.

But that was impossible. Wanting her was illogical. Knowing he was going to do everything he could to have her was illogical. God help him, but even knowing she was a crook was hardly factoring into his desire. Every instinct he'd ever trusted told him that this was right, even though it was goddamned illogical.

There it was, the glaring truth.

At least with stud services he could give them both what they wanted.

"Face it, Sonya, the only reason you're in this bed is because you wouldn't give up that butterfly necklace, right?"

"I'm here because you promised to take me back to San Diego. Besides, do you treat all your devious, underhanded con artists this way?" she taunted.

He raised an eyebrow. "Ah, yes, there's the fact that you're a con too," he noted somberly. "But that's the beauty of having two deals. I get the necklace . . . and sex. You get a ticket back . . . and sex. We get to enjoy both business and pleasure."

She studied him in silence for a few heartbeats. "What makes you think you can keep one separate from the other?"

That was the million-dollar question.

Propped on one elbow, he focused on opening the jar, then leaned over her to place the lid on the bedside table next to the bed. For a moment, her body heat seared the space between them. "They are independent and mutually exclusive deals. The question is, can you separate the business of our traveling arrangement from the pursuit of stud-service sex?"

She calmly reached for the jar, but he pulled it out of reach. "I take my business very seriously, Kai. I expect you to live up to your promise to get me to San Diego."

He nodded. "I take my pleasure just as seriously,

Sonya." And as she'd pointed out, a deal was a deal.

The heat in his eyes made her want to suck in air. She reached for the jar again. "Give it. I can handle it from here."

"Don't be stupid. You can't even reach the bruise to apply the stuff." There was a flicker of challenge in his eyes before his fingers moved to the first button of her pajama shirt.

In a flash, Sonya reacted, her hand covering his to keep him from the task. He looked downright pleased with himself, and a ghost of a dimple appeared in his cheek. Ever so slowly, with her hand still covering his, he undid the button, silently daring her to object.

"The bruise is on my back," she pointed out.

"Yeah. I know."

"Then I don't see how this is helping."

"I'm getting there."

His hand lowered to the next button, her hand still covering his. She had to count to keep her breathing steady, knowing he was perfectly aware of her reaction to him.

"This is ridiculous," she mumbled, but there was no way to keep her pulse from quickening or her voice from becoming embarrassingly breathy. Her hand felt like it was burning against his. If she pulled away, he'd think she was allowing it, and yet how could she fight it when her body wanted it so bad?

A third button followed.

"Just keeping it real."

Then the fourth and final button gave way. Kai shifted his hand so hers slipped from where it cov-

ered his. He parted the shirt just enough so the curves
of her breasts were revealed, but the rest remained
covered. Then, with purposeful intent, he slid his
hand beneath the shirt, moving around to her back.

"Kai, there are easier ways."

"Just be quiet," he said, his voice dark and almost
harsh.

He steadily pulled her to his chest, so they were
face-to-face, with minimal pain to her shoulder.
Once again, Sonya reacted by placing her hand between them.

His heart beat against her palm like busy kisses.
She shifted her hand to his shoulder.

If there hadn't been a bulge under his towel before, there was definitely a bulge now.

He sniffed the air and stared at her with a heated
gaze. "I'd recognize that scent anywhere."

Oh, God, no. . . . He lowered his nose to her
hand, and the pit in her gut clenched. Even with her
fingers curled into her palm, Kai had managed to
sniff out the lingering scents of when she'd started
to masturbate.

He made a show of sniffing her clenched hand,
letting her know that he knew where her fingers had
been.

It wasn't fair! Why should he be the only one to
find release?

Kai pulled her hand closer and flicked his tongue
over her knuckles, making a sensuous sound of appreciation. The wet lick turned into an exploration of
the clenched seam between her fingers. The sleek,
warm muscle of his tongue searched for an opening

to plunge into. It was ticklish and erotic, especially when he gently sucked on her fingers as if determined to lick every trace of her scent.

It was almost too much to bear when he sucked her index finger to the knuckle, sounding for all the world like he'd found chocolate. His velvety hot tongue lapped up and around her finger, the soft suction of his mouth sending crazy sensations up her arm.

He prolonged the torturous moment, then licked and nuzzled the sensitive area between her thumb and index finger. The ache between her thighs gripped and fluttered. It wasn't until he sank his teeth into her skin in a sensuous bite that she realized she'd been holding her breath.

"Open," he whispered.

What? Fingers? Legs? Heart? "No."

He didn't argue, and moments later he licked her fingertips and stopped. Sonya almost whimpered.

Still holding her close, he reached for the jar. She heard the suction of goo, then his hand was back under her shirt, moving up to her shoulder to spread the ointment.

His fingers moved gently, carefully rubbing in the concoction that smelled faintly of mint and eucalyptus. It was unnerving, hypnotic, borderline painful, and intensely confusing to feel Kai's aiding touch as well as his arousal.

"Close your eyes."

She did, not sure she was hiding much of the effect he was having on her.

Unexpectedly, she felt his mouth kissing her knuckles again, but this time his tongue speared between her relaxed grip, delving to touch her palm.

"Kai!" The laziness vanished, and she was caught in his gaze again.

His soothing hand still moved therapeutically over her shoulder, fingers flat, cresting just below the bruise, in careful, swirling caresses.

"Truth or Dare?" he asked.

She stared at him. "What?"

For a moment his gaze was flinty, his expression inscrutable, but his attitude hit her like a wave. His next words were spoken very carefully. "Truth? Or Dare? We agreed to play until one of us won."

The words echoed, full of possibilities and repercussions. She licked her lips. "If I choose Truth, is there a chance in hell you'd believe me?"

Kai didn't answer. Instead he lowered his head and nuzzled her fingers again, his warm breath tickling her skin. "Maybe you should take the Dare."

He had a point. Why should she deny herself? Debating her innocence with him wasn't working, but maybe he would listen to her body. "Dare me, then."

The circles he drew with his hands grew wider, traveling down her spine. "I dare you," he whispered, gently pushing her onto her back, "to lay . . . perfectly . . . still."

Sonya slowly nodded. Heaven help her, but she wanted this.

The dimple on his jaw made a wicked reappearance. His hand came around to cup her breast, caressing it, then holding the flesh in his warm palm. Sonya almost closed her eyes in pleasure when his thumb brushed over her nipple.

Mentally, Sonya did a countdown for control while he slowly stroked her, over and over. Kai arched an inquiring eyebrow.

His hand squeezed again, this time his whole palm trailed over the peaked bud, causing her breath to hitch even more. Whatever remained of the eucalyptus remedy he'd used on her back now tingled wherever he touched. The countdown she'd started now centered on the number of times he traced her nipple. Oh, heavens. . . .

He pushed the pajama shirt aside, returning his hand to her breast. His mahogany brown skin over her lighter brown skin created a vivid blend of color.

"Turn the light off," she said, suddenly uncomfortable with the thought that he'd get her completely naked under the bare bulb. Watching her every expression.

"No."

Sonya tensed uncertainly. "But—"

He lowered his head and took her nipple into his warm mouth, sucking once, then using his tongue to swirl around the very tip.

"Oh!" She stiffened so as not to arch her back.

He watched her a moment more before kissing her bared breast again. This time each lazy open-mouthed kiss was followed by the rasp of his bristly jaw against her skin and ended with soft-lipped nibbles.

She thought he said something, but he could've been growling. His lips moved to her rib cage, kissing his way to her belly button while his other hand absently caressed her covered breast. He nudged his face into her belly, and the textures of his stubby beard, caused by the movement of his masculine mouth and curious tongue, made her shiver.

His kisses and nudges heated a path from one side of her hip bone to the other, leaving a trail of bone-melting nuzzles and bites. Then he licked his way south until he was right against the rim of her pubic hair.

"Let me in," he said, his breath brushing against the trimmed hair before he kissed the curls with an intense slowness, teasing but not quite delving farther.

She hesitated, then parted her thighs and, on reflex, sucked in her gut at the erotic contact that caused more butterfly tremors to quake there. The air was clearly scented with her recent masturbation.

Oh, please, lick me there! Mount me already and get it over with!

Sonya wanted to grab his head and hold him against what should've been a very obvious destination. She felt off-kilter, her skin aching for his mouth, her hands and legs wanting to grab him and hold him against her, but the dull ache in her shoulder reminded her not to make any sudden moves.

Silently she gripped the bedsheets in her fists, dying in delicious misery.

Kai noticed and paused. "Talk to me. Tell me. What do you want?"

Sonya hyperventilated, proud that she didn't actually yell. *"What?!"*

"Where would you like me to touch you? When do you want me to do it? How do you want it, Sonya?"

I want you to kiss me hard, Kai, to feel your mouth on me, the weight of your body on me, feel your cock sliding deep inside me until I can't think anymore. . . .

A remote part of her mind triggered a warning. Was she really going to give him all the keys to her sexual weaknesses without a fight? Should she simply "open" because he wanted her to?

"I'm taking requests. Everything, Sonya. Anything you want. Now's your chance."

Stoically, she loosened her grip on the sheets and with all the calm she could muster said, "You were doing nicely on your own."

His hand stilled against her hip bone. "Sonya, Sonya, Sonya . . . What is it about the way you say 'nice' that makes me want to be really 'naughty' instead?"

In an instant, he moved so he loomed over her, his erection hot and firm against her outer thigh, his hips and torso lying lightly against her. With his eyes holding hers, his hand slid from her hip to the trimmed curls of her sex, covering the heat there with his fingers.

"Is this nice?" he asked, doing nothing more than circling firmly against her heat.

"I, ah— Yes, it's, um, nice."

He licked her bottom lip at the same moment he slipped two fingers into her sex. He paused there, her clit surely pulsing against his palm.

"Do you want more—"

"Yes!"

"Tell me."

"In. More. Please."

He moved much deeper, the downward stroke riding her clit until only the pad of his thumb remained on it. Again he paused, his thumb rubbing her, his fingers thick, his breathing raspy:

"Is this what you want?"

She swallowed dryly. "Yes."

"But?"

"Up a little. . . ."

His fingers adjusted. Sonya quivered.

"Move against my fingers," he whispered.

She did. Tipping her hips and digging her heels into the mattress. *Ohhhhhh, yeeeessss. . . .*

"Look at me."

She opened her eyes, dazed by the delightful sensations and finding his gaze to be so intense, she felt mesmerized by them.

"Do you like this?" His fingers half-twisted, moved inside her, rolling against the walls of her lubricated passage.

Sonya whimpered. "Yes!" Very, *very nice. . . .*

"How about this? . . ." The length and rhythm of his two fingers deepened, marked by occasional thrusts that were pure torment.

"Oh yes. . . ." She couldn't find it in her to be ashamed to beg.

"In the shower," his voice was thick and hoarse, "I saw your reflection on the tile."

Sobriety cut through the haze of lust, and her eyes snapped open. Busted! And somehow, instead of embarrassing her, Kai's words only aroused her further, and she instinctively spread her thighs to his probing touch.

"You were watching me." His fingers kept dipping, rolling, rubbing, his kisses on her lips becoming a little rougher. "And I imagined you with me . . . your hand slick with soap and water . . . stroking me. . . ."

His tongue delved into her mouth again and she sucked it, imagining herself in the shower with him to take his erection in the same way.

Cupping his head in one hand, she succumbed to the kiss. His hand trapped hers and guided it between their bodies to his penis.

His flesh was hot, long, and hard against her palm. Kai groaned in her mouth as she gripped and stroked his shaft, from testicles to the bulbous tip. He flexed his hips, thrusting with tight control.

For each stroke she gave him, his fingers returned the favor, making her forget that she wasn't supposed to move.

"Would you have done that for me?" His voice was dark and so gruff.

"Yes." Sonya gasped for breath against his neck, tasting the clean maleness of his skin. "I wanted to," she confessed.

The caresses of his thumb zoned in on her clitoris, coaxing the sensitive nub with a new caress until she was almost shuddering with need. She moaned ever so weakly, squirming briefly against him.

He paused and demanded, "Why should I give you more?"

"Damn you!" She was panting audibly now, with no way to disguise it.

"Tell me what you want, babe."

A tiny part of her died in mortification, but another part only wanted to tell him and make him suffer the way she was suffering.

Turning her head, she nuzzled against the pulse at his throat, then whispered words she'd never spoken into any man's ear. "I wanted to be on my knees, Kai . . . to take you in-into my m-mouth, all of you. . . . I wanted to feel you on my tongue, against the roof of my mouth, to feel you sliding between my lips and take you down as far as I could . . . to swallow your—"

He growled and stilled, hunkered above her. He turned to her, his face raw with desire. Sonya reveled in the power.

She kissed his chin, a ghost of a kiss, her body aching for him to resume his finger thrusts. "Would you want me on my knees, Kai?" she breathed. "Would you want me facing you? Or away from you?"

The coarse expletive he surrendered was said softly, beautifully. She felt his erection flex against the heel of her palm, clear to where her fingers cupped his testicles. Just saying the words was making her weaker and wetter. Ready to fall apart, knowing she was as much a victim of the lust as he was.

"I'd let you," she continued, still gasping for air. "I'd let you show me what you like, Kai. Everything. Anything. . . ."

His eyes gleamed, and she knew he remembered saying those very words to her earlier.

"Isn't that what you want, Kai?"

"Soon," he whispered. "I will."

He removed his hand only long enough to take hers from his erection and moved it toward her wet sex. Adjusting position, he eased his erection against her outer thigh, punctuating the next moment in a long, hard kiss.

"I want you to finish what you started in the bathroom," he spoke against her lips, his gaze so very hot. "Pleasure yourself for me."

"No!"

"Yes. Show me."

Their hands brushed together, his fingers locking with hers, coaxing hers to stroke with him. They fumbled, their fingers slipping on the wetness as their rhythms clashed, then matched.

It felt surreal. The act that was so intimately hers was now revealed and shared with him, too.

Kai's mouth was all over her face, trailing over her neck, over to take her other breast in a kiss that sparked a new connection.

Behind her eyes, the world tilted and whirled. The quivers started like defective muscle synapses deep inside her gut, randomly at first, then moving to her thighs as they both found the right pace.

"Like that?"

"Yes. . . . Oh, slower."

"There?"

"Yes. . . ."

"Please, Kai . . ."

". . . Mmmm. Yes. . . ."

". . . li'l faster. . . ."

". . . Faster, like . . ."

". . . that! Oh yes. . . ."

His tongue mated with hers, the movement matching their fingers, stroking and tearing at her self-control, strand by strand until—

Kai pulled her hand away and pinned it beside her hip.

"No!" Not again! "*God damn it*!"

"Shh, easy, babe. Don't . . . move." He was breathing as roughly as she was. In a skilled move, he suddenly shifted his body between her legs and slid the loaded length of his erection in one wet, velvet thrust.

Behind her eyelids, the image of his penis as it pushed past her nether lips created a rippling sensation.

The chain of synapses sparked off like flares. The second thrust was rougher, taking her completely and igniting the fireworks in a rapid sequence of liquid gut clenches.

She bucked and there was just enough time to breathe, then . . .

She was trapped in a soundless cry of pleasure, the fluid release stormed and flashed white behind her eyes, zipping in her gut. For an endless moment, locked in the ripe release of orgasm, she came undone, falling . . . falling . . . wrapped so tightly around him. . . .

The echo of it seemed endless.

The aftermath swamped her with bone-weary exhaustion, bringing the world in like shadowy intruders. Little details made themselves known. Somewhere in the bathroom, the faucet was dripping slowly. Outside their window a noisy car took a corner, then sped off. The bedroom walls seemed like guardians in the silence.

There was pure quiet perfection.

It was then that Kai whispered her name and kissed her softly, languidly, with such genuine tenderness that a lump formed in her chest. Kissing him back felt virginal, almost more intimate than the entire intercourse had been.

His nose brushed hers, his eyes mirroring her unexpected emotions. A roll of perspiration moved down his temple to his cheek, nestling where his dimple hid.

As if catching himself in a moment of weakness, Kai stiffened ever so slightly, then casually rolled off onto his back. Moments later, he turned the light out and the darkness engulfed them.

Sonya tried to convince herself that the empty chill that brushed her skin was from the perspiration cooling. But she couldn't deny that her heart felt strapped tight, aching.

Somehow, it was easier to close her eyes to the tears and, in the stillness, pretend to sleep.

The dream was muffled and obscure, the way those memories always were. Her momma was talking to the kind old lady with the white and pink flowered apron. The one who had brought Sonya oatmeal raisin cookies and cold, cold milk.

It was the gentle pat on her shoulders that the lady gave Sonya, along with the timid smile, that had made her bow her head, the weight of something uncomfortable and heavy in her chest. Why couldn't she just be a good girl?

"Quit squirming, Sonya. Do you need to use the restroom?" It was her cue to say yes, but she kept her gaze on her shoes.

"She's still shy for a seven-year-old," Momma explained in the awkward pause. "Do you have to go or not, sugar?"

The warning was enough for Sonya to nod and listen to the elderly lady give instructions.

Sonya moved as if on the moon. Long floating steps took her through the endless dark hallway where the photos watched her from their frames on the walls. She felt as if they would reach out through the filtered light and pinch her ears.

Just like Momma said, she'd found the old lady's purse in the bedroom, and she took the credit cards into the bathroom, where she copied them the way she'd been taught.

Place the paper over the card. Use the pencil lightly over it. Careful, now. Fold the paper for later and wipe your prints clean off it, girl, you got that?

There were so many cards! She'd hurried and done just like Momma said. Paper. Pencil. Wipe. Paper. Pencil. Wipe. Hurry, hurry. . . .

When they left, the old lady had touched Sonya's head with tenderness and it had made her want to cry.

But two days later Momma had been the one crying. She'd been furious, yelling and saying it was Sonya's fault the whole thing had failed.

Sonya had cowered, but Momma's hand was wide and as hard as a skillet. Bolting for the fire escape had been another mistake. Momma yanked her back by the pigtails and Sonya had fought in a blind panic, using her thin arms to block her face, shouting and—

"It's OK. . . . It's OK. . . . Shh, babe. It's going to be OK. . . ." Kai's voice finally began to make sense, the words tumbling together, then wrapping around her like his arms, warm and strong and comforting.

When had she climbed on him? Clutching him?! Damn, there were stupid tears sliding down her cheeks.

"Just a bad dream," she mumbled, but his arms held her, not letting her move away.

"Want to talk about it?"

She shook her head. What was there to tell? That she'd really been a con artist at one time? That she'd helped steal credit card information from anyone kind enough to fall for her mother's scam? After all these years, Sonya still felt like the malicious little girl who exploited people's kindness.

Baby girl, didn't Momma tell you to wipe the cards, goddammit! You goddamned stupid girl!

Her family had fallen apart. Her mother taken away. Sonya and her life thrown into foster care. All her fault. . . .

"No. I don't want to talk about it."

"OK." His hand caressed her head, massaging her scalp through the curls. There was a calm, centered quality to his voice that made her sigh with relief. For a moment, she wished he'd always be there for her if the dream should ever recur—which she knew it would. It always did.

It seemed that no matter how hard she worked toward decency, somehow the stain of the past always showed up again, tainting her, unwashable.

She lifted her head and made out his face in the dark, suddenly aware of his solid body beneath her. The dried tears felt tight on her face. Instinct warned her that she was being reckless, but the rioting need began to bubble inside her, demanding an outlet.

Would you ever believe in me, Kai?

Although her shoulder protested, she shifted upward, brushing her lips over Kai's bristly jaw, sealing her mouth with his.

He began to protest, but she hushed him and instead drank from his lips, quenching her thirst until the comfort of his touch became a caress. Until the flash of desire hardened his erection beneath her hips.

In the muted shadows, she straddled him and slowly danced on his lap, the rocking motions taking him into her body inch by inch, until he filled her, was sheathed in her, moved with her. Leveraging her arms on his chest, she took and gave, stalling every time his hips flexed . . . then riding urgently when the need demanded it.

Kai's hands ran up her thighs to meet at their joining, his thumbs trailed lower, finding the sensitive, swollen clitoris with a touch that made her feel like she was glowing, like a diamond about to rupture from deep, deep inside.

On a choppy breath, she drowned in the mindless orgasm, swaying weakly and holding on, milking him, riding him. . . .

Kai's grip flexed and he bucked beneath her, his cock thickening when he ejaculated. . . .

For a timeless moment, there was the absence of staggered breathing, of pulses still racing, minds still reeling. As intricately as she'd felt her senses twining into sync with his, she now felt them snap and unravel, gradually slipping apart.

Sonya slumped over him, the knocking of his heart was almost deafening beneath her ear.

Much later, Kai carefully tumbled her onto her back, falling asleep next to her, his arm possessively around her waist.

ELEVEN

KAI HAD AWAKENED at the crack of dawn and quietly hit the bathroom, hoping to keep some of the magic of the night between them.

There was something precious about the calm of her sleep, something equally dangerous, too. He'd compromised something he wasn't sure he was ready to admit to. It hadn't been sex for the sake of sex, but—well, whatever happened had happened.

For now it was enough to enjoy the moment and figure out how to deal with the rest later.

He was still mulling the thought when he found himself peering into the figurine where he'd hidden the necklace, his brain slow in jumping to the only logical conclusion. The necklace was gone? "What the—?"

He turned.

On the bed, Sonya slept like a seductive fallen angel tangled up in sheets. One of her breasts and a fair part of her buttocks were exposed, but she couldn't

have looked more innocent and inviting. And yet the
evidence missing from the figurine said it all.

Once again, she'd pulled a fast one on him and
like a dumb ass he'd fallen for it!

Keeping his anger in check, he methodically
searched the room, trying to imagine where Sonya
would hide the necklace. It *had* to be in the room.

When nothing came up, he tried the bathroom.

Nothing there, either.

Every place that turned up empty was like a slap
in the face. He should've expected this! Should've
seen it coming. She was a white-collar con, doing
what she knew best. Stealing! So why the hell was
he feeling so betrayed?! Because he'd let it become
a little more than business?

"Goddammit!" He pounced on the bed, straddling her.

She jerked upright, almost cracking her head
against his. When she flopped back, she instantly
tugged the bedsheets up to her neck.

"Where's the necklace, Sonya?"

She blinked at him, dazed, wild-haired and perfumed like a night of illicit sex.

"The, um, necklace?"

He clenched his jaw and managed to keep his
voice just short of a bark. "Yes."

They faced off for a long unblinking moment.

"Sonya, don't think for one second you can use it
for collateral."

"Why not? I need some guarantee you'll take me
to San Diego."

"I gave you *my word*!"

Her fingers flexed on the sheets at her chest. "I know. And I'm sure you'd keep it, but . . . I-I need more."

More? His fingers itched to encircle her neck, but the frightened-stubborn look on her face assured him she wasn't about to reveal where the necklace was hidden.

"So this is how you're going to play it?"

Her eyes pleaded with him. "I have no choice. Nothing personal."

Just business! Had her nightmare been business? He certainly hadn't consoled her with *business* in mind.

Pleasure versus business. He'd friggin' cautioned her about keeping the two separated and now he could hardly tell the difference. Dumb mistake. She could refer to the game as "stud services," but the way she played, it really was winner takes all.

She was a con.

He had a job to do.

It was best to remember that.

The fact that he'd been arrogant enough to keep the necklace in the room went a long way toward crimping and cooling his anger. What a rookie mistake! He should've worn the damn thing.

"Fine. But this is no free ride, Sonya."

She leaned up on her elbows. "What do you mean?"

Kai didn't have a plan for her yet, but that was beside the point. "It means you're going to put your acting skills to use. I have Romero to catch and you're going to lure him to me."

Her eyelashes fanned, accented against her cheeks when she concentrated on her fingernails for a long moment. "I . . . Well . . . OK, that's fair."

"Just like that, huh?"

Her gaze lifted up to his. "When I signed up for the cruise, I thought I was in for a week-long vacation. This looks like the closest thing to a tour guide as I'm gonna get, so why not? It still meets our business arrangement, right?"

Even though you cried in my arms last night, sweetheart? "Said like a true con."

He raised his hand before she could protest. "I swear to you, if you double-cross me or try to get back at me, I'll make you live to regret it."

Sonya paled for a moment. "I know."

"No. You just think you do." He moved away from the bed, anger still like a viper in his gut.

She made a quiet sound that had him turning around to see her surprised expression. "What now?"

"Nothing." She tucked some curls behind her ear, but even with an untamed, crazy bed head, she looked like luscious sin.

"What?" he repeated, letting his annoyance show.

"I just noticed . . . a tattoo at the small of your back."

She was *just* noticing?

"It's no goldfish-shaped birthmark," he bit off.

"Well, I wasn't exactly looking at your back when we were, you know. . . ."

"Obviously." Kai slipped a shirt on. *Just business, nothing personal.* "I'll let you do what you gotta do." He made an abstract combing motion toward her hair. "Just meet me in the kitchen in ten minutes. We've got business to handle."

🦋

For Sonya, the morning came and went in a hive of activity. Ever since the discussion that morning, it was as if Kai had erected a wall between them. Maybe not a wall, exactly, but he was definitely more aloof toward her. After the night they'd shared, she regretted the change in him more than she wanted to admit.

Kai had produced some flat leather sandals for her that were soft and comfortable. He also left her a buttoned shirt on the bed, but despite them, Sonya couldn't stand the pain it took to put on her bra, so she went braless.

By Kai's raised eyebrows and Rosa's averted face, that little fact did not go unnoticed. Sonya wished for a shawl, a poncho, or even a good old-fashioned Viking corset! She settled for hunching her shoulders.

Kai was talking on his cell phone when she stepped into the kitchen for breakfast. He hung up just in time for Rosa to stuff them with breakfast, then sent them on their way to the market, which Sonya imagined meant they were not to return without new clothes, interior *and* exterior.

The jiggle of her unrestrained breasts soon had her hunching her shoulders even more and crossing her arms over her chest, but it didn't help.

It was easier to dwell on Kai's unexpected tattoo.

Sonya had only caught a brief glimpse, but it was enough to identify the small, unique tattoo of spears across a tribal warrior shield. It resembled one she'd seen on a Kenyan flag. Interesting. Sexy, too. She wondered at the meaning behind it.

Not that it mattered. Details like those were better left unknown. It would be wiser not to know too much about him. Keep him at a distance.

By the looks of things, Kai was back in bounty hunter mode and therefore playing the role of curious tourist. Sonya could sense him casing everyone around them, sometimes using phony conversation to turn for a second look. The day had dawned gray and muggy, which in her opinion was not a good omen.

Kai's pace quickened until he was practically dragging her through the busy sidewalks. He seemed upset, but it was hard to tell if that was part of his bounty hunter act or he thought they were in real danger.

Sonya was starting to get a little paranoid when he led her into a clothing store, firmly tugging her behind some racks. He shifted out of sight, behind a stack of shelves, then instantly returned, handing her several bras with front clasps.

Oh. That.

"Going braless isn't helping us look inconspicuous," he muttered.

Blushing all the way to her toes, Sonya snatched the bras, unable to even glare at him. "Neither is storming into little clothing stores," she snapped.

An attendant showed Sonya a fitting room, giving her the privacy she desperately needed.

Unfortunately, even though the push-up bras solved the jiggly breasts problem, they presented a more bodacious appearance. But having the clasp in the front saved her shoulder the pain of twisting her arm at an odd angle.

She replaced the gaudy-colored bras he'd selected with three simple black ones, then added them to the basket of items.

He frowned and promptly replaced them with a blue one and a gold one.

"What's wrong with the colors I picked?" she asked.

"I'm buying, so I get to choose."

Her eyes narrowed. "You're such an ass."

Kai shrugged.

A few minutes later, it seemed only fair to replace the sensible gray and green boxer shorts he'd selected with ones that had cartoons of tequila-guzzling worms and grinning coconuts. She covered them with an extra shirt and skirt she'd also selected.

It wasn't until they were at the register that Kai noticed, but by then it was too late. The clerk quickly finished ringing up the items and reached for Kai's money before he could object.

When he narrowed his gaze at her, Sonya blinked innocently.

He tipped his invisible hat and reluctantly smiled.

A few more pesos changed hands and Sonya was allowed to use the fitting room to change into her new blue bra, blue shirt, and soft white peasant skirt.

It was amazing how much more feminine she felt with new clothes and fresh lipstick. It lifted her spirits, making her feel touristy and sassy. When she met Kai on the sidewalk, he was checking his wristwatch.

"Thanks for the clothes. I'll repay you."

"Hmm."

"Why are you looking at me like that?"

"You look earthy." His assessment came with a reluctant smile.

"Oh. Thank you . . . I think."

He twirled his finger, so she obliged and spun around once.

"You look like a Caribbean girl, all sunshine brown, about to go into the sugar cane fields."

She frowned, unsure how to take it.

He turned to walk. "Believe me, it's a compliment."

Sonya clucked her tongue and strolled beside him. "You smooth talker, you. I can only imagine what I looked like before."

He shrugged. "Like a million-dollar starlet down on her luck."

Sonya stopped in her tracks. "Starlet? Or harlot?"

"Starlet. A million-dollar one." He kept walking.

For a moment, Sonya wondered what the members of the accounting firm would think of Kai's bold remark. Sonya the geeky accountant turned starlet—whatever the heck that meant! The fine folks would be rolling down the formal aisles of the company, laughing their executive butts off.

She resumed walking and had to speed up to keep up with him. Half a block later, they stopped at a coffee hut where Kai bought them each a cold coffee drink that had the most unique chocolate flavor Sonya had ever tasted.

"Mexican chocolate," he explained. "It's the new iced cappuccino around here."

"Tasty," she said with a nod. She was about to reach for some soda cans, then calculated the price. "Is that right?"

"Yeah. They're pricey, but grab a couple. We're going to need them later. It beats drinking the water."

Back on the street, Kai was back to surveillance mode.

"Think you can run in those shoes?"

"They're not exactly track shoes."

He smiled and touched her cheek as if she'd said something sweet. "See those guys with the shades, loitering in the corner? No, don't turn your head. Wait just a sec, then casually turn. See 'em?"

She smiled, tried to look smitten, too, then casually turned her head as she did a flirtatious tuck of her short curls behind her ear. "Yeah."

"Careful there, you almost flagged down a plane."

She gritted her teeth to keep her smile in place. "Get to it already. Who are they?"

"A couple of the Romero brothers. Not good."

To her they looked like a couple of friendly locals.

Kai's eyes were a dark, maple brown, without a trace of the intimate smile he flashed her. "Relax and finish up the drink. But when I say run, you run. Got it?"

The blood surged in a mixture of anxiety and disbelief. "Run?"

"Come on, now. Smile and look natural," he commanded, doing so himself.

Sonya forced her lips to smile, then took a sip. "Boy, your legendary charm doesn't last long at all."

"In bed it does."

Sonya choked.

He patted her gently on her back, mindful of her injury. "Pretend to go to the restroom," he said under his breath. I'll meet you back there in a few."

"You mean right now?"

"As opposed to next July?"

Smart-ass!

She went to the back as instructed, not expecting him to show up and yank her out the back door and into the alley.

"Run!"

They crisscrossed a few blocks, then stopped behind a van.

"Kai, why are we running?" She gulped for air.

He peered behind the van before answering. "If history repeats itself, they weren't hanging around to chat with me," he replied sarcastically. "By the way, I put a gun in your purse just in case you need it, which hopefully you won't. But for the love of God, if you aim it at someone, you'd better be prepared to fire."

"What?" She hadn't signed up for *this*!

"It's just a precaution."

"I don't want a gun!" she whispered fiercely.

"Too late."

He checked the alley again, then pulled her along with him to a nearby door. When it proved to be locked, he banged on it.

Someone shouted back from inside. Sonya looked nervously about, trying not to think about the gun.

The door swung open, but the man's face soon turned into a fierce scowl. He started to slam the door, but Kai's reflexes were quicker.

"Tony, that's no way to treat an old friend." Kai pushed his way in and Sonya followed. The door closed with a thud behind her.

"Why'd you fucking come here, man?" the man whispered without a trace of a Spanish accent. He looked inmate mean, with a teardrop tattoo at the corner of one eye and an eagle taking up almost his entire neck. By the amount of dough on his apron, she would guess he'd been in the middle of making bread. Sonya slipped her hand into the purse, keeping her fingers lightly on the gun.

"Where's Raul?"

"Don't know. Look, I don't want no trouble."

Sonya glanced around. Two large sacks of flour sat on a counter and the air was rich with the aroma of fresh-baked bread. Several pots, bowls, and utensils cluttered the counter, and trails of flour powdered the floor.

"I just want Raul," Kai said.

The man didn't seem convinced, but Kai kept moving in. Sonya could hear distant voices and a loud TV blaring from beyond the swinging doors. A woman laughed with a child.

In a split second, Tony threw a cup of flour at Kai, but although the cloud hit him squarely on the belly, Kai was able to grab Tony's arm and twist it behind his back. In an experienced move, Kai shoved him up against the wall.

"Why would you want to piss me off, Tony? I told you, I'm not after you," Kai growled. "I just want Raul."

"I'm not a snitch, Armstrong."

Kai pushed further and the man gnashed his teeth in pain.

Kai kept his voice low. "Where is he?"

"If they find out I talked to you, I'm through!"

"Quit whining."

Sonya glanced at the doors where the woman's voice laughed again. Shit!

"Is that your old lady in the other room?" Kai asked.

"Naw, naw, man. Look, OK, Raul's hiding out with his sister, the one that lives by the post office downtown."

"The one by the plaza?"

"Yeah."

"He doesn't have a sister over there."

"Maybe it's another plaza, I don't know!"

"You're lying to me, Tony. You have a kid now, right?"

"Fuck you, Armstrong!" he whispered fiercely.

"Hey, what's your kid's name? Tony Junior?"

Tony remained quiet.

"Yeah, you're right. We should call her in here and—"

"Damn you!"

"I want Raul. Where is he?"

Tony gave up struggling and took a moment to think. "He's hiding out on Herrera Street, at Enrique's Pool Hall. Raul's got a room in the back. But shit, it's Mother's Day. Where the hell do you think he's gonna be?"

"That's the truth?"

"I swear it is."

Kai released him and Tony massaged his wrist.

"If you lied to me, it's over," Kai promised.

Tony sneered and reached for a rolling pin, causing Sonya to grip the gun again, her palms sweating.

"Get the fuck out, Armstrong."

"Yeah. Great seeing you, too."

They left the same way they'd entered. Once they were in the alley, Kai walked briskly up one block and down another.

The adrenaline snaking through her veins turned into a shaky anger.

"You OK?" Kai asked. "You look a little pale."

Sonya sputtered and yanked her hand out of his grasp. She hadn't felt that used in a long time. "Pale? What in sweet heaven were you expecting me to do back there?! You give me a gun—"

"Keep your voice down, would you!"

She smacked his arm. "— and then you pull a stunt like that?!"

"Keep walking. You're making a scene."

Sonya gaped like a fish tossed on a sidewalk, but before she could retaliate, he was cussing again and yanked her toward the marketplace.

"My shoulder!" she winced.

"Sorry, but we've got company again."

They were still in the alley, not far from the crowd, when a shot rang out, clipping the wall beside Kai's head. She screamed, chaos erupted, and Sonya found herself running through the flea market–like maze. The smells of unleaded gas, fresh flowers, and seafood assailed them. She found herself leaping over vendors' wares, the sound of smashing pottery in their wake where the other men followed.

"They shot at us!" Sonya shrieked.

She and Kai dodged several cars and a bus that was bearing down the street. People shouted and farm animals squawked, all clinging as the bus amazingly righted itself and kept going.

"This way!" Kai practically dragged her between several oncoming cars, then through an open plaza.

Kai snatched fruit from a stand and hurled it. Sonya grabbed one of the soda cans from her purse and, gritting her teeth against shoulder pain, whipped the soda can at one of the men.

It clocked the guy on his forehead, and he fell like a sack of rice.

"Jiminy Christmas!" The look on Kai's face was almost comical. "Where'd you learn to throw like that?!"

"Uncle Otis. Baseball coach," she managed, still running.

The diversion was enough to give them a head start, as with a cry, the other brother came after them.

They turned a corner, then doubled back around a large delivery truck, and Kai lifted her in while the loader had his back turned. Kai jumped in behind her and they squeezed behind a bulky stack of boxes, peeking at the activity outside through the large planks of wood that made up the sides.

"Shh." Kai placed a finger over his lips, signaling to a little kid who watched them through the slats of the truck.

Outside, the remaining Romero brother skidded to a halt in the middle of the street and started looking around. A number of people quickly moved out of sight when they spotted his gun.

Someone slapped the side of the truck. "Manuel, *ya vámonos!*"

The idling engine was revved, and seconds later the truck pulled forward, making its way over the pocked street.

After several angry shouts, the Romero brother ran frantically around, spotting them at the last minute.

He started shouting in Spanish as he ran and leaped onto the tailgate to climb into the truck.

Kai immediately went to push him off, but Sonya reached for the remaining can of soda, gritted her teeth again, and flung it. It bounced neatly off the man's head and he fell backward into the street.

Kai's ferocious expression turned into one of surprise. "You've got a helluva throw."

Sonya exhaled and sagged against the back of the truck, her heart still racing. "They shot at us!"

He made his way to her. "Just a couple of bullets."

"A couple of . . . !" She poked at air, wishing it were his chest. "This is insane! I didn't sign up for this."

"You sounded sure enough this morning."

"Adventure, yes! Bullets, no!" This time she reached farther and poked at his chest with her finger. "I don't have the first clue of what to do with a g-gun. I didn't care to witness you roughing up someone I've never met before, much less to be shot at!"

He shrugged, dismissing the hurricane of fear wailing in her chest as a minor detail.

" 'Roughing him up' is a bit of an exaggeration," Kai said. "I was only questioning him. Tony is a reliable snitch. We have an understanding."

"You were twisting his shoulder out of its socket!"

"I say tom-ay-toe, you say tom-ah-toe . . ."

She gritted her teeth.

The truck honked, and the driver shouted and promptly stomped on the brakes. The momentum pushed Kai's body into hers as the truck slowed to a hard halt. The contact brought a rush of memories. Although Kai's eyes looked slightly haunted, Sonya hoped she was mistaken about the bulge that pressed against her hips.

Sonya stammered in amazement. "Are you—"

His frown wasn't in the least convincing. "How can you even think of sex at a time like this?"

"*You're* the one with the . . . *I'm* not the one thinking of sex!"

"You brought it up."

"No, apparently, you did!"

He chuckled, but it died quickly when the truck surged back into traffic and he had to hold on to the knotted rope to keep from tumbling on his back. Sonya slammed against him, jarred them together again. Her breathing took a slippery dive.

"We have to stop meeting this way," he murmured.

"Kai!" she fumed.

"It's a switchblade." He pushed his hands into his pocket, then showed her the crude knife. His eyes squinted in a frown. "And I'd like to think my package is a little bigger than this, thank you very much."

"Do you even care that some lunatic was shooting at us?"

"Look at it this way: We're alive."

A couple of potholes shook the truck as it moved along.

She still trembled, wanting to lash out. "You're crowding me. Scoot back."

He pocketed the switchblade. "Can't. A box is blocking me."

His voice was gruff and he watched her with narrow eyes.

She peered around him, pretending to look through the slats at the street, all the while aware of Kai's body practically flush against hers. If he could be calm and collected after being chased and shot at, she could, too. "So, what's the plan now?"

"We get off at the next stop."

Interesting choice of words. She nibbled her bottom lip, wondering if maybe resorting to a mindless quickie was better than this horrible panic.

He grinned, his voice gruffer. "I just love how you think."

🦋

Kai couldn't help the rioting emotions that were going scattering through his system.

Things were wrong on so many levels. Flying bullets always made him reflect on whether the job was worth it, but at the moment that wasn't happening.

Sure, it had felt like his heart had completely stopped back there, when he'd thought the bullet was going to rip through Sonya, but here she was, safe in his arms. Kinda.

She hadn't thrown a fit of hysterics yet. It was as if she didn't know what to do with the adrenaline and jumble of emotions and was holding them tight. On the other hand, even though he was trying to ignore it, he knew exactly what his body wanted to do.

Goddammit, she was finger-poking his chest again. "You have no idea how I think, Kai! If you could read my mind right now, you'd—"

He kissed her, blue flames of need licked over the rush of adrenaline and erupted into hot orange. She groaned, shoved him away, then just as quickly snatched him back, sucking hard into the kiss.

What started out raw and desperate burned itself down until her lips became softer, tasting of such a timid fear that she trembled with it.

He kissed her long and hungrily, working her breath out of every sigh, moving her against boxes, against the vibrations of the vehicle, against the warnings that blared in his mind.

She moved, too, arching gently like a cat, pulling him closer and angling her head for more depth. No matter how much he sank into the kiss, it drew from him, taking back just as strongly, dragging his thoughts south.

He pulled away, deciding to taste the limber length of her neck instead. She moaned and quivered lightly.

The delivery truck suddenly came to a stop and the loud rough-idling engine was killed.

"Shit." He peered out between the slats, his heart still knocking off-kilter, reality seeping in. It looked like the loading dock of a hotel. Sonya was panting warmly against his neck.

The driver jumped out and called to someone, but there weren't many people around. Kai squeezed out from between the boxes, pulling Sonya along.

By the time the bay door rolled upward, Kai was ready to bolt. The young man stepped back, exclaiming in surprise at seeing them.

"My woman, you know," Kai said in Spanish.

The man laughed but reprimanded him roundly as they left. Although Kai was certain Sonya hadn't understood a word, her face was flaming again.

They walked briskly toward the sounds of the surf, finding the beach scattered with tourists wearing straw hats and sunscreen.

The tall cathedral landmark at the center of town stood with the glory of a lighthouse in the distance.

"Can't be more than four miles," Kai said, sure he was lying.

"Uh-huh. So, what do we do now?"

"If we stroll down the beach we can get away with looking like tourists and shortcut to the south plaza. That ought to buy us some time."

"What about the rain?"

He gave the gathering gray clouds another glance, then shrugged and started down the beach. "More than likely it will be a quick drizzle," he lied again.

TWELVE

AT FIRST, THE water stung the tiny blister on Sonya's left foot, but the pain soon receded. The sandals she wore were comfortable, but they still rubbed the wrong way a little.

The breeze was getting stronger, becoming the breath of a forming storm.

They strolled along the shoreline in companionable silence. If there really was a parallel universe, Sonya imagined that instead of having her hair-raising adventures through the streets of Puerto Vallarta, she'd probably be at her desk, working the numbers while trying to decide what frozen dinners she still had in her freezer.

What a vacation.

When Kai finally interrupted her thoughts, she wished he hadn't. She stopped in her tracks, the water lapping around her heels.

"Are you serious? You want me to pretend I need help with a car battery?"

"Raul is a sucker for women in distress, not to mention tight clothes."

She ignored the additional tidbit. "You don't think the fact that I'm black will tip him off that I might be in cahoots with you?"

"He'll suspect, but it's a chance I'm willing to take."

"How reassuring."

"Don't overanalyze this. I don't plan on giving Raul Romero time to think."

"There's all sorts of holes in this. For starters, where would you get the car with this alleged battery problem? How do you know Raul will be where you think he'll be? How do I know he won't just shoot me on the spot and ask questions later?!"

"Relax. Mother's Day is big in Mexico. He'll go to his mom's, guaranteed. As for the car, I'm working on it. And even if Raul thinks you're with me," Kai continued, "he won't shoot. He'll play along for a while, flirt a little maybe, perhaps try to trip you up on a lie. That kind of thing."

"That's comforting. Do you want to paint the bull's-eye on my forehead now?"

"You'd do that for me?"

She growled.

She caught him grinning and it irked her even more. "I guess if things don't go according to plan with Raul, you'll be rid of me without breaking a sweat. Sounds like a win-win situation for you."

"Atta girl. Way to put a positive spin on it." He sounded too cheerful.

She was clenching her teeth on a snide remark when a fat raindrop fell across her cheek and stopped her in mid-thought. "Oh no."

She looked around at the sprinkling of rain, suddenly aware of how close the storm was. The turmoil of sea waves frothed as they reached the shore, the breakers crashing like bottles of champagne against the cliffs.

"Come on," Kai said, "before you get struck by lightning."

"I thought you said it'd be a drizzle!"

He grinned. "I lied."

The wind rustled through the palm trees, tossing them around like anemones. A boom of thunder bellowed from above, so jarring that Sonya bolted for shelter.

Kai's strong grip found her hand and pulled her along to match his longer strides. At least he had the uninjured arm this time.

The rain chased and overtook them, forming a silver curtain that obscured the distant hotels in a hazy blur.

Running, they wove through the trees and headed beneath the scaffolds of a half-constructed building.

Once they were inside, they carefully stepped over wooden planks that littered the ground, and by the time they were in the heart of the building, Sonya was slick with rain, her curls drooping on her forehead.

The unleashing storm deafened overhead, the wind whistled as it rushed between boards, and the scent of sea and storm became infused with that of fresh wet plywood.

"What is this place?" she asked.

"Looks like a hotel lobby, I think."

The abstract carved artwork nearby, she decided, was probably intended to be an elaborate fountain of some sort. She looked around, noticing the tiles and walls with gaps in the planks that, from the correct angle, afforded a view of the street.

"For now, it'll do."

The enclosure made brief echoes of Kai's words, the cool breeze raising a shiver over her skin. The tone of his voice made her look over her shoulder at him, and she caught him looking right at her rear.

One glance at her gauzy white skirt was explanation enough. The rain had made the material translucent to the point of being porn-worthy. If the view was anything like the front, he could probably even see the peach color of her thong.

Thank God the navy top was not opaque, although the cold had raised her nipples against the tight material.

Sonya crossed her arms, but it was too late. Kai's grin turned the shiver that went through her to one of heat. The word *wet* plastered itself on her mind. Wet fantasies. Wet whatever.

"How long does the rain last?" she asked.

He shrugged. "Who knows?"

He placed the backpack near his feet and leaned back against a plank as if waiting for a valet to arrive. The position only served to emphasize the bunched muscles under his wet clothes, delineating the bulge in his crotch. Definitely not a switchblade this time.

The overcast light blended with the rain on his skin, accentuating his leanness, his sheer maleness.

She glanced away. "Is there a reason you're not springing for a taxi out of here?"

"Yup. We're not that far from town, and frankly, we don't have that much money left." He rubbed his jaw in thought. "Let's go over the plan again."

They took a few minutes to recap. Kai tugged at his clingy wet shirt with a frown of discomfort. Then while he talked, he began to unbutton it, stripping it off his shoulders.

Sonya watched the material peel away from his skin, revealing the roll of his shoulders, the tightness of his chest and abs. The sparse sprinkling of something gleamed just above his waistline, drawing her eyes lower still. His words rolled on in a jumbled tone.

Sonya swallowed audibly. *And the Striptease Award of the Year goes to . . .*

"Hey, lady. Up here." He pointed to his grinning face.

She cleared her throat and looked away.

"Want to see more?" His hands went to his belt, and she held her breath. The buckle made a small clinking sound, then the black leather was slipped through the hoop and—he stopped.

"Are you trying to put on a show for me?" she asked.

His dimples deepened and his low chuckle carried like quiet thunder. "Truth or Dare?"

Even though deep down she squirmed, Sonya stood stiffly. "Not if you're going to play this out like a bad porn flick."

"There's no such thing as bad porn," he said.

She held her hand up. "No, please. I'll take your word for it. Actually, I was going to point out that the flour Tony threw at you is melting into your, um . . ." She gestured toward his pants.

He glanced down and touched some with the tip of his finger, then raised it to his lips, eyebrows rising as he tasted it. "Powdered sugar."

Sonya licked her lips and caught herself in the act. The mischievous gleam in his eyes told her he'd read her mind, loud and clear.

His smile faded slightly, replaced by quiet intensity. His eyes reflected only pure challenge. "Wanna taste?"

"Don't you ever think of anything but sex?"

"This after you stared at my crotch?"

"I was just glancing around."

"Hmm."

She started to pace, then caught herself. "We were talking about the plan, remember?"

"Don't try to pull that prudish accountant act again, OK? I thought we were beyond that."

"I *am* an accountant."

"Crooked, sure, but I'm not buying the prudish thing."

"I'm not crooked!"

"Look, I follow the evidence, but to tell you the truth, I really don't care whether you are or not. I just want the necklace. Still do. But I also want you.

There's no point denying it. We're hot as hell together and that's enough for me right now."

It bothered her to hear him summarize everything so nonchalantly. "This deal for sex—"

"—is not subject to change." The intensity of his eyes captivated her. "You don't have to be coy, Sonya. What is it you want? Call it."

Old insecurities erupted. A part of her, the accountant with traditional preferences for sex, was tempted to cower. What if she wasn't able to please him the way she wanted? Was it really a good idea to play out a fantasy this way? After all, there was a raging storm outside, there was powdered sugar melting all over Kai's torso, and for the voyeur, there were gaps in the planks to think about.

A heavenly growl of thunder jolted her, bringing back the panic of being shot at, of escaping with Kai.

Carpe diem.

"Truth or Dare," she whispered.

He contemplated her for a moment. "Dare."

Exhaling carefully, Sonya approached him and placed his hands on the planks behind him. With her feet she nudged his apart.

She stood inches from him, feeling his breath fan against the raindrops still clinging to her face. Even as she debated kissing him, a trickle fell from the unfinished ceiling, down on his shoulder, trailing a path to the remaining powdered sugar, turning it into a shimmer of glaze.

"Don't move your hands," she ordered, sounding more nervous than in charge.

"Copycat."

Dammit, how did he always get the upper hand? "No talking! Except to forfeit. Ten words max."

"Damn. Only ten?"

"Seven now."

Another droplet on his shoulder drew her eyes and Sonya leaned in to kiss the spot, reveling in the almost inaudible hiss that escaped his lips.

He smelled of rain and clean male sweat. His skin tasted wet and slightly salty as she licked the rivulet of water from its origin on down his chest. Just above his belly button, the sweet flavor of sugar made her hum in anticipation. His muscles tightened beneath her lips.

Sonya got on her knees and nipped her teeth into the soft skin of his belly.

"Zipper," she said softly.

His hands left their grip on the planks and began to unzip the front of his shorts.

"Good boy," she teased.

His eyes lit with a million replies, full of hot promises of paybacks.

She started licking his flat belly button, lapping up the sugar there, rolling her tongue against the texture of tiny sweet granules and hot skin.

His chest billowed with his breaths, his eyes all but commanding her to do more.

She licked some more while trailing her hands up his knees to search farther under his shorts. When her fingers reached mid-thigh, she raked her fingers lightly down his legs.

His low growl said far more than words could.

She winked at him, then moved her mouth lower. Her hands moved back up under the shorts, then reached into the juncture of his thighs to fondle his testicles.

"God. . . ."

Six words left. She worked blindly, cupping and stroking him through his underwear, but still not removing his shorts.

When her lips encountered the elastic band of his underwear, she stopped and rubbed her cheek against the bulk of his straining erection, nuzzling and all but purring against it.

The scent of him was pure sex, male and virile, blending with the other scents of wood, sugar, and ocean.

He made a choked sound deep in his throat.

Using her teeth and hands, she tugged his shorts down, kissing arbitrary inches of skin that appeared, until his penis jutted out, straining in all its glory. The tiny smears of damp powdered sugar on his penis mesmerized her. Talk about icing on the cake.

She glanced up at him. Kai was breathing faster now. But then, she was, too.

The rude sound of a clattering plank cut into the moment and Sonya instantly jumped up and took a step back. She looked around, squinting at the gaps in the planks for signs of a voyeur.

Kai hadn't moved except to jerk his head to pinpoint the sound, but she sensed he was on the verge of action. Several seconds went by with nothing but the flow of wind and rain.

She could feel his attention return to her, watching her, drawing her gaze to his.

"Someone could be watching," she whispered.

He raised an eyebrow, daring her to continue.

His erection twitched.

Maybe the wind or the rain had knocked a plank over. Maybe it was something else. Someone else. It didn't keep her from wanting to taste him.

Kai groaned and closed his eyes, gripping the plank hard.

Sonya stepped up to him again, pushed back her worries, and sank to her knees before him. Her clothes felt tight and wet, clingy and cold where her body burned. She wanted so badly to touch herself. To touch him. . . . The hell with maybes.

"Please," he whispered.

Five words.

With deliberate slowness, she flicked her tongue out and licked his penis right under the plump tip. Nice. Different.

Kai tensed as if held at gunpoint.

The taste of sugar and rainwater had her licking again, swirling her tongue lower, placing indiscriminate open-mouthed kisses along the way. He moaned, barely suppressing the sound.

She cupped the weight of his testicles in one hand, then licked the length of his cock, using her other hand to gather the rivulets of rainwater from his belly, rubbing them on his sex. Her fingers encircled him, moving to stroke him, methodically working her mouth upward, too, almost to the shiny tip of his penis, licking around, then back downward, then up again . . . around . . . then down. . . . Over and over, shyly at first, then enjoying the experiment too much to care.

She could see the taut muscles in his arms, his heavy gaze all but begging. The moist noises of her suction blended with the storm. Sonya hummed, making sure her lips grazed lightly on his skin when she did, exhaling gently on the places she'd just licked. And when it seemed that he couldn't possibly get any harder, she took him in her mouth, working her jaw to take more with every try.

"God. . . ." Kai threw his head back and arched, straining with each dip of her head.

It was like sampling erotic dessert, lapping up the sugary, watermelon-like flavor and feeling his muscles respond to the most intimate kiss.

He groaned again, panting hard.

She let herself get lost in discovering him, finding out that several catlike licks on the head of his penis made him grit his teeth. Rubbing his sac while she serviced him made his moans sound like sweet agony. She hummed and he trembled.

He groaned, his head tipped forward, eyes half-mast as if he'd been flogged.

His expression was so open, so raw, she reveled in being able to read him. Really read him. He hid nothing.

It suddenly became critical to know the truth. To know what this man, bounty hunter and lover, thought of her.

"Do you think I did it, Kai? Do you think I'm guilty?"

He groaned, shaking his head as if to clear it.
Flecks of rain spilled down on her.

She sucked on his tight plump tip, just barely, in a
lazy kiss intended to keep him on the edge of release.
She licked his rigid length again. A suckle turned
into a deeper kiss. . . . Then she paused once more.

"Kai? You don't really think I embezzled the
money from—"

"Yes."

Their eyes clashed, the naked truth splintering
like hard, angry lightning between them. In an in-
voluntary reflex, she squeezed him in her hand, and
he moved against the stroking motion with a groan,
as if he couldn't help himself.

Something brittle cracked sharply in her soul,
leaking.

Kai's jaw clenched and he tensed as if to gather
the remains of his discipline. He closed his eyes.

"This is just a game." His words were filled with
urgency, anger, and so much more.

If that's what he really thought, then she wasn't
about to lose this battle.

She kissed him on the hip, then worked her way
to his erection again, blowing softly on the tip.

Kai groaned and jerked, submitting almost involuntarily when she parted her lips further, leaned forward, and mouthed the last strands of his control in
a succulent kiss,

Kai's control snapped and he thrust, spilling his
hot semen with a spent grunt.

Sonya took that and more, licking and kissing until his knees almost buckled. After a moment, he

shifted his weight more securely against the planks and she released him.

Sonya turned slightly to lean her forehead against his thigh, trying to cool her own sexual fever.

She should've made him suffer. He'd been ripe for breaking. And yet . . . she hadn't been able to do it.

When she finally had the strength to move away, it was to turn her back to him and step closer to the strange wall sculpture, into the circle where rain was falling. She touched the back of her hand to her swollen lips, feeling as if she were steaming, dying, every nerve ending crying out for relief.

There was no way to cool the storm that was threatening to erupt inside her, waiting to burst and dissolve into a million pieces! God, how could Kai trust her so beautifully with his body and yet not believe a word she spoke? And how could she want him still?

With both hands, she pushed back tendrils of hair from her face, feeling the water fall on her eyelids, wanting the rain to wash away her tears as well.

She ran her fingers through her frizzy curls, finger combing them. Behind her, there were the rustling sounds of wet clothes, then the sharp closure of a zipper. She kept her back to him, feeling hollow and used.

The longest five seconds in the world went by.

Without turning, Sonya felt Kai behind her. He kissed the side of her neck, a touch that zapped into the well of wetness between her legs. She wanted to scream and to shove him away almost as much as she wanted to ease her ache with his body.

She hardly struggled when he pulled her backward until she settled reluctantly against his chest.

"I don't need you," she said. It was a lie.

"Shh. . . . Come for me," he whispered, his hands already pulling up her skirt.

No. . . .

But his touch delved into the core of her sex, past her swollen labia, into the juicy ache. She tightened her thighs around his hand, her body suckled his invading fingers.

Yes, yes, yes . . . oh yes, please. . . .

He kept murmuring words, unrecognizable words, until she was way past resisting. He shifted a hand over her heavy breast and pulled her farther into his lap, delving deeper between her thighs.

Sonya closed her eyes and leaned her head back, surrendering softly to Kai's impending magic.

🦋

Kai held her with one arm around her waist and stroked Sonya's clit. She was slick, his fingers sliding over her folds.

It awed him how perfectly her body responded to him, how easily and instinctively he responded back, like a piano player fondling a familiar melody in the dark.

No woman had ever felt so soft and sinful. She was the only one who moved to the rhythm of his hand like a dancer. The echoes of her broken gasps seemed like voyeurs in the background. Her neck tasted like tears, but damned if he couldn't be sure. It was enough that his gut tightened at the thought.

By the time he nipped her earlobe, she was cresting, coming undone in a breathless stretch of sound, her hands against his thighs, gripping his shorts in clenched fists, straining.

As she spiraled toward ecstasy, he delved deeper and her secret softness suddenly twitched around his finger like hard colliding pulses, her jumbled breathing seemingly breaking . . . slowing . . . falling apart in the quietest gasp . . .

So damned perfect.

Undeniably perfect. He *knew* he was the first man to ever make her feel that way. He didn't care how cocky that made him, he just *knew*!

It was the biggest turn-on. A lifetime from now, he'd probably still react the same way to her. Nothing about sex with Sonya was even close to run-of-the-mill. It was stripped and bare and elemental.

For a while he held her that way, repressing his own impulses as she lay against him in lax satisfaction.

When she finally moved away, now stilted and so obviously embarrassed, Kai felt a cut of guilt. How could that be? She'd satisfied him, and he'd returned the favor. He'd taken the Dare and thrown in the Truth to boot.

"You OK?"

She didn't say anything for a while.

"The rain is letting up," she finally said softly, her back still to him. She was straightening her clothes, but the effort was futile.

He reached for the backpack and pulled out the khaki pants and yellow shirt he'd bought her. "Here."

She turned and took the clothes from him. Kai watched her struggle to slip off the skirt, hands tugging it down as she bent at the waist.

The sight was temptation enough to reach for her again, right then and there, but a new tension stood between them, more effective than any physical one they could construct.

What the hell did sex have to do with innocence or guilt?

He crushed back the questions spinning around in his head and busied himself tidying up the backpack while covertly watching Sonya. The pants he had bought her sagged low on her hips when she used the cloth khaki belt to pull her hair back. She turned and caught him watching. God help him, she still had the grace to blush, looking for all the world like the shy accountant she claimed to be.

With sudden uncomfortable panic, Kai realized he was losing perspective. Since the beginning he'd been intrigued by the mysterious combination of her wiseass spunkiness, passion, and demureness. Now he couldn't get enough of it.

And at that moment, he knew he was in big trouble.

🦋

"Ready to roll?" Kai asked.

"Yeah."

The rain had dissipated enough for them to walk the silent streets to the house of one of Kai's acquaintances.

Sonya sighed. Being miserable, cold, and wet simply did not qualify as an adventure. Waiting for Kai to use her as bait was not exactly the thrill of a lifetime, either. Was hot sex and the thus far elusive promise of adventure really worth it?

The silence between them was caged and edgy.

There was a measure of relief to be welcomed into the house of Kai's buddy. The man knew of a friend, who knew another friend, who could get them a junky car for the evening. After twenty minutes, some burritos and enchiladas, Sonya found herself in a Volkswagen Beetle relic that was dented, battered, and looked junkyard bound.

The rear window was cracked, the interior had a strong oily smell, and—she found out after a brief moment of horror—the brakes had to be pumped furiously to work.

Her nerves were stretched thin by the time they arrived at Hector's house. It was all she could do not to kneel on the street and kiss the sidewalk in gratitude.

🦋

"Listen." Kai raised his voice again to be heard. "I wish we had more time to rehearse this, but we don't, so just play it like we planned."

"It's not much of a plan."

"I won't let anything happen to you."

It was hard to respond to that, especially when he was pumping the brakes again, the paint on her door coming inches from another concrete wall.

"Kai, slow down!"

"I'm getting the hang of it," he said defensively.

Sonya was relieved a short while later when he'd parked on a solitary street, allowing her only a moment to catch her breath before he began giving her instructions.

"The snitch says Raul is with his two brothers. Just pretend you don't know what's wrong with the car—"

"Not exactly a stretch."

"Just look under the hood and keep talking until he gets close enough. I'll handle the rest."

"That's it? You want me to just look at the engine?"

"Yeah. And stay out of arm's reach. I'll have Raul bagged, tagged, and headed for the border in no time."

"Where exactly will you be?"

"Nearby. Come on. They'll be here any second now."

"And how will I know which one is Raul?"

"Thin as a reed. He's the one who's not a twin."

Kai was out the door and seemed to disappear into thin air, but more likely into the shadows of the nearby alley.

"Excellent," she grumbled as she stood. Her back and legs were unsteady, as if she had endured hours in a vibrating chair.

She did as instructed and stood next to the popped

hood, waving her hand to ward off the fumes that arose from the engine.

She didn't have to wait long to hear their voices. "Want some help, little lady?" There was no trace of a Mexican accent at all.

She turned, hoping she looked helpless and clueless. Raul Romero was as handsome as his twin brothers were equally ugly. He was also as thin as they were stout.

"Oh, thank goodness!" She leaned forward, pushing her breasts against the low shirt to show off her cleavage. "I was wondering how I was going to get help."

"What's the problem?"

"It made a squeaky, clunky sound and now I think it's dead."

"Squeaky sound?" Raul squinted at the engine. "You know what the problem is? I think—"

The rest of his comment was suspended by the distinct sound of a gun cocking.

"The problem, boys, is that Raul's gonna take a trip up north," Kai said from behind them, his weapon pointed at Raul's head.

The smiles on their faces deflated and Raul in particular looked angry.

"Get in the driver's seat, Sonya," Kai ordered.

Driver's seat? She tried to assure herself that Kai had an intelligent plan, even if it did involve a gun.

When she didn't immediately move, he nodded his head in the car's direction. "It's the one with the steering wheel," he said with a wink.

"Kai . . . it's a stick shift."

His smile was anything but genuine. "You can't drive a stick?"

"If you'd have asked me—"

"You made that crack about driving blindfolded!"

"I was making a point!"

He sighed and nodded toward the driver's side. "No big deal. I'll walk you through it."

"Still the pro, huh, Armstrong?" Raul sneered.

"Come on, pretty boy. The guys in jail need fresh meat."

Sonya closed the hood and scrambled to the driver's side. Moments later, Kai had handcuffed Raul Romero and shoved him into the backseat, while successfully keeping his brothers at bay.

"I wouldn't try that," Kai warned, waving his gun at one of the brothers. He settled into the passenger side.

"Listen. It's real simple," he said softly to her. "Step on that there, push this to where it's labeled one, then when I say 'go,' stomp on the gas, and slowly release the foot pedal. Repeat to shift through the gears."

In the rearview mirror, Sonya could see the brothers give each other a look. She exhaled nervously, took the stick shift in her hand, and once more followed directions, praying all the way. The gears made an awful grinding noise, and before Kai could give the word, the tires squealed and the car jerked forward like a racehorse bolting from the starting gate.

"Ho' shit!" Kai was slammed back against his seat, and from that point on Sonya could do little more than focus on the driving.

It was like a nightmarish video game where the object was to avoid hitting anything, because *the brakes didn't friggin' work!*

"Clutch!" Kai shouted.

"What?"

"Step on that one!" He pointed to the pedals.

"Oh." She stepped. He yanked on the stick shift.

The car picked up more speed, the grinding sounding less terrible.

"Again!" he hollered.

She cringed, but stepped. He moved the stick shift again.

By the time he was done, the car was blazing down the street, rattling like a box of nails down a hill. She spared a quick glimpse at Kai and found him grinning as if he was enjoying himself tremendously.

Half a mile away, Sonya started pumping at the brakes again, hoping to make a curve in the road.

"You should've asked if I knew how to drive this piece of crap!" she hollered, ignoring Raul, who was banging and yelling from the back.

"You're doing great!" Kai leaned over his seat and Raul's yelling was soon muffled.

"No power steering! No brakes! What the hell were you thinking having me drive this?!" The length of the khaki belt she used as a hair band flapped at her right ear.

"Go that way." Kai pointed to a street that required more brake pumping and steering wheel wrestling. Her leg muscles were getting a workout.

It was with some relief that she realized they were headed into a more rural area.

"OK, pull over."

Downshifting was an interesting lesson, which ended with the car abruptly stalling.

Kai wisely kept his mouth shut, but when they traded places, he gave her butt a teasing pat. "Awesome driving."

"Bite me!"

"Maybe later."

She strapped herself in the passenger seat and took calming breaths.

Raul, at least, had given up on his muffled shouts and backseat kicks.

Under Kai's hand, the car seemed to ride a whole lot smoother. He drove for hours, until her heart returned to normal and the town had faded in the background. She watched drowsily as the night began to creep over the sky.

Sonya realized she'd fallen asleep only when the noise and vibrations stopped.

"Wake up, sleepyhead. We're here."

"Here" turned out to be a little isolated house with cactus in the yard and the neighboring house at the horizon.

Kai stepped out and stretched while Sonya rubbed her face. As she reached to undo her seat belt, she noticed Kai's phone, almost under his seat. All that jostling and bumping around must've jarred it out of his pocket.

Heart pounding, she palmed the small device and slid it into her pocket, then calmly gathered her purse and backpack before stepping out of the car.

❧

"Hallelujah," Kai exhaled a short while later.

Things were going smoothly. Well, with the exception of the shaky car and Sonya not knowing how to drive a stick shift. Minor oversight.

He leaned over the engine, trying to figure out what had been making the awful clunking sounds, but at this point it was anyone's guess.

The stillness of dusk had him glancing at the safe house, wondering if Raul was still handcuffed under the sink and if Sonya was smart enough to keep her distance.

The hood creaked when Kai lowered it, and he headed indoors, tempted by a couple of hours of sleep and some of the tamales Rosa had packed for them.

He'd barely opened the door to the kitchen when he heard Sonya speaking.

"What exactly did you do?"

"I made a mistake," Raul replied, sounding like the drama king he was. "I was in a car accident and I had no insurance."

Kai stood by the door and watched Sonya's lovely back as she leaned on the counter to hear the rest of the story. He frowned when he noticed his phone by her hand. Dread started up his spine.

"That was it?" Sonya asked, baffled. "No insurance?"

"I was just twenty years old. I wasn't a U.S. citizen. I couldn't think of spending the rest of my life in jail, so I ran."

"I'm sure they have attorneys or special groups that could've helped you."

"And how was I supposed to pay them?"

"I don't know. If worse came to worst, maybe you would've ended up just doing a couple of months in jail, or maybe—"

"Maybe he's not telling you the whole story," Kai interrupted, making his presence known.

Sonya twitched in surprise, then straightened, her hand closest to the phone trembled slightly.

"Tell her the rest of the story, Raul," Kai prodded. "Tell her how the *accident* was really a hit-and-run *crash* that involved a ten-year-old boy on a bike. Tell her how you were so drunk you threw up all over the backseat of the police car. And don't leave out the part of how your good friend, Bronco Alvarez, put his house up to bail you out, because he believed in you when you gave him your sob story. He thought you were the real deal, right? *El mero mero!* So, he treated you like his own family and came up with the bail. Did I leave anything out? Oh yeah." Kai snapped his fingers. "Almost forgot to mention the part where you not only cracked a bat over your pal Bronco's head, but you robbed him and his family of the last two cents they had to rub together. Then just like the spineless coward you are, you hightailed it across the border to hide behind your mama's skirt."

Sonya carefully looked back and forth.

"Did I leave anything out?" Kai asked.

"I wasn't thinking, man!" Raul said in exasperation. "I made one mistake! What did you expect me to do?"

"Time. I expect you to do time."

Raul cursed vividly and fluently.

"Save that for your jail buddies." Kai walked over, pulling out his plastic gloves, preparing to shove the rag back into Raul's mouth.

"No! No, no, man. I'm sorry, OK? I'll shut up."

As casually as possible, Kai pocketed his phone and then dug through the grocery bag of items that Hector and Rosa had packed for them.

"If you're hungry, I can throw something together," Sonya volunteered.

"Cool. Thanks." What better chance to drug them, huh?

Sonya started searching through the cupboards, so Kai went to the bathroom and felt his heart hammering when he looked at his phone. His gloves came off and he tucked them into his rear pocket.

The last call he'd made had been to his brother. The last call the phone displayed was to a number he didn't recognize.

"Damn, damn. . . ." When had she snatched the phone? At Hector's house? In the car? More likely the latter.

He pressed a button to redial the number, hearing it ring several times, then bounce to voice mail. A cheery Otis Drummond announced he wasn't available but to please leave a message at the beep.

Kai hung up, then immediately dialed his brother.

"Hey." Dre sounded tired.

"Bad news. Sonya Drummond called her uncle—"

"Is that why his phone keeps chirping?" Kai could hear the deep honk of an eighteen-wheeler cruising by in the background.

"You've got him?"

"Yup, caught him sleeping in the car. I'll be pulling into San Diego in less than an hour."

"Money, money." Kai sighed in relief.

"How's the cruise going? What's this about Sonya?"

"Long story. Can't talk much right now. I'll catch you up later, OK?"

"Sure. Hey! You haven't forgotten the necklace, right?"

"Right. Meet you in San Diego."

Kai hung up and massaged his forehead. The only reason Sonya would have to call her uncle was to warn him either about the money they'd stolen, or the necklace.

The word Old Lady Miller had used came to mind. *Thwarted.* He'd almost been played again. It wasn't game over yet.

Sonya had made her move.

He had to be careful how he played his next hand.

🦋

The guilt of borrowing Kai's phone to call Uncle Otis gnawed at Sonya as they finished their reheated dinner and went about preparing for the night.

Her uncle's voice mail had kicked in, but the conversation she wanted to have with him wasn't ex-

actly something suitable for voice mail, so she'd
hung up.

Of course, Uncle Otis was innocent, and chances
were that he'd laugh with her when she explained
the embezzlement story that Kai had told her.

On the other hand, having to face the possibility
of Uncle Otis's guilt was a precaution. It didn't
mean she had to like it. *If* Uncle Otis admitted to the
crimes Kai accused him of, and *if* he confessed his
reasons to her, well . . . she would find a way to deal
with it. Somehow.

*Didn't Momma tell you to wipe the cards, god-
dammit!*

Sonya flinched, hearing the words as clearly as if
they'd just been spoken. *Oh, Lord. . . .*

She kept herself busy, cleaning the dishes—
stepping over Raul to do so—then putting them away.

The last thing she'd expected was to turn around
and find Kai leaning against the wall, with a look in
his eyes that clearly read: *My turn. . . .*

There was something about the depth of his eyes,
too, a darkness there she couldn't read. With a nod
toward the bedroom, he went down the hall.

Heart pounding, Sonya followed, suddenly aware
that the only doors to the house were the ones to the
bathroom and those leading outdoors. Otherwise,
the rest of the doors were missing.

"Um, what happened to the doors?" she asked as
she examined the hinges.

"They were removed."

"Yes, but why?"

He shrugged. "Your guess is as good as mine."

He fell on the bed, and it gave a tiny squeak.

Rising up on one elbow, he gave her a look that declared both war and seduction. "Handcuffs," he said quietly.

Oh no. "Look, Kai, we don't have doors, it's been a long trip, and—"

"And?"

For a second there, his gaze was piercing, and she was sure he knew she had used his phone.

"Can we skip sex tonight?"

There was a calculating look in his eyes, something just short of anger and yet not enough to override the sexual awareness.

"I wouldn't do anything that you won't like."

She crossed her arms. "I won't like whatever you're thinking of, so just forget it."

"How do you know?" His gaze lingered on her lips. "I haven't started yet."

She walked around him. "I'm going to take a shower."

"Fine."

She should've guessed he'd follow her in.

Of course, the handcuffs didn't do much to calm her, either.

He wouldn't hurt her, she told herself. He was just after another wet fantasy, good old raunchy sex, and the ambitious pursuit to win.

"Are you guys getting freaky over there?" called Raul from the kitchen. "You can't just leave me here tied up this way, Armstrong!" A loud bang that followed sounded like Raul had kicked a stool over.

"Let me handle this." Kai left her, already pulling the plastic gloves from his back pocket.

Sonya seized the opportunity to lock the bathroom door. At least now she'd bought herself some time, she hoped. She'd undressed and was in the shower when she heard Kai trying the knob.

He knocked.

She ignored it.

She was covered in soapsuds when she heard a jingle, then the shower curtain was pulled aside. Kai stepped in, gloriously naked, cuffs in hand.

"The door must've accidentally locked after I left," he said, his grin making the statement a lie.

"Strong wind," she replied. "Came out of nowhere."

"Hmm." He took the soap from her hands and set it aside, then he pushed each wrist behind her back, the shower knobs bumped against her buttocks and hands.

"What are you doing, Kai?"

"You'll see."

Warm water rained over them, giving her a sense of déjà vu.

With a *snick* the deed was done, handcuffs locked into place, her hands locked to the knobs.

He looked good wet. But the tension emanating from him was intense.

"Maybe we should talk about this first," she suggested nervously.

"Hmm."

He picked up the soap she'd been using to lather

herself and took over the job, his hands intimate and familiar.

They slid over the curve of her neck, slick with soap and suds, his fingers resting at her racing pulse, his eyes watching her intently.

She closed her eyes, but when he leaned in for a kiss, she avoided it. When she peered at him through her lashes, his gaze drifted downward to her breasts. His hands followed, spanning her waist, her hips, then the curve of her rear. Their breathing entwined, the heavy sound of it working like a hypnotic meter.

This time, when she leaned in to kiss him, he avoided it. His fingers dipped into the ache of her sex while his lips nuzzled her neck.

Sonya shivered and moaned at the unexpected tender rawness of her vagina.

"Shh. . . . Don't want Raul to hear you, do you?" Kai's fingers caressed again. And again. And again. . . .

Every time she thought he would delve deeper, he withdrew his hand to her hip. His mouth moved to kiss the flesh of her shoulders, down to the valley of her breasts, where he ravished each one until it was puckered and hypersensitive.

"Got something you want to tell me?" he growled huskily in her ear, his erection against her inner thigh.

Sonya felt wary, lust-drugged, and found it hard to even think straight. "Hmm?"

His chuckle was gruff, half-broken.

Then once again, his fingers were stroking her,

making her aware of every inserted thrust. "Mmm, Kai. . . ."

"Did you use my phone?"

Sonya stiffened, her body clenching around his fingers as the first waves of pleasure threatened to break over her. He withdrew and she whimpered.

"Did you?"

Her gaze was locked with his hard, unrelenting eyes, and she suddenly realized that beneath his tightly controlled passion, he was angry. Maybe even furious. The sexual inquisition wasn't going to be over until he had some answers. The pads of his fingertips caressed her clitoris, teasing the bud from its folds, the pleasure making her toes curl.

"Who'd you call?"

Oh, Kai, please understand. . . . She spoke between panting, trying to convince him. "I tried to call my uncle."

His fingers continued teasing. "What did you tell him?"

Sonya endured each caress, trying to control her focus on her breathing, her moans, but it was impossible.

"N-nothing."

"Sonya . . ." He narrowed his eyes, then moved in to lick the pulse on her neck, sucking it gently.

Oh, Lord have mercy. . . .

"What did you say to him, Sonya?"

"He didn't pick up," she managed. "I didn't leave a message."

"You are such a lousy liar."

"I swear to God, Kai—"

Kai cut off the rest of her words with a kiss that fairly exploded with pent-up emotion.

When her knees trembled as if about to fail her, he turned the water off and stepped back. His hard arousal was proof enough that he was denying himself as well.

"The game ends tonight," he growled. "Don't bother with the Dare. Take the Truth tonight."

"No. I'll take the Dare."

He moved in close until he was just inches from her nose. "Did you talk to your uncle?"

"No. That's the truth!" She glared back. "And I said I'd take the Dare."

He slapped the wall next to her head. "Damn you!"

She could feel the insistent throb of his hot erection against her thigh, could feel his chest grazing her breasts with every harsh breath.

"Why?" he finally asked. "Why'd you call?"

"I need to know," she confessed, hating that her voice choked up a bit. She jerked her chin up. "If he's guilty, I need to hear him tell me why. I need to hear *him* say it."

Kai's gaze remained on her, the passion mixed with bewilderment.

"I'm not lying to you, Kai."

❦

Kai felt the slipknot of doubt unraveling from what should've been a tight, sure thing. Every instinct in his gut told him she wasn't lying, but shit, his instincts had started failing him the day he'd met her.

What happened to all those distinct shades of gray?

"I have a one-time deal for you," he whispered. His large hands moved up her bare back, past the handcuffs and faucet knobs. For a second, her fingers brushed his knuckles as his hands wandered. He did it again.

Her skin was a radiant blush of mocha. It was a color he'd forever associate with Sonya being aroused.

She licked her lips and his erection twitched.

He whispered an insane sum of money into her ear. "I know you have it. It's a reasonable price for your freedom."

Her eyes widened, the shock complete. She shook her head. "You'd let me go if I pay up?"

"Mind you, it'll just give you a head start," Kai explained. "Run off to Brazil or wherever. But if I find out you and your uncle are anywhere near my turf, I'm gonna come after you. Guaranteed."

She tugged against the handcuffs, eyes blazing. "Listen up, you thick-headed, judgmental, blackmailing . . ." she struggled for the perfect words, "jerk! I'm innocent!"

"You left out stud-service provider."

"Ha! For all the good that's done—"

Kai twisted the knob on the hot water, so only frigid water flowed over her.

She shrieked.

Kai could hear Raul kicking something in the

kitchen again. Obviously the sleeping pill Kai had slipped him hadn't taken effect yet.

"You—" Sonya gaped in astonishment.

"See, that's how I know you're a liar. You couldn't fake your way through sex if your life depended on it. Not with me anyway. Sometimes you even begged—"

"I never begged!"

"*Begged* for it, like you were in heat."

Despite the goose bumps raised on her skin, she didn't look cold. Rivulets of water slid down her corkscrew curls and highlighted the gleam in her eyes. The last thing he expected was for her to launch herself at him, but her handcuffed hands tugged her back.

The tiny hiss was the only indication that she'd pulled on her injured shoulder.

Kai instantly felt the pain as if it were his own. Heck, if her shoulder pain was fake, she deserved an Emmy for that. Still glaring at her and cursing under his breath, he reached for the key and looped his arms around her to unlock the cuffs.

She turned her face into his chest and bit into the muscles of his shoulder, just hard enough for her teeth to make an imprint.

"Goddammit!" he roared as he backed away.

More banging spilled from the kitchen.

Sonya massaged her wrists, letting the handcuffs clatter to the wet tiles. She snatched a towel by the curtain rod and tried to step out, but he caged her in place with his body. Despite it all, his dumb, narrow-minded cock remained like a loaded shotgun.

Kai glowered at her, his shoulder throbbing. She

clung to the towel, chin up and eyes blazing with hues of frustrated passion and enough fear in the depths of her eyes to deflate his own temper.

"For the last time, Kai, I'm not guilty of anything," she repeated.

"The evidence speaks for itself. This deal is your first and last chance. Take it and run." His gut clenched at the lie. He wouldn't let her go.

Couldn't.

She remained mutinous.

He tucked a long curl from her cheek. "I can hear your accountant brain trying to do the math on this. Think of it as a long-term investment."

She shifted her stance ever so slightly. "Get this through your head. I'm not guilty!"

Stalemate.

Kai felt like heat was steaming from his skin, and yet she stood puckered and shivering. The thought of pulling her flush against his body was driving him crazy.

"Move," she said.

When he didn't, she ground out, "Please."

"My turn isn't over. Unless you forfeit right now, I plan on watching you not 'fake it' half a dozen times before the night is through."

For the next few seconds, only the falling droplets could be heard.

"And if I don't?" she asked.

"Hell, if you 'fake' it even once, really fake it, I'll not only forfeit the game, I'll send you off with traveling money, the necklace, and pay for any other expenses!"

It was a big mistake, Sonya realized from the bed, to blurt things out in anger without thinking things through. Challenging Kai to an orgasm? Was she nuts?

Whatever had possessed her to be so reckless?

"Rule number two," Kai whispered calmly. "If your hands leave the headboard, we start over."

Rule number one had been to keep it down, which was why Kai had been whispering since they left the bathroom. Raul hadn't made a sound, but Sonya was determined not to give the man an earful.

Besides, faking it meant not making a sound, right?

Get to the next rule already! She faced the wall, keeping her eyes right over the crest of the headboard. Her knees straddled the pillows, which Kai had fluffed and placed ever so conveniently for his head, so close to her sex that the breath of his words caressed her skin.

She nodded, determined to endure.

"Rule number three. Guess the letter and say it," he continued. "Any questions?"

"No."

"Good." His hands moved up her thighs, over the flanks of her buttocks to pull her closer. He inhaled and hummed.

Sonya gripped hard, refusing to look down.

"Last, but not least, all these letters lead up to a word. You've got to figure out the word to win."

Sonya took a deep breath. "Do I get any time-outs?"

She hated to admit that her legs hadn't stopped trembling since the shower. From experience, she knew his oral skills were superb, and the reckless fit of temper she'd had in the shower stall had disappeared, leaving only anticipation.

"Two," he said generously.

His nose nuzzled her clitoris, inhaling . . . exhaling . . . long and steady. . . .

He licked her, slow and velvety. Right on target. Sonya arched instinctively, sucking in air.

"Relax," he said in a soothing tone. "We're just getting started."

His tongue swirled, looped around her clitoris, then curled around again and stopped. Sonya panted.

He paused, then repeated the motion. Sonya bit her lip and strained to focus, but it only made her imagine his tongue in action. What in the world was he writing? *Oh, mercy, that curve right there . . . ohhhh . . . !*

"*E!*" she whispered huskily, stiffly enduring the third delicious motion.

Kai hummed his approval, the contact vibrating on her sensitive skin.

"T-that's cheating!" she accused.

"What? This?" He hummed again.

Oh, oh, ohhhh! "Yes!" she hissed.

"We don't have rules against that."

"Just give me the next one," she panted, hoping and praying he hadn't picked the longest word he could think of.

He licked and kissed her noisily, torturing her with his tongue through a delicious flat-licked *U*,

then moved on to a *T* that zapped her nerves with
pleasure every time he crossed the letter. The following letter, *S*, was the most delightful, sensuous,
spine-tingling *S* she'd ever had to succumb to.

Deep in her gut the mini-orgasms gathered force,
coiling and tensing at the oral spelling bee. Her
mouth felt dry, thirsty for kisses, her breasts ached,
and she knew she would shatter if she didn't con-
centrate to hold them back. . . .

By the time the next letter was carefully swirled
and drawn on her sensitive sex, Sonya was close to
grabbing his face in her hands and rocking against
his mouth until she found relief.

Oh God! Uppercase? Lowercase? "What the hell
kind of font is that?!" she demanded, sounding entirely too desperate.

Between slick-lipped kisses, he murmured, "Old
English. Cursive."

"Damn you," she gasped. More like wept. The
pleasure was that intense!

It took all her willpower to follow the movement
of his tongue. One crazy lick upward. A satiny loop!
Sweet mercy. . . . Oh . . . my . . . another loop . . .
down and . . .

"Time-out," she said breathlessly. She hovered on
the edge, her mind fighting the vortex of what could
only be one of the best orgasms she would probably
ever have. She gripped the headboard and panted,
for the first time becoming aware that Kai's harsh
breathing was causing his chest to brush against her
inner thighs.

She looked past her aroused breasts, down to

him, and their gaze held. Even in that, their wills warred.

She looked over her shoulder to where his erection was straining, veined and hard. Good!

"Time's up," he said.

Dammit. He must've seen the smile she'd tried to hide.

Before she could protest, he was back to stenciling intricate fonts with his tongue.

"B!" she shouted, only half-sure.

For a second, he seemed baffled. "You're good."

"Here's the last one," he said, then dived right to it. Sonya got it on the second try. Barely. Gritting her teeth and holding back the instinct to buck against his clever mouth.

"D!"

He acknowledged it with a very definite exclamation mark. Flat, quick flick of his tongue, followed by a definite dot. . . . Desire brimmed and trembled inside her, close to overflowing, threatening to spill—

"Time-out!" she squeaked.

His fingers flexed against her buttocks, and his groan was both disappointment and deprivation.

Sonya gulped in air to clear her brain. For several torturous seconds she couldn't remember what letters she'd called out. Little by little, they bounced around in her hazy mind, vying for order.

"Time's up."

Just like that, the letters grouped and formed the only word that made sense. Sonya laughed in a heady rush of victory and jagged pleasure. "BUSTED!"

Sonya's husky burst of laughter taunted and delighted him. He slanted his mouth over her sex in a final possessive kiss, swirling his tongue like a pen as he lavishly autographed his name on her beautiful, slick sex.

He tasted the last strands of her remarkable control just as he crossed his *t*.

"Oh . . . ! Oh!"

Even as she unleashed, he slid his fingers into her vagina, plunging, aiming for the G-spot, finding instead the tremors of her release. She gasped loudly, dropping unsteadily against his hand, then rocking against his fingers, crying out with shaky force.

The second wave hit, slick and hard, and she clenched so tightly around his fingers that he wished fiercely that it was his cock inside her. Each quake that came after it seemed to suckle his fingers farther into her sex.

Unable to hold back his own needs, Kai pulled his hand away and tumbled her onto the bed, leaned over her, and positioned his strained, engorged erection at the wet folds of her vagina.

Sonya's eyes were half-shut, her face was a mask of lingering ecstasy and innocent passion. She sighed in open-mouthed rapture. "Kai . . ."

It was less than a whisper, but enough for him to tumble her and surge between her parted thighs, sheathing himself to the hilt, groaning at the intense enclosing pleasure. Slick. Wet. Hot. Perfect grip.

He tried. God, he tried holding back, but he was unable to stop himself from surging again in wild, rough thrusts, demanding more than giving, barreling and crashing into his own orgasm. It assaulted and gripped deep in his testicles, snatching his breath, squeezing his soul.

He felt as if he had turned to stone, locked with her in his arms, sculptured in an eternal erotic embrace.

Then he breathed, dizzy with release, hearing her cry blend in with his.

The aftermath swamped and lapped like a full-moon tide, timed by the quick pulsing of her heart against his, of his breath billowing where he'd buried his face at the crook of her neck.

He rolled her on top of him to keep from suffocating her with his weight. She shifted slightly in her new position, her legs still entwined with his. Their perspiration made her belly slide against his in a sensitive contact of skin on skin.

For the tiniest moment, he caught her eye, then she tucked her head lower, out of sight.

Kai lay there, tangled up in her and stabbed by the feeling that he'd just behaved like a horny, savage brute. Shit! Had he hurt her? Had she cried out in pain or pleasure?

"Sonya?"

"Shh."

"Honey, I just wanted to know—"

"Not now."

"But I—"

"Please." It was said quietly, with tired finality.

Did she think he was going to gloat? God in heaven, he had to know if he'd hurt her! She wouldn't cuddle next to him this way if she was hurt, would she?

"Hey," he whispered.

Silence followed.

Doubt churned in him, shrouding the cockiness that had been flourishing earlier. Calling himself all kinds of names, Kai finally reached to tip her chin up to where he could see her face.

She had fallen soundlessly asleep.

The night seemed endless, and the question of whether he'd hurt her whirled back and forth, keeping him awake.

Hours before twilight, Kai finally cuddled up to her and slept. It felt like no sooner had he closed his eyes than something woke him up with a start. At his side, Sonya was curled up with her back to him, wearing his T-shirt.

When had she put it on?

A faint chirping persisted out of the stillness and Kai realized it was his cell phone logging a voice message.

Moving carefully, he left the bed, tugged on his boxer shorts, and went into the kitchen for some bottled water.

Right off, he could see that things weren't how he had left them. Not only had someone—no doubt Sonya!—delivered a beanbag to Raul for his comfort, but the stove's night-light had been left on as well.

Kai worked around Raul's dozing body to double-check the handcuffs and found them secured in place. Either Sonya was a soft touch, or she was extending hospitality to Raul because she had ulterior motives. More doubts reared their ugly heads.

Kai guzzled water and contemplated them for a moment, then went for his cell phone. Dre had left a message, sounding groggy and a little ticked off. "Old Lady Miller called twice. If you've got the necklace, let's collect on it, Bro. Call her back, would you?"

He went back to the bedroom, picked up his wristwatch he'd left on the bedside table, and checked the time. There were still a few hours left before dawn.

He went to the bathroom, washed his face, and brushed his teeth. As he dried off with a towel, he ran his hands over the faint bite mark that Sonya had left on his shoulder, then caught himself wondering again if he'd hurt her.

He'd been like a possessed beast. But had lust pushed him over the line, or had she also been lost in the ecstasy?

Disgusted with himself, he turned off the light and sat by the side of the bed, nursing his bottled water and watching Sonya sleeping serenely.

For what it was worth, she wasn't twisting with nightmares tonight.

Kai suffered the foolish urge to simply hold her.

The devil in him was twirling its pitchfork and not-so-subtly reminding him that if he'd picked a word like *embezzlement* instead of *busted*, he would've had the whole fandangled thing over with by now.

In the bed, Sonya sighed in her sleep and snuggled more comfortably into the sheets.

Kai was just about to crawl into bed with her when he heard the low idle of a car and the careful crunch of gravel.

THIRTEEN

SONYA JERKED BENEATH the hand that clamped over her mouth and the weight that was smothering her. For a second she struggled, but Kai's words were urgent in her ear. "Get dressed. Quietly."

He was already dressed and shoving items into his duffel bag. By the time she was dressed, he had already arranged the pillows under the sheets to look like bodies.

The duffel was strapped across his chest commando-style, freeing his hands to lead her into the kitchen. His gun gleamed faintly in the sliver of moonlight that poured through the window.

Raul was sleeping peacefully, seemingly unaware of Kai moving the handcuffs to his back. The nasal snores ended abruptly when Kai taped his mouth and tugged him up.

"Is that really necessary?" she hissed.

Kai replied with a ferocious frown and pulled Raul to stand. Raul wavered groggily, his eyes barely staying open.

"What's wrong with him?" she asked.

"Nothing. I gave him a little sleeping pill is all."

"You drugged him?"

"Keep your voice down."

The knob of the front door made a faint rattling sound.

Kai hefted Raul over his shoulder and tugged Sonya to the garage door. He pressed buttons on the keypad and they stepped into the dark garage just as another door squeak was heard in the house.

They walked out of the garage just in time to see a figure moving around the corner.

"Shit!"

Kai's comment barely reached her ears, but when she looked past him, her sentiments matched his perfectly. The tires of their trusty, dusty Volkswagen Beetle had been slashed.

"Romero punks," Kai growled.

He readjusted Raul's weight on his shoulder and they hurried to peek around the corner where the idling car could be heard.

The night wrapped around Sonya like a cold sweat as they crossed the yard to hide behind an anemic saguaro cactus.

The night was frigid!

The man in a relatively new Cadillac was smoking a cigarette, his focus completely on the silent house. They hunkered down by the trunk, the exhaust choking them but warming her legs.

Suddenly it seemed like the world exploded into action. With a deafening blast, the house alarm Kai had rigged began to shriek. From inside the house several shouts were heard, followed by gunshots.

Sonya watched Kai collide with the driver, who had started to bolt out of the car. The man whirled and grabbed her, pushing a knife at her throat and shouting something in Spanish.

Even with the deafening alarm, it was impossible to mistake the sound of Kai's gun being cocked.

"I'll kill her!" the man threatened.

Sonya held still, feeling a quick painful nick, then the warm roll of blood trickling down her neck. Raw panic gummed her mind. *No! Not like this.*

"We switch," her captor barked.

She'd never seen Kai look so calm. The gun he aimed at her captor didn't even waver. "Sure, but first she needs to tell me where the necklace is."

Sonya choked on her outrage. "What?!"

"Switch!" the man insisted.

"The necklace," Kai said, "or I'll let him keep you."

Sonya sputtered. Even her captor's grip slackened.

Raul groaned, and in the blink of an eye Kai had shoved him down and snatched the knife from where it pressed against her throat, pulling her away. Her attacker tried to turn the blade on Kai but failed and instead took a hard punch to the ribs.

Suddenly several gunshots were fired inside the house and the wail of the security alarm was abruptly killed.

Sonya scrambled into the driver's seat just as the shouts started to leave the house.

She stepped on the gas pedal and the car lurched. Kai dived into the backseat in the nick of time. The car fishtailed wildly, scattering gravel and dust before she got control of it.

The blinding fear was mind-numbing, but Sonya gripped the steering wheel and strained every muscle to keep the car headed down the road. She only allowed herself a breath when the angry shouts and the sounds of the gunshots grew faint.

Kai's amazed grin abruptly covered the scene in the rearview mirror. She watched him shuck off the duffel bag. "Hot damn! That was amazing!"

The need to punch him surged out of nowhere, but her fingers seemed glued to the steering wheel and the warring thoughts resulted in the car swerving to the right.

"I'm going to *kill* you!" she vowed viciously.

"Aw, now, honey, I wasn't really going to leave you back there."

The car swerved again and once more she overcorrected. Her blood felt like molten lava in her veins.

"Slow down, Sonya—"

"Shut up!" she commanded. "Just shut up so I can drive!"

Sonya lifted her right hand and began to angrily swat and slap at Kai as he slid into the passenger seat.

"Hey!" Kai backed away, leaning against the door until his head was almost out the window. "Just a minute! Calm down, will you?"

"No! I will definitely *not* calm down!" She did, however, stop hitting him. It was the only way to keep the car on the road.

She could feel Kai watching her as if she'd grown horns on her forehead. It didn't help that her throat was in the grip of what could only be tears. "You! You . . . shit!"

"Sonya, just calm down, OK, sugar?"

"Shut. Up."

He sighed, sounding somewhat exasperated.

She wished she could sigh, but there was the little fact that her heart was crowding her lungs, not to mention the hyperventilating, the angry seething, the wicked twitch in her hands to reach over and rip his throat right out!

After several minutes, she found that she could finally sigh. Not deeply, but just enough. The cool breeze streaming in from the open window felt good and she began to wonder where in the hell she was going. The road stretched out before her and disappeared into a murky dark horizon.

"Better?" Kai asked.

She gave him a quick glare. Roughneck! Meeting him had been the worst thing that had ever happened to her. "What you need is a bad boy," she mimicked Lisa under her breath. "Preferably one with a tattoo or an earring."

"What's that?"

She ignored him. "New clothes, new look. What for?" She didn't need to look at her hands to know that even the polish on each and every nail was ruined. Of course, that was far better than having her throat slit by a stranger in the Mexican desert, but at the moment ruined nail polish seemed like a vital and important detail to dwell on. The fact that she was also shaking was only pissing her off more.

"Pull over, honey."

"I don't think so." Nope, no way. She was going to drive this stupid, big, badass, Mexican mafia Caddy until she was back in San Diego, damn it!

She was just about to explain that to Kai when he suddenly reached over and pulled hard on the steering wheel, sending the car on a spin.

Sonya reacted by slamming on the brakes and the car screeched to a halt. In the back, what she hoped was his duffel bag thumped as it rolled off the seat and to the car floor.

Sonya gripped the wheel and gaped at Kai, words failing her.

"It's over now, babe. Take a moment to relax, OK?"

She swallowed roughly but couldn't dislodge the tears. "You're such a jerk!"

"I know," he said quietly, which somehow made it worse.

She bit her lip and glanced away, trying to hold it together.

She looked back in time to see Kai yank the key from the ignition and pocket it. With a final glance at her, he let himself out of the car.

Kai walked over to the driver's side, simply stating, "Scoot."

Sonya drummed her ruined manicure against the steering wheel. "Give me the keys. I'll drive."

"Don't think so."

He simply squeezed his body in, his sheer size effectively sliding her over to the passenger side.

She shoved.

He moved quickly, lifting her onto his lap and keeping her hands behind her back before she could think to pummel him again.

Now, close up, she could see into the dark pools of his eyes, to the emotions clashing there. "Look, I said I was sorry about what happened, but I wasn't planning on leaving you back there, OK?"

"I don't believe a thing you say!"

"Christ."

"You were going to let that man slit my throat for that necklace!"

"I had to let him *believe* that, Sonya, but I wasn't about to leave you behind." His voice was intensified by gruff tightness.

For a moment, Sonya was aware of his grip on her wrists, of the way his eyes trailed over her face, down to the cut at her neck. A pained frown creased his forehead, but the shadows in his eyes moved too quickly to decipher. With a muttered oath, Kai lowered his head and touched the raw cut with the faintest kiss.

She held perfectly still when he did it again, his tongue a gentle velvety texture.

"I swear to God," he whispered the words as if he were muttering only to himself. "I never meant for you to get hurt."

Sonya swallowed dryly, her anger dwindling at the tender assault. She wanted to believe him, could see his eyes pleading with her to trust him, but she simply couldn't. How could he expect her to when he'd all but made a getaway without her?

She suddenly ached for him to be the honorable, debonair man she'd met on the first day of the cruise, when she'd been dazzled by his charm and sincerity. Every time she saw glimpses of who he'd been, it made her heart tumble just a little further into despair. That man had been too good to be true.

A chill raised goose bumps on her skin. The empty yearning for adventure she'd felt on her birthday all those nights ago suddenly seemed as safe and comfortable as winter home fires.

"I can't trust your promises anymore." She tugged her trapped hands. "Let me go."

He studied her face. "Did I hurt you?"

"You're hurting me now!" she said. It was a lie.

His hands slackened, but he continued to hold her. "I didn't mean to."

"Save it."

"All right," he said, letting go of her hands. He leaned back, letting his large hands rest in his lap. "We need a plan to get Raul back."

"What?" she asked, thrown by the change of subject.

"I'm not leaving Mexico without him."

Sonya had always thought of herself as reasonably patient and kind, but she found herself holding back a feral growl.

"That vein shouldn't be popping out of your

forehead like that," he said. "Take a deep breath and relax."

Suddenly Sonya found herself deposited back in her seat.

"Seatbelt," he cautioned right before he jammed the key back into the ignition and maneuvered the car back onto the road.

❦

Kai was relieved to see Sonya finally relax. He'd driven for half an hour now and he couldn't get the taste of her from his mouth. All of her: doubts, sex, skin, and that thin cut at her neck.

Kissing her wound had meant tasting her, and he realized it had been like a primordial vow. Beyond words. In fact, he kept reliving that moment, seeing the nick, seeing the trickle of blood. . . .

He'd failed to protect her.

Shades of gray had turned to red. Crimson. Completely out of his league. What the hell was she doing to him?

He spotted a dip in the landscape and turned the car around, heading toward it.

"What are we doing?" Sonya's voice was filled with panic.

"Going back."

"Going back?"

"It's better to nab Raul now before the sun comes up."

"Can't you cut your losses—"

"No. It's all about the principle now."

"Principle?"

He scratched his chin. "Have you noticed you're repeating everything I say?"

Peripherally he saw her spine stiffened and her arms crossed over her breasts. When he glanced at her, her eyes were blazing once more and her lips were pressed together tightly.

"Not to worry," he assured her, "you can stay in the car until I get back."

She opened her mouth to speak, then shut it with an audible click of her teeth.

It seemed that almost too soon he was coasting to a stop. With the engine off, the silence was disturbing.

He reached into his duffel bag for his gun, checked it, then handed it to her. "If I'm not the one trying to open the door, shoot and ask questions later."

He kissed her before she could react.

"I won't be long," he promised.

"I'm coming with you."

"No, you're not. You're staying here."

"Watch me."

He glowered at her to make his point, then turned and left. Seconds later, she was right behind him.

"Sonya—"

"If you think I'm going to stay there twiddling my thumbs while I wait, you are sorely mistaken!"

"Sonya—"

"I'm not going back."

Her jaw was stubbornly set and that more than anything wore him down, but he gave it one last try.

"Watch where you step. Snakes can curl up in the oddest places."

Her fingers tightened on the gun. "Right now, one snake isn't that much different from another."

🦋

Sonya followed Kai, sure that the world could hear her heart knocking in her chest. The dry riverbed they'd parked in was low enough to hide the car. They peered above the rim to the house. Their position afforded a view of both the front and the back of the house. There were a few lights on, which projected silhouettes of movement on the windows. In the front of the house, a man was talking on his phone.

By her count, there were at least three Romero thugs, not including Raul.

Kai settled against the elevated riverbank. Behind him the sky was a spectacular cloak of blue-washed ink drizzled with tiny stars. If only she had a campfire and a sleeping bag to snuggle up with him. . . . Instead, she was trying to hold down an anxiety attack.

"So what's the plan?" she asked.

"I go in while you stay here. I come out, jump in the car, and you drive like hell."

"*This* is your plan?"

"Yeah. I learned it in Basic Apprehension 101." He handed her the car key and leaned forward.

She pulled back. "Don't do that."

"Do what?"

"Kiss me again."

"Come kiss me, then." Even in the dim light, she could see his dimple. "For good luck."

Her fingers itched to cup his head for a tonsil-tingling kiss, but she held back. "How about I just wish you good luck?"

He winked, grinned, and quickly moved through the sparse darkness farther down the riverbank before heading toward the house.

She felt her blood turn cold as she watched Kai finally make it to the back of the house, weapon in hand, his back flush against the wall.

From the front of the house a huge dog strolled a path to the man with the phone.

Sweet Jesus, where did the beast come from?

She held her breath as she watched Kai peer into the back door, then let himself in. The man in the front yard pocketed his phone and rubbed the dog's massive head.

Sonya strained her eyes, her ears trying to pick out sounds and movements that were too far away.

"Come on; come on. What's taking so long?" she muttered under her breath.

It felt like an eternity went by before she saw the back door open again and Kai sneak back out with Raul thrown over his shoulders like a bag of potatoes. He'd just made it to the edge of the riverbank when Sonya noticed the dog's head perk up. The man had tried to open the front door and was now banging on it. He sprinted to the back of the house in time to see Kai.

The dog bolted like a shot, the man chased him, and Kai started shouting, "Start the car!"

She ran to the car, shoved the key into the ignition, and turned the engine. She backed up fast, sending pebbles and dust in all directions. Kai slapped the side of the car when it reached him, dumped Raul into the backseat, and dived in after him.

Kai shouted out when the dog managed to bite the bottom of his jeans and wouldn't let go. Sonya turned in her seat, grabbed one of Rosa's burritos from Kai's duffel bag, and threw it at the dog.

"Just drive!"

Sonya turned back around, slammed her foot on the accelerator, and the car leaped forward. Kai slammed his door shut and she saw the dog in the side mirror, chasing them with his owner not far behind.

"A burrito?" Kai asked her.

"You have your ways, I have mine."

She gripped the steering wheel, trembling from nerves and afraid she'd slam into the side of the gutted river at any minute.

In the backseat, Kai started laughing, his amusement booming until she could practically see his molars in the rearview mirror.

"I was trying to help."

He only laughed harder.

"Well? What did you expect me to do?"

The riverbed dipped, bouncing the car. Kai was all but clutching his ribs.

His infectious laughter cut through the panic

and Sonya found herself fighting the bubbling urge
to join him.

"Oh, God. You're killing me," he groaned.

She allowed herself a muffled chuckle, which gave
way to laughter. The tension drained from her shoulders and suddenly she was sure that everything
would be OK.

$$\text{🦋}$$

Several minutes later, when the car was out of the
riverbed, Kai asked Sonya to pull over so he could
drive.

He was about to pull off when he suddenly put
the car in park.

"I just thought of something."

He got out of the car, opened the back door, and
dragged Raul out of the backseat. Kai hauled him
over to the roadside, where he started frisking Raul.

"What are you doing?" Sonya asked, staring with
her mouth open.

"His brother said they tracked us, and there was
no place to hide. So it has to be on him. . . ." Kai's
hand fisted around the necklace and abruptly tugged.

The thin chain gave and Kai studied the little
cross. He reached into his back pocket, pulled out a
switchblade, then used the tip to pry out a tiny round
device from the center of the cross.

"GPS," Kai grumbled, squinting at it for a moment before tossing it over his shoulder.

Global Positioning System. No wonder they'd
been tracked.

Kai dragged Raul back to the car and unceremoniously dumped him into the backseat once more.

Kai and Sonya both got back in the car and drove until the sun came up.

was damaged. Raul has the cuffs key... Get out, Sonya.
Slowly uncurled him, and they're coming after us...
Kai and Sonya hurried close to the car and now in...
the McIntyre downs...

FOURTEEN

DRIVING IN THE dull, dead heat was wearing on Sonya's nerves. She'd just flicked a glance at Kai when suddenly she saw Raul lunge at him.

"Aaaargh!"

Both cuffed hands slammed toward Kai's head, but he managed to move and the blasting thud hit the headrest. The car swerved as Kai half-turned to ward off Raul.

A punch flew, another connected, and the car swerved again, veering off the main road.

Sonya watched the swing of strong arms moving mere feet from her. She clung to the door, too stunned to interfere.

With driving force, Raul head-butted Kai, then clipped the handcuffs hard against Kai's throat. Kai gasped and keeled forward, managing to step on the brakes and bump the gears into park. The car shook and stopped in its tracks like a shot bull, leaving only the sounds of an idling engine and Kai's strangled breathing.

Raul doubled his fists and pounded the back of Kai's head with a grunt of satisfaction, then quickly climbed into the front seat.

"Fucker!" Raul opened the door and kicked Kai out. Kai held on to Raul's leg and received another kick in the chest. Kai was half-crouched and tried to catch his balance, but the kick sent him sprawling in the dirt.

Sonya tensed and reached for her door handle, but Raul had already slammed his door shut and, still handcuffed, threw the car into drive and edged it back onto the main road.

The car had started to eat up the stretch of road when Raul let out a crazed, victorious yelp. He grinned at her and hooted again, shouting a torrent of Spanish.

Raul practically bounced with joy. "Give me your water."

Sonya did as he demanded. He awkwardly steered with his knees while he guzzled her precious ice water. Heart thudding, she reached into her purse and fumbled for the gun Kai had given her the day before.

Raul had tossed the empty plastic bottle into the backseat when she cocked the gun, her hands trembling. "Stop the car."

"Aw, fuck!" His face became a mask of anger.

"Pull over!"

"I don't know what the hell you're doing with him, but even I can see it's not exactly a love match."

Her hair band snapped in the wind, but all she could think was that Kai was back there. Alone. Injured. "Pull over!"

"You're not going to shoot me—"

Sonya aimed and fired out the driver window. The sound was deafening. Raul jerked and the steering threw the car off the road again. He tried to lunge at her, but she recovered first, aiming the gun mere inches from his nose.

Her aim twitched and wavered. She tried to loosen her grip, praying she didn't accidentally discharge the weapon. The car slowed as it bumped over uneven ground.

"Raul, I swear to God, if you don't stop this car . . ."

"First chance I get, I'm gonna—"

"What?" She centered the gun at his forehead.

Revenge gleamed in his eyes.

She trembled, more frightened than she'd ever been in her life and bluffing with everything she had. "Get out."

For several seconds she thought he wouldn't obey, but finally, he did, slowly, casing for an opportunity.

He started muttering in Spanish.

"Back!"

She waited until he was a safe distance from the car, then she slid into the driver's seat, gun still pointing at him, dropped her foot on the gas pedal, and peeled out.

With numb fingers, she turned the car around and headed back to where the outline of Kai was about four inches tall at the horizon.

Sweat trickled down her neck, but she felt marginally calmer. Kai had a tiny limp, but as she neared, he stopped in a hard stance, his clothes scratched and grimy. His shaven head gleamed in the sun.

She parked the car next to him and stepped out. Her knees weakened, but she locked them, realizing she still held the the gun in her hand. It slipped from her fingertips.

Kai swallowed, and at that moment Sonya wasn't sure if she was any safer with him than she'd been with Raul. His anger seethed, rolling from him like a fist.

"Where is he?" Kai's voice was as coarse as gravel.

Not trusting her voice, Sonya pointed.

"Did you shoot him?"

"No."

Every breath she took was hot. She felt both light-headed and freezing inside. *Did she shoot him?* No, but she almost had, and that was too much!

She turned to walk over to the passenger side, but before she could take a step, Kai whirled her around and pushed her up against the car.

His eyes searched hers and with a guttural sound he sealed his lips to hers in a hard, forceful kiss. She couldn't turn her face away, could hardly deal with his strength.

There was a wildness in his eyes that frightened her. She tried to push him away but couldn't. The whirlwind of panic grew and she squirmed and shoved against him again.

"Christ!" His voice cracked in the whisper and the mood shifted. The wildness in his eyes ebbed and his lips softened slightly, his arms wrapping around her until their bodies touched from shoulder to thigh. She felt the slight tremor in the tendons of his arms as he pulled her closer still. This time his lips were tentative against hers, unsure.

It touched the frightened part of her, dispelling the fear. She stopped fighting him and kissed him back.

Then once more, with something stronger than fear.

The kiss slowed until tongues and lips touched, yet didn't move. A breath later, she inhaled greedily, her body shuddering, the ice melting in her bones.

He whispered something low and gruff.

Then, just as suddenly, he'd whirled away from her. Her body sagged against the car, holding her up when she would've slid to the ground.

"I owe you one."

She pressed her lips together. They felt overly plump and swollen. His words remained jumbled and incomprehensible.

His breathing was still uneven. When he reached for the door, Sonya snapped into action and forced herself to move to her side of the car.

Without a word, Kai pulled off while she strapped herself in.

He gunned the engine until Raul was back in sight. For a moment Sonya thought Kai might run him over. Instead, Kai stopped a few feet away, pulled the trunk latch and stepped out, walking right up to Raul.

Raul swung his handcuffed arms. Kai dodged and threw a kick that connected with Raul's inner leg.

With a shout, Raul went down, holding his knee and howling in pain.

Despite the cries, Kai dragged him to the car and threw him into the large trunk, closing it shut with a thud. He immediately began banging and shouting.

Kai slid back into his seat, fastened his seat belt.

"Kai, it's got to be over a hundred degrees in there—"

A muscle twitched at his jaw. "Not another word, Sonya."

He started driving again.

🦋

"You OK?" Kai asked her.

"I'm fine." She was glad to see far-off houses and trees. "I wish I'd booked a vacation to a tropical jungle instead."

"No joke."

The banging in the trunk had stopped and Sonya tried not to think about the man sweltering in it.

A short while later, they crested the outskirts of the city of Ensenada.

She'd been waiting for Kai to reveal his destination, but he remained wrapped up in his thoughts as they drove through the service entrance of a quaint mission-style resort that announced it was the Oasis.

She followed Kai past the flourishing garden to what was obviously the workers' entrance.

"Señor Armstrong!" They were met by a tall, lanky man with a smile and mustache that dominated his face.

"Francisco, my man. How's it going?"

"Life is good! Hector said you might come this way." He was dressed in a sharp business suit and appeared to be in charge.

"Hector is worse than a mother hen."

Francisco chuckled, then slapped Kai on the back with familiarity.

"So, you are Kai's woman!" Francisco asked after a break in conversation.

Before Sonya could answer, Kai put his arm around her, molding her body next to his possessively. "Amazing, isn't she?"

"Absolutely," he agreed.

Kai abruptly patted her butt in what could only be a show of macho possessiveness.

Sonya flinched, but Francisco was already leading the way into a boisterous kitchen.

"Come in, come in!" Francisco waved them in with his hand.

Sonya glared at Kai and gritted her teeth. "If you grab me like that one more time, I'll field-kick your family jewels over the border before you can think to apologize."

Kai laughed as if she'd said something sweet, then winked at her.

A firm squeeze on her shoulders warned her to play along. So, she pasted on a smile and held it in place.

The kitchen was filled with bold scents of Mexican

cuisine. The fire from the stove whooshed, and the heat emanating from the stone oven rivaled the heat outside. Everywhere, workers were moving. It instantly reminded Sonya of the waiters on the cruise.

Once they left the maze of the kitchen, they entered a small, modest office that looked out to the parking lot.

"Forgive me," Francisco said to her, "but I conduct business much more efficiently in Spanish."

"By all means. Go ahead."

Kai and Francisco immediately started speaking Spanish, leaving her to feel much like a potted plant.

Francisco picked up the phone and placed a call. When Sonya stifled a yawn, Kai casually touched her thigh.

The contact sent invisible spirals up to her breasts.

"Tired, hon?" Kai asked casually.

Not anymore! "A little."

"I have a surprise for you."

Uh-oh.

Francisco hung up, and soon after, a maid knocked on the door.

"Please, please." Francisco stood to escort Sonya to the maid. "Your surprise awaits. Enjoy the comforts of the Oasis, compliments from us on your recent engagement!"

Engagement?!

Kai brushed a kiss on her lips before her jaw could form the gaping denial. "Go on, honey. I'll catch up with you in a minute. Enrique and I still have some business to discuss."

"But what about Romero?" she whispered.

"Taken care of," he whispered back. What the heck did that mean? When Kai squeezed her hand, she realized he was waiting.

"That was very kind of you, Señor Francisco," Sonya said. "Thank you." Sonya flashed the chintzy smile again, forcing it into play a little longer. The maid led her through a beautiful lobby, past what looked like an indoor chapel, then on past a gift store where dildos, vibrators, and negligees were prominently displayed at a fifteen percent off sale price.

Oh, sweet Mary! It was like an elopement chapel in Vegas.

"Would you like to see?" the maid asked in heavily accented English.

"No! No, no."

The maid smiled diplomatically, then continued on.

Farther down the hall, the maid produced a key and opened the door, ushering Sonya inside.

Sonya took one step through the threshold and blinked in disbelief. The room was huge, the decor a mixture of a sheikh's palace and Tarzan's jungle.

"This can't be our room!"

"Absolutely, yes. Your fiancé wished you to be surprised."

"Believe me, I am." A warmth spread in her gut and she found herself genuinely smiling. "Is that an indoor pool?" Sonya pointed to the smooth trailing water surrounded by several tropical plants.

The maid nodded, as if the replica of paradise was an everyday thing.

Sonya glanced around, hesitating over the lush Persian veils that covered a king-size bed, revealing only the impression of pillows and colorful sheets. A few bowls of fruit caught her eye and made her stomach rumble.

"The kitchens are open until eleven thirty. We also offer laundry service and have a hot stone mahseuse for your convenience."

Hot stone massage? After being in the desert? No thanks. Laundry service? Yippee! Her skin fairly itched to rip her grimy clothes off.

"How would I use the laundry service?"

The maid pointed out the discreet basket chute, then pointed to the schedule when the clothes would be back. Turnaround was only a few hours.

"If you wish for anything else, please ring the lobby."

The maid executed a curtsy and left the room. For the first time since signing up for the cruise, Sonya felt like twirling around in glee.

She raised her arms and did just that, then sniffed her armpits and cringed. Laundry definitely had to be done. But first there was the issue of hunger to deal with.

She perched next to a bowl of fruit and popped several grapes into her mouth. Using the knife provided, she sliced up part of a papaya and ate it, groaning in satisfaction. She sliced some mango, which she also ate while shedding her clothes.

If Kai showed up while she was stark naked and salivating over fruit, then fine. There was no help for it. Chances were that the night would end with one or both of them naked. So, why not set the advantage?

"Hussy," she chided herself.

Nude, she tagged and dumped her clothes in the basket chute, pressed the button, and heard the suction that took them away.

She selected a large towel, picked up a bowl of fruit, then went to the shore of the lagoon-like pool.

If she stayed in the small cove, the leafy plants and the two large silk curtains could partially hide her from the view of the front door.

Looking around once more, she placed the bowl of fruit nearby, then carefully walked down the gradual slope into the pool.

🦋

"Are you sure you don't want the video? They are quite discreet and controlled remotely. It can be your souvenir to enjoy time and again, yes?"

Kai knew that Francisco meant it as a gift. After all, the man ran one of the most successful role-playing resorts in Mexico. Whether it was a dungeon, an Irish bar, or a tropical jungle fantasy, he could create—and professionally film—a couple's trysts every step of the way, for the right price.

Yet the suggestion raised Kai's hackles and almost made him vault from where he sat.

Anger.

Possession.

Passion.

Oh, the thought of seeing Sonya's lush naked body moving against his, caught in instant replay . . . Hell, as of the moment, it topped his Christmas list.

But she's mine.

And no matter how professional the gift, Kai wasn't about to share any part of her, image or not, with anyone.

"No, thank you." Even to his ears, the words sounded curt and menacing. When Francisco paused to light a cigarette, Kai tried to remedy the situation. "You've already been more than kind."

Francisco studied him through the smoke he exhaled. "OK, we shall do business then."

It wasn't until their discussions were over, deals made, and handshakes completed that Kai finally left in search of his room.

Halfway there, he finally admitted it was guilt that had driven him to get the room for her. Guilt over the possibility that he might have been too sexually rough the night before. Guilt because he was starting to doubt her involvement in the theft. Guilt because the game was all but over and he wasn't ready for it to end quite yet.

Hell.

He wondered if Sonya realized she'd been locked in. If so, the rooms were either soundproof as hell or he was about to get his head chewed off the minute he stepped through the door.

He paused with the key in the lock. He was tired but looking forward to being with her, regardless of whether it meant a war or an orgasm. It wasn't the kind of thing that fell into any shade of gray at all, and frankly, it was scaring him a little that he didn't know what to do about it. He wasn't even sure he wanted to.

Repeating that she was a con wasn't having its desired effect anymore.

Jeez.

He turned the key and opened the door.

🦋

Sonya had been floating on her back, chewing on a tangy-sweet guava, when the front door opened. She immediately scrambled to hide, grateful when it proved to only be Kai.

He locked the door behind him, placed a chair against the knob, and scanned the room for her.

She slinked back down, barely keeping her shoulders above the water level. He still spotted her instantly. A smile curved his lips, and the charming dimples appeared. "I leave you alone for a second and you're already naked."

She shrugged. "Don't you want me to be naked?"

"It's my favorite way to have you."

His words caressed her like a phallic stroke, so unexpected that she clamped her thighs together. Once again, the intensity about him was arresting. How did he do that? How did he take the upper hand away from her?

As he strode toward the pool, he tugged his shirt off and threw it negligently over his shoulder. Then his hands went to his belt.

"Kai . . ."

"What?"

She gripped the edge of the pool, trying to deny that her heart was racing and her body warming. What indeed . . . ?

"Francisco seems like a nice man."

"On occasion, he is." Kai kicked off his shoes. So damned cocky.

"Where's, um, Raul?"

Kai's smile stayed in place, but the heat in his eyes cooled. "Still worrying about him, huh?"

"Nope. Just wondering."

The zipper made a sharp, brief sound as Kai's hands worked it down with a flick of his wrist. "He's still alive and kicking."

Kai's hands remained on the tab of his jeans, waiting. "Any other questions?"

"No."

"Good." Kai shucked his jeans down, along with his underwear.

He looked lean and natural, man at his most elemental. His manhood was half-erect, bobbing with each step as he entered the pool, slow and predatory.

"No. Absolutely not, Kai. I don't want any sex tonight."

Kai swam closer, nearing until she could feel his body mere inches away, his heat pulled to her as if in slow motion through the cool water. Despite the light scent of flowers and fruit, Sonya could smell him. Maleness, sunlight, and desert sweat.

"Did you hear me?" she asked.

"Yup."

With a ripple of water, he lifted his arm, and she thought he meant to touch her face, but instead he reached for the bowl of fruit she'd perched nearby and selected several grapes. He popped some into his mouth. His jaw flexed, the muscles in his bristly jaw moved.

"Um, when I made the comment earlier about a tropical paradise, I didn't intend this."

"I had business with Enrique and he just happened to have a room. No big deal."

"Liar." Her smile widened when he frowned.

"Whatever."

"Is this because of what happened today with Raul—?"

"No." His eyes narrowed.

God, he was making this so difficult! "It's very nice of you. Thanks."

He scowled. "Do you have to talk everything through?"

"When it deserves an explanation, yes."

"Fine. I, ah, wanted to thank you is all."

"For what? Not shooting Raul or not leaving you in the desert?" Seeing his frown deepen made her want to grin.

"You're not going to make this easy for me, are you?"

"Didn't think I'd have to go waving guns about and shooting out windows, you know?"

"Dammit, you're ruining a perfectly good seduction with needless conversation."

She struggled to hold back a chuckle. "My bad.

I just thought that given the circumstances between us—"

"I thanked you. Just tell me I'm welcome and change the subject."

"Not yet. I think I may be cut out for this business. Maybe not the shooting part, but I could handle the rest."

Kai glowered. "Forget it."

"Of course, I don't know how to twist an arm out of a socket or anything like that."

Kai popped a grape into her mouth. "Woman, you don't know the half of it."

She chewed and swallowed. "I'm just pointing out that—"

"Shh."

"Kai, you—"

Another grape was pushed past her lips, but this time he leaned over and silenced her with a rushed kiss, taking the grape from her tongue and biting it between his teeth.

Sonya flicked her tongue, toying with the grape. "No fair."

The pupils of his eyes darkened and a ghost of his left dimple appeared.

When she did it again, she licked his lips, too, nibbling there, then moving on to gently bite into the fruit. Water lapped quietly around them, playing back Kai's unsteady breath when the tips of her nipples barely grazed his chest.

The wet spark of contact bloomed in her pulse, racing until it settled between her thighs like liquid honey. She could see it in his eyes, in her own reflection there. Emboldened, she kissed him again, determined to speak with her body as she could not with her words.

She kissed him with her eyes open, the velvet flick of his tongue released the grape, and it became a continuation of the kiss. His lips tugged at it, only hard enough for her to slant her mouth over his and steal it back. They dueled with it until it fell apart and all that remained was the undisguised kiss, and the slow, delicious struggle to dominate it.

Somewhere along the way, Sonya realized that Kai had maneuvered her, edging her toward the lower end until her toes barely touched the bottom of the pool. With a skillful turn, he blocked her retreat physically, her body brushing against his so that she swore the sparse hair on his leg was barely brushing her inner thighs.

He braced his arms against the edge of the pool behind her and moved in, the surrounding water becoming a part of him. Sonya resisted riding his thigh, but her parted thighs could feel his warmth, and her nether lips tingled at the swirling water, cool, then warm.

The kiss broke apart long enough for her to gasp for air. Kai's attention went to the way her breath caused her breasts to rhythmically crest the water.

He seemed so hesitant and cautious. Unsure why and unwilling to wait, Sonya closed the distance between them, riding his thigh like it was the back of a dolphin.

Kai stiffened and quietly groaned, grinding his

erection against her. She wrapped her arms around his solid shoulders and licked his earlobe, rubbing her body upward, then sliding down.

"Nice," she breathed. The intimate rub of his muscular thigh against her clitoris was some kind of madness.

"No sex tonight, huh?" he murmured.

"Shut up."

Every nerve ending of her sex felt alive and caressed by the sensation. Desperately trying not to clench his thigh, she rode him again, flexing her hips on the ride up, then grinding slightly on the way down.

"Are you sore?" he asked.

"A little."

He paused, looking into her eyes. "Was I too rough on you last night? I mean back at the house. In bed."

It bothered him, she realized. That wild sex had pushed several of her buttons, but it had been exquisite. "I wasn't complaining."

He lowered his head again and kissed her, his hands cupping her buttocks and tugging her even more firmly against him.

She groaned and the kiss suspended between their mouths, breaths torn, anticipation quaking. The world tilted as she shimmied upward, locking against his thigh so snugly that she could feel his pubic hair blend with hers. He held her there, in a slow, grinding groove that made her clitoris tighten and ache. Next to her hip, his erection blocked and twitched, begging to be caressed.

She obliged him, loosely gripping his penis and

stroking as she slid downward. His face was beautiful, taut with concentration and weakness. When she kissed him, he moaned and reacted by covering his hand over hers. Together they stroked and rocked, creating small waves that lapped at the edge of the shore.

It wasn't clear when it was no longer about who could outlast the other. It simply became too much, the only possible outcome fused by their challenging passions.

Sonya felt as if Kai's arms were everywhere, cupping her head for an onslaught of mindless kisses, holding her so close that not even water was between them, his thigh riding her until she felt about to implode.

His fingers carefully teased her clitoris, mindful of any touch that caused discomfort. His fingers tenderly cupped the slick lubrication, caressing the sensitive edges of her nether lips, pressing and caressing circles over her clitoris.

The fringes of awareness were both softening and spiking. The world seemed to shrink and spin, and yet each breath made her feel like she was holding perfectly still. His body moved and she moved with it. He sighed her name and she felt lost in the depths of his eyes.

"Kai . . . Oh . . ."

She bit her lip and held her breath when he suddenly pushed both her thighs apart, carefully thrusting his erection against the folds of her sex, then to her clit, caressing back and forth. The area was raw from the last time, and yet the careful contact wasn't nearly enough.

She squirmed to get closer.

He gripped her hips and sheathed his rigid length deeper inside, locking their bodies and holding the position as she absorbed the invasion. As she was still abraded from the previous night's sexual challenge, the entry was slightly raw, yet incredibly accurate. She clenched him with her muscles, heard him groan in response.

As if the spinning world clashed with the silence of the union, Sonya hovered there, at the brink of something visceral, infinitely more devastating than sex.

She could see him searching her eyes, fighting his own desires for whatever it was she couldn't hide.

"Sonya . . ."

She closed her eyes and rocked against him, using the thickness of his flesh to overwhelm her.

"Look at me," he whispered.

If he looked into her eyes, he'd know!

All her body needed one thrust—two—oh . . . She buried her face in his neck and the pit of her gut jerked at the impact of her orgasm. She squeezed him, clenched, and rocked against him again.

"No. . . ." His whisper fell apart at the final thrust. Sonya felt the bittersweet victory of his ejaculation deep inside her.

🦋

Kai felt limp as he leaned against the edge of the pool, certain that if he tried to move, they'd slide underwater and die without much of a struggle.

As the seconds passed, the devil in him tapped impatiently at his clock. *Time to pull apart. Set some barriers. Remind her that no matter how good the sex—and there was no doubt it was* excellent— *we still have rules to play by.*

But with her body nestled so close to his, with his semi-limp penis still inside her, he couldn't do it.

He stroked the fine slender curve of her spine.

Man, he was losing it.

🦋

For Sonya, the rest of the night was like another fantasy. The privacy of the veiled bed and the exotic throw pillows made it even more surreal.

Kai ordered room service; then, wearing just little more than towels, they ate like they'd been on the brink of starvation.

With her hunger sated and her body still tingly from sex, Sonya rubbed her belly and slouched against the couch. "If I eat another bite, I'm gonna explode."

Kai rubbed his flat belly and let out a sigh. He was about to answer when his phone chirped. In the span of a second, the bubble burst and reality intruded. The clash of his gaze was enough to make her look away first.

Kai went and picked up his phone next to where he'd dumped his clothes in the laundry chute earlier. "Armstrong."

He kept the phone to his ear and gave monosyllabic answers.

Sonya straightened out of the couch and wandered around the room, stopping at a large jeweled box by the bed. The words *Chest of Delights* were embossed on the cover.

Since she had her back to Kai, Sonya took a peek and found condoms, mini-whips, and several other sex toys. All plastic-wrapped and for sale.

Good God! A kinky treasure chest! It even came with a checkout list, just like a motel mini-bar, she thought in amazement. She turned the labels to read them. The Secret of the Five Veils? Wasn't that supposed to be Seven Veils? They looked like satin scarves. Pretty ones, too. Maharaja condoms . . . to "Sheath Your Scimitar"? Oh, brother! She browsed on. A String o' Pearls. Huh. Probably not something one wore to dinner. Hmm, Lickable Lotions . . . interesting. . . . Edible underwear, one size fits all. . . . *Really?* Her fingers paused on a familiar pink device, almost identical to her birthday gift. The Lotus Butterfly. Oh, boy!

"Find anything you like?"

Sonya slammed the lid shut and whirled around, realizing she'd been too caught up in her thoughts to hear Kai sneaking up on her. "No!"

He reached around her to flip open the box. "I find that hard to believe." Even though he chuckled, a faint flush suddenly ran all the way up his scalp when he looked in.

His eyes twinkled. "Nothing at all, huh?"

"I'm *not* that kind of girl."

"I'm not that kind of guy, either, but if ever there was a golden opportunity . . ."

"No, thanks."

"Carpe diem. Isn't that your motto?"

Sonya felt as if she'd lost her balance. "How do you know about carpe diem?"

"You mentioned it on our first date."

"Oh." *Crap.* She'd been tipsy, but she didn't remember saying it.

Kai reached in and pulled out the pack of scarves. "Secret of the Five Veils. Sounds harmless enough. Want to try a little bondage?"

"Like I said, it's not my thing."

"Tell you what. There's five scarves. I'll give you two."

The prospect left her speechless and unexpectedly giddy. "That would mean you get three."

"Boy, you're a whip with that math."

"Top of my class, I'll have you know."

"Kudos. That didn't sound like a no, though."

She blushed even more when he chuckled.

"If you want me to tie you up, all you have to do is ask," she retorted.

"Actually, I was planning it the other way around."

"Were the handcuffs too boring?"

"Too industrial. Not as erotic."

Before she could respond, he picked her up and carried her to the bed.

When he set her on the bed he groaned and she knew his bruises were making themselves known. Compassion cut into the moment.

"I get the first scarf," he said, already tearing into the plastic and pulling it out. He leaned on his side, the mirror above her giving her an interesting view of the tattoo on his back, his lean buttocks, and his beautiful physique.

With the orchid pink scarf in hand, he quickly tumbled her so she was draped over his torso.

"Straddle me," he commanded.

"What?"

"You heard. I want to watch you riding me." He leaned upward, pushing her into sitting against his erection. His eyes challenged and his dimples added to his smirk. His voice was damn near hypnotic. "Pretend you're in my palace, my latest concubine sent to pleasure me."

She rolled her eyes at him. "Ha! How about *you* are in my Amazonian palace as my sex slave, sent to do my bidding?"

"Did you say bidding or binding?"

"Possibly both."

He pretended to think about it. All of two seconds. "I like my idea better."

Her heart raced and she decided his dimples were the most adorable thing about him. "That's impossible," she whispered. "I can have no master."

He sat up quickly, catching her wrists and binding them behind her back. She barely put up a fight. It was hard to when his mouth began sucking and nibbling on her neck.

"Oh yes, you do. You just don't know it yet," he breathed. His erection nudged against her clitoris like a bully. Kai rubbed his thumbs over her nipples, gliding back and forth over the hardened peaks. "I shall have to show you the secret of each veil until you learn who is your master."

She lowered her head and licked the male curve of his collarbone. "Resistance is futile, Kai." She nuzzled and licked him again. "If you submit now, I will show you mercy."

He covered up his chuckle with a cough. "The secret of this veil, my concubine, is obedience."

She looked up. "Obedience?"

Kai's breathing was about as uneven as hers. "Yeah, let's go with that."

"Dream on." She worked her mouth down his chest, using her head to gently push him back to the mattress. Little by little, she shifted and kept moving down the expanse of his firm stomach, over fine soft hair that formed an arrow to his rigid cock.

She glanced at him, but his focus was on the mirror above and she knew without a doubt that she now had all the control.

"I'll ride you," she breathed on his spearing sex, "when I'm good and ready. You shall wait on my command."

Kai's hand flexed on the sheets and his erection strained toward her lips. His gruff response was rushed. "Sure, babe, whatever you say."

She flicked her tongue over the tip of his cock, the little licks teasing around the strained flesh, tasting her wetness where she'd straddled him.

Kai moaned and flexed his hips, but she continued the tongue-licking all the way down the veined length to his testicles.

"Sonya . . . Good God . . ."

She placed a French kiss at the base, then gave

him one big fat lick all the way back up to the tip, taking the plump head into her mouth and suckling it like a juicy treat, rediscovering its textures and firmness with her tongue.

Kai groaned and flexed his hips again. His right hand reached for her, then fell back on the bed in unspoken surrender.

His erection twitched in her mouth and she took him in earnest then, working her jaw to accommodate as much of him as she could. With every oral stroke, she felt his control slipping. His hand came off the bed twice and her own muscles strained from the imposed position, but she didn't stop.

"Enough!"

One minute she had him in her mouth and the next he'd dragged her up and over him. With surprising strength, he lowered her onto his cock, sheathing himself between the folds of her slippery wet vagina until she had impaled herself completely on him.

She arched her back and gripped his hips with her thighs, needing to move, to ride.

For a moment the passion blinded her, but when his thumbs moved toward her aching clit, she moaned and opened her eyes to the image of their reflection.

She moaned his name and rode him, matching the slow rhythm of his thumbs rubbing over her sensitive nub. "Now!"

She'd just started to feel the encroaching orgasm when Kai pulled her completely off and scrambled behind her. With one tug, her bindings were undone, and she braced herself just as he slid into her vagina from behind.

He curved over her, his hips molding against hers while his hands cupped her breasts, squeezing and caressing.

"Come for me," he whispered, his breathing harsh. "Come for me now. . . ."

His hand tightly cupped a breast, the fingers of his other hand massaging the pearl of her clitoris. The world faded under the command of need. The orgasm hit like a wave, rolling her and shattering her breath for an endless moment.

Kai stiffened, his ejaculation twitching deep within.

They collapsed on the bed, his hand still palming her wet sex, his bellowing breath flowing over her shoulders.

She winced a little when he withdrew from her, but then his arms went around her to pull her to his side. She felt soft and replete in his arms, dozing off on nothing more than a sigh.

🦋

She woke up when she felt a tug on her leg and realized that Kai had her spread-eagled and had loosely tied both ankles to the footboard.

Kai was leaning on his elbow beside her, watching. The bedsheets half-covered his erection, but he was more preoccupied with running a scarf back and forth over her breasts.

The fabric felt both silky and scratchy against her abraded nipples. The sensation coaxed a shiver of pleasure with each contact. "What are you doing?"

Kai shifted and started on her other breast. "I'm initiating you to the Secret Veil of Submission."

She bit back a grin. "If you insist on making such ridiculous statements, I will have to get rough with you."

This time he rolled his eyes.

"Amazons can control their sex slaves with their minds, did you know that?" She said the whopping lie without so much as blinking.

"You've got that going for you, huh?"

"Powers you cannot fathom."

"Fathom this." In two moves, he slid the bronze-colored silk under her back and strapped it tightly across her breasts. Crouching over her, he softly bit into her left nipple, dragging out a moan of plea-sure-pain from her. It was twice as erotic to watch his reflection in the mirror above. When she thought he'd stop, he suckled her until the fabric was wet and almost coarse, then worked his tongue under the silk to toy with her again.

"Do you submit?" he asked, his voice dark and haunting.

Yes. Sure. Anything you say. "Never."

"Upstart concubine."

The other breast withstood a similar assault, the areola treated to rough suction and slow, remorse-less kisses. Sonya realized she was clutching his head to her breast and forced her hands away.

Her fingers encountered the stack of scarves and she grabbed one. The more she pulled on the neon blue silk, the longer it seemed.

The desire in Kai's gaze was tinted with amusement. "I think the secret to that veil, babe, is not to grab more than you can handle."

She tugged some more and the last of it finally left the packet. "I definitely can handle it."

Kai brushed his lips over hers, the weight of his hardened penis nestling between her thighs, familiar and impatient. In the mirror his tattoo wavered with the movement of his muscles.

"What are you going to do with all that fabric?" he murmured against her chin. "You're already tied up. Might as well let me finish the job."

"Not so fast!" She wracked her brain for something tempestuous to do but came up with nothing. On impulse, she threw the thin scarf over his back, sliding it down over his hips. Only when one of Kai's kisses made her lose her grip on the material did a new idea occur to her.

She arched up, aligning her pelvis to his but denying him the entry his penis was spearing to make.

Kai made a delicious growling sound and she had to refocus not to let him have what they were both dying for. She moved her hands down his back, adjusted the veil lower still, then used it to strap his muscular thigh to hers.

She licked her lips, feeling wet and needy. "You move only when I do," she managed, trying to shift the remainder of the scarf across his back.

"Really?" Kai grinned in tight restraint and slid the plumlike tip of his penis between the lips of her wet folds. She instinctively flexed her muscles, needing to feel his length inside her.

"Ahhh. . . ." The scarf started to slide over his buttocks and between their legs. Sonya caught the tail end before it slipped from her grasp and held it firmly. Damn! If he kept distracting her, she'd never get her part done!

Kai lowered his forehead to her shoulder and she could feel the strain of his muscles.

"Sonya . . ."

"Wait. I'm not done." She tugged on the scarf to finish the job and Kai immediately stiffened.

"Hold up! It's looped around my boys."

Her lips twitched into a shaky grin, and even his ferocious frown couldn't make her hide it. "Of course. Just as I'd planned."

He looked a little nervous. "Don't think that will work."

"Don't you trust me?" She licked the bite mark she'd left on his shoulder and took advantage of his immobility to strap their other legs together, hoping she left enough slack so as not to harm his "boys."

"That," she said, stroking her hands up his back, "is the Veil of Domination."

His head lowered and his mouth clashed with hers in a long languid kiss, before he finally replied, "You think so?"

"I know so." It was a bluff. A challenge. A little white lie.

His thighs moved intimately against hers and she felt the flex of his muscles as he sheathed himself deeper into her wetness, tantalizing and snug.

"It takes control to dominate," he whispered, nipping her bottom lip ever so slightly.

And trust to submit.

Good God, the length of his cock plundered with the skill of a tall lollipop easing in and out of a willing mouth. Her wet passage worked around him like tongue and throat, clenching and working him deeper.

When she least expected it, he stopped and took the last of the scarves from the packet.

Her breathing broke to the same rhythm as his, revealing how close she was to giving him anything he wanted from her. She could see his pulse racing at his throat, and one look at the mixed emotions in his eyes told her he intended to win with this final scarf.

For her, it wasn't about winning a game of obedience, submission, domination, or control. It was only about trust.

Four desires against one hope.

He reached for her wrist, but she countered and gripped his. He whipped the vivid red around her wrist twice, but she quickly twisted her hand around and wrapped the rest of the scarf around his wrist, effectively tying them together.

Stalemate. Again.

She licked her lips. No retreat, no surrender.

Not yet, at least.

Trust me, she silently begged. *Trust me.*

❦

For an endless moment, the battle of wills and desire remained trapped . . . then Kai moved, unable to help himself. Sonya's body was so lush, soft, and tight, so slick and wet, that he thrust all the way in and held it there when the beast in him wanted so much more. Despite the satin grip of the scarf around his testicles, the motion was incredibly pleasurable, cupping him like a hand job.

The devil in him laughed. She's got you by the balls.

Kai ignored it and experimented with another thrust, delighted to see Sonya moaning, her eyes drifting shut in pleasure.

"Kai . . ."

He clasped his tied hand to hers, his larger palm to her smaller moist palm. He devoured her mouth while cupping one of her strapped breasts in his other. He rocked again, learning the limits of all the restraints—ankles, thighs, loins, breasts, and hands—synchronizing them.

She whispered and kissed him back with an innocent finesse that never failed to blindside him. So he hardened the kiss, giving in to the beast of lust, then fighting to rein it in.

The bindings creaked.

Sonya muffled her gasps against his skin.

Kai's heart pounded like a tightly wound clock.

Her half moan, half chuckle touched him like a caress and in desperation Kai reached for the last of his arsenal. The Lotus Butterfly.

He stilled and ripped the wrap with his teeth.

Her eyes widened in surprise. "Oh, God."

Kai moved between her thighs again, trying to keep her muddled in desire.

"I saw you this way once," he confessed. "You walked in when I was searching your house and I hid in your closet."

"No," she gasped, and blinked hard, as if trying to focus her scattered senses.

"Yes." Kai slid the remote into their tied hands and with a flick, turned it on. In his other hand, the tiny butterfly wings fluttered, the body vibrating like a hummingbird looking for a flower's nectar.

"Yes. The way you played with that pink vibrator, the butterfly just like this one, touching and stroking yourself."

She closed her eyes and tossed her head in denial, but she licked her lips and arched into him.

He danced the vibrator over the swell of her breasts, swirled it over her fabric-covered nipple, drinking in the myriad of emotions that crossed her face.

"God, I wanted you to come," he said gruffly. "I wanted to be deep inside you when you did. Hell, I would've settled for that taste of your wet slit under my mouth, your body . . ."

He eased partially out of her and placed the humming butterfly over her clitoris, then thrust until his body held it in place with his hips.

The humming vibrations almost set him off.

"Oh! Oh, Kai!!" The jagged edges of her orgasm began to spasm against the tip of his erection when he surged in again.

The need to ejaculate clawed from deep within, swelling almost painfully. "Sonya . . . oh, babe, not yet, honey. . . ."

". . . please . . ."

He didn't know whether he flicked the remote on high or she did. But the new vibration was almost too much to bear.

The world threatened to dissolve. Somewhere between the pleading sounds of her words, he heard the broken swears in his breaths and he tried desperately to gain control.

He didn't care who won or lost anymore. It only mattered that it had to be this way, restrained so deliciously by her, together, lost in the storm of silk and skin.

He struggled to separate the pieces . . . the softness of her hips, her sinewy legs strapped to his, her full restrained breasts against his chest, her secret innocence that still, even now, was so apparent that it seared into his senses in a wave of wild panic.

"Nooo . . ."

He tried to outrun it with a blunt thrust into her body, but she strained against him, against the bonds, grinding as if she could reach him through wet skin and wild cries, as if her soul was branding into his.

And suddenly the cradling movement of her hips stilled, flesh and bone locked and arched. She breathed quickly, quivering silently within, her inner muscles holding him in a soft, greased grip.

He groaned, the telltale hitch of her cry marking her prim orgasm, her womb fluttering, so damned exquisitely.

"Ahhh . . . love," he groaned. "Don't move . . . don't move!"

The thought imploded and his mind suddenly dimmed, emptying with the surrender of his ejaculation, suspending the world in a timeless fracture.

Little by little, awareness crept in and unfolded like smoke. Kai flicked off the remote and rolled onto his back to keep from crushing her. With her freed hand, she removed the vibrator, and it ended up on his chest, in the center of her hand.

Kai fought the encroaching exhaustion but watched as Sonya's eyes slid shut. He exhaled.

A million questions vied for attention, but he didn't want to face a single one of them. Not if it jeopardized the moment.

Anyway, Sonya was snoring ever so softly. Weren't women supposed to be the ones who wanted to cuddle and talk all night?

He studied her in the mirror above. Perspiration turned her skin the color of roasted coffee beans, a sensual harmony against his obsidian flesh. Her legs lay spread and tied to his. The soft curves of legs and buttocks, arms, trapped in the colorful bindings . . .

Hell, maybe she hadn't noticed that he'd called her *love*.

Dawn was peeking over the horizon when Sonya woke to Kai moving quietly in bed. She felt as if she were glowing from deep inside, as if she'd been smiling in her sleep.

The bedsheets, his body heat, and the peacefulness were the kind of stuff that she'd only dreamed of.

Their lovemaking had left her chafed and sore, but without a single regret. Maybe faint bruises, but not many.

She kept her eyes closed and pretended to sleep while he crept into the bathroom. When the faint drizzle of the shower had been going for a little while, she sat up in bed and stretched.

She was tempted to flop back amid the secret of the jewel-colored veils, but she was suddenly embarrassed by the role they had played the night before.

Well, Kai had actually started the whole thing.

Thinking of him, she headed toward the bathroom to join him, then noticed his wallet and belt on the dresser and slowed to pick them up.

Guilt crept up her spine, and the glow in her chest tightened and began to fade. There were no words for it really, just the knowledge that it was time to give Kai the necklace and trust him to understand what it meant. It wasn't about blackmailing him to get her out of Mexico or admitting her uncle was a possible crook. It wasn't even about the necklace anymore.

She laid the belt back down and sighed.

It was about her heart, and no amount of psychoanalysis or Lisa's warnings could've prepared Sonya for the moment.

The teeth of the hidden zipper in the belt gritted quietly when she opened it. Her fingers encountered the razor-thin blade and followed it down, but to her surprise, nothing was there.

Nothing but black leather. No money. No necklace. Just a thin, dangerous knife.

"I was wondering when you'd get around to that."

Sonya jerked, startled by Kai's voice. He was standing in the bathroom doorway with a small towel around his hips, his eyes lifeless, his features chiseled in stone. Mr. Bounty Hunter to the core.

"I, ah . . . You . . ." No words came to her rescue. She felt like the intruder, as if *she'd* broken into his room and was caught prowling though his personal items. Like a little girl scribbling in the bathroom. Hurrying, hurrying. She fought the urge to cover herself, desperate for a bedsheet, a towel, anything.

Kai didn't so much as move a muscle and yet she felt crowded by him.

"When did you find it?" she finally asked. What was the point in denying it?

Kai took his time arriving at his answer, watching her like a predator eyeing limping prey. "That's irrelevant now."

"It's not what you think. After last night, I realized that—"

"Careful. Don't drag the sex into this. It was great, but that's all it was. Sex, plain and simple. I'm sure you have an entertaining explanation, just do us both a favor and leave out the sob stories, OK?"

Sonya felt as if he'd slapped her, and the verbal attack caused her to take a step backward.

"Go ahead," he taunted. "I'm waiting."

Riding her anger, she took a few steps to the bed and snatched the sheet, wrapping it around her with numb fingers while she gathered her composure. "You want the truth? Well, here it is." Her voice warbled, which only made her angrier with herself. "I was a thief once. A long time ago. Before I was even a teenager. I was too young to understand the implications of what I was doing, but I knew it was wrong. Believe me, I paid my dues the hard way, but all I ever wanted was . . ." *a little love.* She shook her head.

"A little cold, hard cash?"

"You wouldn't understand," she ended weakly.

"I told you I played to win."

And obviously he'd won the day he'd found the necklace. So what was he playing for now? The pain in her chest increased, as if her heart were being squeezed hard by a fist. She hurled a pillow at him, but it bounced harmlessly off his chest.

"No matter what you think, Kai, I was going to give you the necklace right now."

A muscle twitched at his jaw. "Don't insult my intelligence, Sonya. You played a good game, but I played a better one."

He turned his back and walked back into the bathroom. "Get dressed. We leave in an hour."

FIFTEEN

SONYA SAT IN the car, the departure from the night in paradise still a blur in her mind. The ache in her chest had increased, feeling as if her heart was crystallizing against the fist that gripped it.

She deflected her thoughts to the new sports-utility vehicle they drove. Her guess was that Enrique had traded with them and handled whatever paperwork was necessary. She thought of Raul, curled up in the huge suitcase in the trunk, and wondered whether the secret ventilation was going to be enough for him. At least he wasn't snoring.

On the other hand, Kai didn't look worried at all. In fact, he looked excited, as if they were headed for a theme park rather than Tijuana. In his neat, clean clothes and shaven head and dark sunglasses, he was the perfect portrayal of a tourist on his way back from a day trip with his wife. Female companion. Sex slave. Whatever.

She absently rubbed her wrist and caught Kai

following the motion. She immediately stopped and looked away, the heat wave of recent memories scalding her cheeks.

Nothing was said. Once or twice she noticed him watching her from the window reflection, but even then, his sunglasses hid whatever he was thinking. Only when they reached Tijuana did he hand her a manila envelope with her ID in it and tell her to "start praying."

She held her breath when the inspector unzipped the suitcase Raul was in, but the top layer was filled with clothes and the inspector did little more than a visual evaluation.

Kai pretended not to speak a lick of Spanish but flashed his sizzling dimpled grin and in shorter time than she'd expected they were on U.S. soil, cruising down the freeway toward San Diego.

❦

"I know you have business to attend to, so why not stop the car and I'll find my way home? I won't even bring up charges," Sonya said.

Kai clenched his jaw and let out some of his frustrations by strangling the steering wheel. "You happen to be part of my unfinished business."

"What's left? You won the game. You've completed your promise to me. Pull over."

"No can do."

When they stopped at a stop sign, she reached for the doorknob, but he clicked the auto-lock first.

She bristled. "It doesn't have to be this difficult, Kai."

"It's the only way," he said with regret.

In his peripheral vision, he saw her cross her arms, her anger coiling like a snake around her, poised to strike. Things were going to get ugly, but hell, there was just no other way.

"If you don't unlock this door in the next two seconds, Kai, I *will* bring on a scene like you won't believe."

"Winner gets a wish granted."

She calmly looked out her window and recrossed her arms, all but ignoring him.

"I want you to give me the next hour without attempting to run off."

"Am I free to go after that?"

He nodded, conflicting emotions knotted in his gut. "Free as a bird." Or a butterfly.

The silence in the car became almost suffocating.

By the time he entered the parking garage where Dre was waiting to take custody of Raul, Kai felt like he was being smothered. Part of him was convinced he was doing the right thing in making her face her victim. Facts were facts, and the necklace incriminated Sonya. But his gut instinct howled that this was wrong, that he'd been wrong about her all along.

Wrong or right, he had to know!

He parked close to the door level to their office space to find Dre leaning on the wall, waiting impatiently.

"'Bout time," Dre greeted him.

"Hey, Bro. Good to see you, too." Kai stepped out of the car and endured a stout hug and slap on the back from his brother, who was smelling of cologne and dressed well enough to hit the clubs for the night.

Kai tossed him the car keys and caught the set of keys Dre tossed his way.

He heard Sonya close her door and walk up to them.

"And you," Dre said, pausing to give an appreciative look, "must be the one and only Sonya Drummond. It's a pleasure to finally meet you."

Sonya's features softened enough for a friendly smile. Dre flashed back with the same smooth-operator face he'd been practicing in the mirror since he was twelve. Back then, Kai had laughed. Now he wanted to punch Dre.

"Stop drooling, Dre." Kai grimaced. "It's embarrassing."

Dre barely spared him a glance. "A cruise. A hottie. I definitely got the short end of the stick on this one, man."

Kai steered Sonya to the building door. "We can argue about that later. Right now I need you and your short stick to go take care of Romero for me."

Dre lowered the sunglasses he wore to peer at Sonya, then back again at Kai.

"And what are you and Ms. Hottie gonna do?"

Kai narrowed his eyes at Dre and threw him a mind-your-own-business vibe.

Dre shrugged and winked at Sonya. "Fine. I'm out." He clasped the keys and headed for the vehicle.

Kai opened the door and Sonya walked through it. Her chin was held high, her shoulders tense.

They went past the stark reception area to the holding room, stopping short of opening the door. For a moment, neither of them moved. Kai felt rooted on the spot, trying to remain impartial, and failing.

"Kai, open the door."

"Let me explain."

"A little late for that, isn't it? Just let me get this over with."

"Not yet." He fought the urge to hold her then. His bones itched with the need. By the look on her face, it was the last thing she wanted from him.

She licked her lips in a nervous gesture, but stubbornness crowded the sorrow in her eyes, shouting at him.

Defiantly, he leaned forward to place a kiss on her cheek, pausing to inhale the scent of her that would haunt him for some time. She stiffened.

"Don't touch me!" she whispered urgently.

Kai froze, then stepped back, the scent burning in his lungs. He brushed the back of his hand roughly over his lips in an absent gesture to rid himself of the need for contact.

Keep it business.

He abruptly turned and unlocked the door, flinging it open with more force than he'd intended. An old man who had been lying on the small couch sat up abruptly.

"Uncle Otis!" Sonya flung herself into his arms.

"Sonya? Is that you, girl?"

Her smile was wide. "Yeah, it's me."

"Darlin', your hair! You cut it off! And . . . look at the rest of you!"

Kai sat on the corner chair and let them have their family moment. Outside the door, he could hear movement, doors opening and closing. Probably Dre taking care of things.

The chatter between the two finally gave way and the smiles sagged at the edges.

"What's this about a necklace?" Sonya asked in a whisper, as if Kai weren't in the same room, only a few feet from them.

Mr. Drummond turned his head to Kai, raised his peppery eyebrows and asked, "Mind if I talk to her for a moment?"

There was defeat written all over the old man's face, but Kai didn't want to give an inch. The silent plea from Sonya broke him.

"Tell her the truth. All of it," he said, and left the room, watching not far from the door.

🦋

Sonya wanted to cup her uncle's face and see his denture smile again. She'd never seen him look so weary. Instead, she kept her hands in her lap and searched his face.

"I never dreamed you'd get involved in this," he mumbled, almost too low to hear.

It felt surreal and disorienting, like a bad elevator ride going down. His rheumy eyes remained focused on his shoes. "I only meant to give you a birthday present you'd love, 'cause the minute I saw that necklace, I knew you'd love it."

He clasped his leathery hands together and rubbed them in a dry sound. "I never meant any harm. Don't know what I was thinking."

"Tell me you didn't do this for me, Otis. You know you didn't even have to buy me a card, much less get me a necklace."

His focus shifted from his shoes to her face. "I stole the necklace. I . . . have a lot of apologizing to do." He lowered his head again and his shoulders hunched downward. Before her eyes, the man she'd admired and secretly held up as her noble mentor tumbled off his virtual pedestal.

"Look, I can help you out. We'll get an attorney that will straighten this whole thing out."

But he was already shaking his head.

"It's no reason to give up!"

He took her hand in between his and tried to work up a smile. "I guess I should tell you the rest. I have a little, um," he sighed, "problem."

"How little?"

Outside, footsteps approached the door, and it wasn't until Sonya turned to the doorway that she realized the additional sound was a walking cane. A petite black woman stood as if in a spotlight. She wore a purple business suit, leaned on a cane with one hand, and with the other touched the butterfly necklace at her throat.

"Mr. Drummond, I presume this is your niece?"

Sonya sat up. "I am. And you are . . . ?"

"I'm certainly not the helpless old lady your uncle thought I was," the woman retorted.

Sonya inwardly cringed and forced a smile. "I'm sure this is nothing more than a big misunderstanding—"

"Embezzlement and grand theft are not a misunderstanding, young lady!"

"Mrs. Miller," Otis began, "I said I'd pay you every cent back."

"You bet you will." She glowered at him.

"Grand theft? Embezzlement?" Sonya turned to her uncle.

Uncle Otis squeezed Sonya's hand in his. "Remember that problem I was mentioning?"

Sonya braced herself, really seeing him for the first time.

The words seemed dragged out of him. "I used to have a gambling habit when I was a kid, hanging out with your mother. Back then I ended up with a loan shark and things got real bad. Pastor Nelson got me out of it, took me to Gamblers Anonymous, and I was clean. For over twenty years I was clean. Then three years ago I . . ." he ran a hand over his balding head, "I thought I'd do a little harmless gambling on the computer. I bet on baseball, 'cause you know that I know my baseball, right?"

His hands gestured helplessly. "I lost. Big. I swear I was only going to borrow the money, pay my debt, then pay it back. I didn't even have enough money for your birthday present."

"The necklace? You stole to cover up your gambling problems?" It didn't make sense. Uncle Otis was an upstanding, rational man! He'd taught her right from wrong. He'd stood beside her when her childhood had been falling apart. How could he resort to stealing to cover his gambling debts?

He squeezed her hand again and took a steadying breath. He looked from one woman to the other. "I'm sorry. I'm so very sorry. Sonya, these folks think you had something to do with it, but the truth is," he turned to the doorway, "she didn't. You couldn't incriminate her even if you tried."

Mrs. Miller tipped her head to squint intently at them through her bifocals. Beyond her, Kai's expression was as stark as a statue.

Sonya's throat was in knots. Fear, disappointment, and sadness overwhelmed her like she hadn't felt since she was a seven-year-old child in a giant courtroom.

When her uncle started to sniffle, she gave him a hug, shielding his tears against her shoulder as he had once done for her.

SIXTEEN

KAI WAS DRUNK and he knew it. It was pathetic to be so drunk and still know that it wasn't enough. For instance, it was bugging him that Dre had parked his butt on the coffee table to talk, when he knew damned well that Kai didn't allow feet nor butt cheeks on that particular piece of furniture.

"Damn, Bro. Is this a bachelor pad or a pigsty?"

"You're blocking the TV. And get off my damned table."

Dre didn't even shift. "How many bottles of beer does that make?" He started gathering the ones littered nearby. "Ever heard of canned beer? It's cheaper and you don't risk slicing your feet when you drop them."

Shit. Kai hadn't been able to look at a can without thinking of Sonya's great aim. She threw like a pro. So the choice between bottles and cans was a no-brainer. Besides, a little cut never killed nobody. Well, the one Sonya had received at the base of her neck still made him bristle. That cut would probably become a permanent scar. If he ever saw it again.

He remembered kissing the nick and the way Sonya had responded with that little vulnerable sound. . . . He wondered what the cut looked like now.

"Kai? Hellooooo."

"Leave me alone. Go practice your, you know . . ." Kai tried to imitate the smooth-operator look.

"What the hell is wrong with you?" Andre demanded.

Kai tipped his bottle, but only droplets hit his lips. "Fuck. Hand me another brew, would ya?"

"No."

Muttering curses, Kai struggled to his feet and stumbled over the bottles to the kitchen, where he flung open the fridge.

Aha! Four more beers left. And some mayo. Some soy sauce packets. And some lunch meat, which was either pastrami or possibly some really bad smoked turkey.

Maybe after the next beer he'd take a sniff and see what was what. He twisted off the cap from his beer bottle, tossed it over his shoulder, and walked around his brother.

"Did you ever consider she was innocent?"

Kai stopped guzzling beer. "Who?"

"Wow. Stupid *and* drunk."

"I'ma knock you out, Dre." Drunk or not, Kai was suddenly spoiling for a fight. "Don't know why I ever gave you my spare house key."

Andre's eyes sparkled like a dog with a meaty bone. "You can't even talk about her."

Kai growled, cussed some more, and stalked back to the couch.

"You know, Kai, when I first saw the surveillance shots of her, I thought she was all nerdy and whatnot, but man, with that tight shirt on, she's like, *bam*! And her butt is like, *kapow*! Makes a guy want to grab something."

"Shut the hell up."

"Can't lie. She has a behind that makes me want to sink my teeth into—!"

In a flash Kai swung and missed. Barely. Alcohol turned into volatile fuel in his veins, stoking his anger. "You're crossing the line, Dre. Don't fuck with me."

"Look at you. Talk about crossing the line! Do you even know why you are trying to get drunk?"

Kai's heart felt like the devil had lanced a red-hot pitchfork through it. He'd been in anguish since the day Sonya had walked out of his office without a backward glance.

From that moment on, his heart hadn't pounded quite the same. His mind veered to thoughts of her every chance it got. He missed the way she laughed and ran through the rain. Missed the way she sipped her hot chocolate like she was the Queen of Courtesy herself. She'd been honest to a fault, loyal as a bleeding heart, and damned if he didn't miss her!

Hell, he was afraid to wear the goofy tequila-worm boxers she'd selected because they reminded him of her. He'd begun to look for her traits in everyone around him but kept coming up blank. And worse yet, his nights had become sensual replays that haunted him and left him feeling empty and craving every dawn.

No matter how many beers he poured down his throat, the taste of her was still on his tongue, and his body still craved to sink into her, to wake up next to her. See her smile. Watch the happiness in her eyes whenever she looked at him with love and trust and hope. All the things he'd ripped to shreds.

Forever. Oh God . . .

Kai slumped back on the couch. A headache pounded against his temples and he was pretty sure the hangover hadn't started yet. "Dre, take your annoying Dr. Freud ass out of here and don't let the door hit ya where the good Lord split ya."

Andre stood and crossed his arms. "If you want to mope, that's your business. My business is to maintain a professional reputation. I don't know what went on between you guys, but whatever it is had to be your fault. I figure I'll give you a couple of days to apologize to her and if you don't, I'm going to do it myself, then come back here and give you that fight you want, got it?"

Kai lowered the beer. Dre looked like he meant every word of it. "Stay out of it."

His brother shrugged. "I said what I came to say. Now it's on you."

Andre slammed the door on the way out.

Kai guzzled his beer, then swallowed past the pain and hurled the bottle into the empty fireplace.

"Have a nice weekend, Ms. Drummond."

"You, too." Sonya waved at the receptionist who blew past her office, ready for the weekend.

A couple more co-workers left and Sonya found herself tapping her pencil and staring at her monitor, dreading the moment she'd have to face her empty apartment again.

The phone rang, startling her. She reached for it, then stopped, her heart knocking like a fist. Was it Kai again? He'd left half a dozen messages at home and several more at work, but she refused to call him back. She couldn't think about him. Even Lisa knew not to bring up the subject since their last phone conversation.

"So how was sex with a bona fide kinder-and-gentler gigolo? Did you have lots of wild and crazy romping?"

Sonya had been curt. "No." OK, it had been a little wild. Crazy? Well, um, that word was so subjective.

"Are your eyes glazing over, because I'm not hearing anything," Lisa complained.

"Lisa, it was an uneventful vacation." So what if that lie was a doozy?

"Are you saying there was no bondage, no sex in public places? Not even a butt spanking?"

Sonya couldn't even force a chuckle. Well, at least the butt spanking hadn't happened. Not exactly. There was that one time when Kai was asserting his machoness to ward off Enrique. Or did that even qualify? Either way, it probably wasn't what Lisa was looking for.

"Fine, don't tell me. But on a scale from one to ten, how did he rank?"

"Lisa, I'm not going to do a play-by-play."

"But you agreed to tell me the details!"

"No. I most definitely didn't."

"Come on."

"No! I went on vacation. I had a lousy time. I'm back. End of conversation!"

"Oh no!" Lisa gasped. "Oh, honey, you didn't. Tell me you didn't get your heart mixed up in that man."

Sonya groaned. "Not the lecture, please!"

"The rule is to love 'em and leave 'em, go where you have never gone before, lose your inhibitions . . ."

Sonya listened to about two more minutes, then interrupted. "Lisa, I couldn't do that. My heart was in it. Still is in it. Way deep in it. And telling me I-told-you-sos right now isn't going to help a bit." *Because, dammit, I love him!*

Her heart gave a broken, helpless tug again and a shrilling phone brought her back to the present.

Yes, she loved him. God, would the pain ever end?

Another suit flew by, waving a hand, calling as he headed to the elevators, "It's just you and Lora in Personnel and she said she'd be out in thirty seconds."

"Thanks, Boyd." With a deep sigh, Sonya leaned back and rubbed her face, pushing her curly bangs from her forehead.

She ought to be running for the door, too, except there was no reason to. The singles-bar scene held no appeal. Her house was as empty as a tomb these days. The future loomed like a galactic hole. Who was she kidding? She might as well get woolen socks, ten cats, and spend the rest of her life living in a rickety old house with them.

With Kai at her side, she'd do it in a hot second!

Oh, hell!

The elevator dinged and Sonya turned her head toward the sound. It was way too early for the janitor. She turned back to her computer but stilled when the heavy footfalls approached her office.

She'd just begun to stand when Kai stopped in the doorway, his presence breaching the distance like an open-mouthed kiss, taking her breath away.

Kai!

He was dressed in a sharp black suit, like her lover on the cruise. In one hand he held a gift bag, and with the other he smoothed out the tie against his chest, his hand pausing as if he were swearing allegiance.

His eyes held hers and the nonexistent kiss burned clear to her soul.

He shifted his stance just slightly. "Hi."

"Hi." She drank in the sight of him, locking her knees to keep from throwing herself at him. Working to recover her composure, she caught herself before she straightened out her burgundy dress in a nervous gesture. "This is a secured building. How did you get in?"

"Charm." Kai's eyes beguiled warmly, and a ghostly show of his dimple made her heart do a flip.

"I'll have to have a talk with Security."

He stepped farther into the office and Sonya was thankful for the large desk between them. The overhead lights made his skin radiant, reminding her of all the strength and smoothness of his flesh. Damn him.

He placed the gift bag on the table and shoved his hands into his pockets as if he had all the time in the world.

"I should start by saying I'm sorry. I made a mess of things and—"

Sonya threw her hands up. "Stop right there. I don't want to hear any more. You were doing your job and I understand that now. It's over, so let's just move on, OK?"

"I'll move on only after I've said my piece."

"We both know that's not necessary, Kai."

A flash of hurt appeared in his eyes at the sound of his name. He walked around and when he was close enough to touch, close enough for his subtle cologne to wrap itself around her, Sonya retreated to the comfort of her executive chair. "Say what you have to say already."

He reached into the gift bag and pulled out a knot of colorful scarves, all bright, brilliant, and bleeding memories.

"I can't get you out of my head." He combed his fingers through the scarves, separating them. "From the very beginning, I didn't want to trust my instincts about you. I only knew I wanted you."

"You wanted the necklace," she interjected.

"Yes, that too. But it wasn't nearly as important."

Carefully, he pulled the bronze-yellow scarf free and let it fall on her lap. "I miss your bright smile."

His voice was gruff and low, his eyes revealing a loneliness that mirrored hers. Sonya's throat went dry, her fingers itching to reach for the scarf. "Sometimes, when you were fighting not to laugh, you'd get a little crooked smile. I miss it."

She didn't know what to say. Her heart felt like it was thawing from a deep freeze.

"I miss your body." Another gruff confession, professed with the long royal purple scarf. "I can't tell you how many times I've reached for you in my dreams."

She shook her head as if she could deny it.

"And your laughter. I miss that a whole lot." Orange silk fluttered down to her lap, too, barely weighing anything. She could only watch him, afraid to reply.

"I miss your touch at night. In the morning. And every couple of seconds in between." He crushed the blue scarf in his right hand as if he couldn't release it. In his other hand, the red scarf also remained in his grip. "I want my friend back. I want my lover, too."

She couldn't take her eyes away from him. With every passing second, her heart beat more recklessly, her breath billowing in her chest.

He leaned forward and kissed her, softly, with infinite tenderness, the soft contact of the scarf grazing her cheek.

"I guess what I'm trying to say is that I miss you. God, I miss you. . . . I feel like I've been missing you my whole life."

Sonya blinked to keep the tears from brimming in her eyes.

"Please tell me you missed me, even just a little," he begged.

"Oh, Kai." She touched his cheek to keep him from kissing her again. "This won't work. We won't work! It's impossible."

His Adam's apple bobbed. "Why, hon?"

She closed her eyes at the endearment, rushing with her explanation. "I took a big risk on that cruise, acting as if I knew how to be a player. That woman you met was part of my makeover. You don't know the real me. I'm mostly a quiet, level-headed, conservative person—"

"Who can throw a mean overhand."

She peered at him, desperate to make her plea. "I have this blind faith in people that—"

"You have strong loyalties and are braver than some men I know."

She suddenly wished he had hair to tug on instead of a smooth scalp. "I don't do crazy, adventurous things—"

"Oh, yes you do."

"That was different. I was in Mexico and—"

Kai dropped the blue scarf in her lap and cupped her breast in a sweet caress that fluttered deep in her belly. "Are you saying you wouldn't do those things here?"

Her protest faltered in her throat.

"I really like the woman I got to know." His hand moved up to her cheek, his voice growing more hoarse. "I admire lots of things about her. About you.

And even if I don't deserve it, I want to spend a lot more time getting to know you. If you'll have me."

She could feel her heart tattooing onto his palm, joy bloomed like a tangled vine despite the tight rein of caution she was desperately trying to maintain. She made herself say the words before they could choke her. "Great sex is not enough to base a relationship on, Kai."

"Agreed." He tugged her up. "I want more than sex. I want to know why you like peach-colored underwear, who your favorite musician is, whether you sleep in on weekends, your favorite wine, the worst movie you've ever seen. . . ."

Joy bubbled over, thrilling her into laughing.

"OK." She grinned, wanting to rain kisses all over his face.

". . . I want to wake you up from your nightmares and hold you when you're cold. I want to see if you can pull a fast one on me again, to make me live for rainstorms, to sit in the sun and do nothing at all. Anything and everything about you. I want to know you more. . . ."

She brushed her lips over his to silence him, her heart near to bursting. "Kiss me."

He did, passion and laughter blended into a new hunger that rapidly got out of control. It brewed between them until caresses became more urgent, and they grappled to shed each other's clothes.

Kai's jacket fell to the floor unheeded.

All the buttons down the front of her dress were undone in record time. The front clasp of her bra made a small snapping sound and flew apart.

Kai buried his face in her cleavage with a groan, then sought out a nipple and suckled it. Sonya arched back, surrendering with a purr to the erotic sensation. He pushed her on the edge of the desk and she drowned in the whirlwind of his mouth, feeling branded by every place his lips touched.

The need to feel her breasts against his chest had her tearing at his shirt. A button flew off and one clicked when it hit a picture frame on the wall.

But finally there he was, his hot skin on hers, his mouth and hands ravaging, creating sensual shivers up her spine.

When his erection pushed against her sensible white panties, she wiggled closer still. His hand moved between them and his fingers delved in with familiar skill. Sonya flexed into the contact, so aroused and wet that she was faintly embarrassed.

"Sonya," he whispered her name over and over, between kisses.

She wrapped one leg around his hip, then realized she had to remove her panties.

"I need you," she whispered. "Please."

"God, yes."

She practically climbed him to shimmy off her panties and still maintain the kiss with him. The clink of his belt buckle soon followed. His teeth had just nipped her upper lip when he pulled her against him and entered her in one slick, hard thrust, lodging all the way in with a groan.

She gasped his name and trembled at the perfect fit.

Kai managed a pained half laugh. The blazing passion that burned so fiercely suddenly tempered, thickened, and liquefied.

She turned her face up to his, seeing the beautiful intensity of his face. His lips moved just as she confessed, "I love you."

"—I love you."

Their words echoed. His face imprinted by awe and unforgettable tenderness.

"You do?"

Truth and desire made it hard to speak. "Swear to God I do."

The tautness in his face gave way to a dimpled grin. He withdrew and thrust again, slowly. "I'll hold you to that."

Her orgasm frothed with each flex of his hips, words and their meaning fading as she and Kai made love.

She leaned into the strength of his arms, moving with him in the timeless dance of lovers. When the need became too great she cried out his name and came undone in his arms, her legs gripping his hips as she rode the last of it, trying to suspend the moment just a little longer.

Moments later, Kai clasped her close as if to fuse her completely against him. He grunted against her neck and his ejaculation spilled hot in her womb.

The aftermath rolled in like a receding tide.

He kissed her neck, his cheek against hers. "Love you. Shh, don't say it just yet. Let me look in your eyes."

He lifted his head and she let him stare into her eyes, seeing everything her heart could hold, even the lingering tears of joy. *I love you, love you, love you. . . .*

After an endless moment, she kissed the tip of his nose.

"I forgot to give you one more thing," he said.

"What's that?"

He held out the red scarf. Dangling at the end was the butterfly necklace, the item that had brought them together. "I tried to buy it from Old Lady Miller, but she refused to sell it to me. But when I told her what it meant to us, she decided to *give* it to me, telling me that only a fool in love deserved it."

Sonya grinned and touched it. "A fool in love, huh?"

"Only for you, babe." Kai tangled the scarf and necklace around Sonya's neck, tugging her in to seal his vow with a kiss.